The
Phineas Fletcher
Mysteries

The "Spencer's Mill" Series

Cherie Harbridge Williams

Round Mountain

Publishing

Any scriptures referenced in this book are from the King James Version.

ISBN-13: 979-8-9874296-1-7

DEDICATION

This book is dedicated to the memory of my maternal grandmother, Carrie Jackson Reese, who could spin a tale with the best of them.

It is also dedicated to the memory of my paternal grandmother, Frances Dalton Winget, who loved a good mystery.

ACKNOWLEDGEMENTS

Grateful thanks to my husband, Conway Williams,
for his support and patience as I invested time
and resources into this work.
Also to Jeanne Boyce, Janice Shoe, and Gail Anderson
for reviewing the manuscript and their kind suggestions.
Thanks to Jessica Ryn, my editor, whose input helped
put a polish on Phineas.

TABLE OF CONTENTS

Note: An earlier episode, "The Unlikely Jewel Thief" is
available for free download from
www.CherieHarbridgeWilliams.com

THE VANISHING WHOLESALER

March 1887

Phineas Fletcher grinned as he picked up the morning newspaper from the kitchen table. His son-in-law Danny had already gone to work at the general store, and his daughter Charlotte, the village schoolteacher, had gone to school with the children. It was the most enjoyable time of day for Phineas. He had the entire house to himself.

He brewed a pot of coffee and scrambled some eggs, then opened the paper, giving it a smart snap to unfold the pages. He hadn't made the headline this time, but an article on the second page reported the part he'd played as a private investigator by recovering some precious stolen jewelry and capturing the thief. Not only that, but he'd also restored two sisters to each other, and that adventure had come on the heels of his success in capturing a murderer. Reading reports about his success filled his heart with joy.

Perhaps it was time to claim the title of Investigator and order business cards from the printer. These adventures had added some spice to a rather dull life. His newfound celebrity was almost as intoxicating as that new brand of ale they served at the Golden Lamb.

Phineas smiled, thinking his local fame was more than a former salesman had a right to expect. The sun's rays poured through the window as he lifted his fork. He had a feeling it was going to be a great day.

After finishing his eggs, he scrounged through Charlotte's sewing supplies for her scissors, then carefully clipped out the article to save with the headline from last week's paper. *I need to get some frames for my clippings, or at least make a scrapbook,* he thought. For now, they would have to remain in his bureau under his socks.

On the back page of the paper, an ad caught his attention.

Wanted: Information on the disappearance of
Mr. Marcolus Banks of Banks Wholesale Supply,
missing since Friday last. Reward offered.
Contact Mrs. Banks at 321 Metcalf Street, Lamar.

Phineas paused, put his coffee cup down, and read the ad twice. There may be an opportunity here. I need a case to work on.

The calendar on the wall marked March 14th, and the temperature in Ohio was just below average for that time of year. It would be a cold, blustery ride to Lamar, so he bundled himself into his heavy Inverness coat with the fur collar and put his felt top hat on his head. After hitching Dancer, his horse, to the carriage, he hopped in, covered his legs with quilts for extra warmth, then began the hours-long drive to Lamar.

The icicles on the naked tree limbs dripped water along the sides of the road, and the recent late-winter snow on the roadway had turned to dirty slush. Despite the chill, he was in merry humor, anticipating an adventure.

The road condition slowed the horse, so Phineas occupied himself by humming the tune to "I'll Take You Home Again, Kathleen." His quiet humming gradually transformed into boisterous singing resonating through the woods, which didn't matter since no one was within earshot. Then he broke into an enthusiastic rendition of "Sweet Betsy From Pike." The solitude was wonderful.

It was about noon when he arrived in town, so he stopped by the bank to take care of an errand. As he left the bank, he ran into an old friend, Edison Duncan.

"Ed," he said, "I haven't seen you for at least a year. How are you and your family?"

"We're doing pretty well. Say, I'm meeting my wife at the Old English Tea Room for lunch. Would you care to join us?"

"I'd enjoy that." Phineas agreed and made his way to the restaurant with his friend.

The restaurant's warmth welcomed them as they stepped inside.

He kept his opinion of the décor to himself. Despite the excessive frou-frou, they served the best food around.

The two of them joined Mrs. Duncan, who had already secured a table. She was a shy red-haired lady, so the conversation was mainly between Edison and Phineas. He told them about his new avocation of investigator. "I'm going to see if I can get hired to find a businessman, Marcolus Banks. He's disappeared."

Edison's chin dropped. "Marcolus Banks, you say? I went to school with him years ago."

"What kind of fellow was he then? Was he irresponsible and flighty?"

"No, he was solid. If you had a need, Marc was there to help a friend. I can't believe he'd just disappear without saying anything."

"He could have had a heart attack somewhere. Or it could be foul play, I suppose. I'll have to talk to his wife once we finish our meal."

After an enjoyable and satisfying lunch, Phineas said goodbye to his friends and left the town square. He headed his horse down Market Street and took a left on Metcalf. The address in the ad was a small frame house, much to his surprise. He had expected something more imposing for a major downtown business owner.

He tied his horse to the rail and walked up the path to the door. The brass knocker was shaped like the head of a lion, a small icicle dripping from its nose as if the poor metal beast needed a handkerchief. Phineas grinned at it and rapped three times, knocking the icicle to the ground.

A humorless-looking woman of about forty years opened the door. Her brown hair was pulled back into a tight bun, except for a few strands hanging loose. She had a distinctive mole to the left of her mouth. Phineas thought she was attractive in a stern sort of way.

Yes?" she said.

"My name is Phineas Fletcher, ma'am, and I saw your ad looking for Mr. Banks. May I come in?" He spoke as warmly as he could out of compassion for her difficult situation.

"Have you seen him?" she asked.

"No, ma'am, but I may be able to help you find him. I'm an investigator."

She eyed him suspiciously but invited him in. "Please, sit down. Tell me what you have in mind."

Phineas took a seat and unbuttoned his coat. He groped in his pocket for one of his new business cards and handed it to her with as charming a smile as he could put on his face. "You may have read about me in the paper. Last month I solved a murder in Florissant. Last week I recovered a client's missing jewels and reunited her with a sister she hadn't seen in two years. I'd like to offer my services in finding your husband."

She took a moment to read Phineas' card. "What is your fee?"

"Four dollars a day plus expenses." He had just given himself a raise. "Hopefully, I will find Mr. Banks quickly, but there are no guarantees."

"I believe we might be able to work together." She took a chair herself and sat with her back ramrod straight. For a moment, she looked preoccupied with her thoughts. That wasn't surprising to Phineas, considering the anxiety she must be going through. He admired her control over her emotions but thought he detected a crack in her bravado. He wanted to reach out to her to express his sympathy but thought better of it. A woman as rigid as Mrs. Banks may not welcome bringing emotion to a business transaction.

"Ma'am, it wouldn't take a good detective to see that you're quite distressed. How long has your husband been missing?"

"It's been five days now. Let's see, he left for work early on Monday, and now it's Friday. Yes, five days. Nothing was out of the ordinary then, but that was the last time I saw him. One of his employees came to the house Monday morning to find out where he was. He said he never made it to work that day. It's like he disappeared off the face of the earth." She dabbed at her eyes.

Phineas took his notebook and pencil from his pocket and prepared to write. "Let me jot down the basics first. Then we'll talk more in detail. Where is his business located?"

"From the town square, you go two blocks east. It's a large warehouse on the south side of Market Street."

"I'm sorry to have to ask, ma'am. Is the business doing well, or is it in financial trouble?"

"As far as I know, there's no problem. I'm sure he would have mentioned it."

"What is his daily schedule? What time does he normally go to work?"

"He normally leaves the house early, maybe seven o'clock, so he gets there before the employees."

"I see. And how many employees work for him?"

Mrs. Banks absent-mindedly fingered her necklace as she spoke. "I believe he has twelve people on the payroll. Maybe more. I'm not sure."

"Do they get paid once a week?"

"Yes, he calculates the pay for the previous week on Monday. Then he goes to the bank and withdraws the correct amount of money, and the employees receive their wages in envelopes on Tuesday. They're already three days past their payday now. Some of them are threatening to quit. Who can blame them? But if they leave, the business won't be able to survive."

Phineas admired her emotional restraint as she calmly told him that her husband's livelihood was in immediate danger. "Then it's essential that we find him very quickly. Let me ask a few more questions. Tell me about the operations of the business. Who are the suppliers, and who are the customers?

"Mr. Banks doesn't share those details with me. I suggest you go to the warehouse and question the employees."

"I would think, madam, that in your husband's sudden absence, the employees will probably be reluctant to give out details of the business. Would you agree to go with me and permit them to share information?"

"I will if you think it would help."

"Could we go now?"

"Yes, of course. I'll get my wrap."

Shortly afterward, she returned from another room, wearing a brown wool cloak and a hat secured to her head with wispy black tulle tied under her chin. The thin tulle covered her hat and entire head, including her face.

The two seated themselves in the carriage and headed to Mr. Banks' warehouse. It took less than ten minutes.

"Do the employees know you?" Phineas asked.

"No, except the one who came to the house. I've never been inside the warehouse before."

"Hm. This may be more difficult than I thought."

He pulled his carriage up to the rail, tied the horse, and helped Mrs. Banks out of the carriage. They entered the door to find employees busy stocking shelves with new deliveries and other employees with papers in hand, pulling orders for customers. A small man wearing a gray work uniform occupied the desk at the right of the door. From there, he had a view of the whole operation. He had documents stacked on the desk and opened letters as they walked in.

Phineas cleared his throat, and the man glanced up, surprised that someone was there. "I'm sorry, sir; I didn't notice you come in. What can I do for you?" he asked.

Phineas laid one of his cards on the desk in front of the man. "I'm Phineas Fletcher, a private investigator. We want to speak to the person in charge about the whereabouts of Mr. Banks."

"I've taken over responsibility for running the warehouse in the owner's absence. My name is Leslie Peters." He hesitated, then stood and offered his hand. The men shook hands while Mrs. Banks stood with her gloved hands folded. "I'd offer you seats if I had chairs . . . Wait, I think I know where I can get some." He disappeared between two stacks of shelves and came back with two straight-back chairs. "Now, would you like to have a seat?"

Phineas and Mrs. Banks each took a chair.

"I'll get right to the point," Phineas said. "This is Mrs. Banks. She has hired me to find her husband."

Peters turned to her. "I'm sorry for this turn of events, Mrs. Banks. Whatever I can do to help. We want him back, too."

"When was the last time you saw Mr. Banks?" Phineas asked.

"A week ago. When he left here last Friday, that was the last we saw him."

"Did he seem upset about anything or unusually nervous? Maybe preoccupied?"

"No. Say, these are questions the sheriff already asked us. Maybe you could get the answers from him. We're overwhelmed trying to get orders out without Mr. Banks."

"Please, I'd rather get the answers first-hand from you. It's important. I might learn something the sheriff overlooked. What kind of products do you sell?"

Peters smiled. "It would be easier to tell you what we don't sell. You name it; if our customers want to buy it, we figure out a way to get it. You can look over at the shelves and see some of the products. We have household goods, toys, farm tools, medicines for doctors' offices, bolts of fabric, and other things we sell to the general store. Then we stock food and drink for the restaurants and taverns."

"It would be helpful if you would allow me to see your lists of suppliers and customers."

"I don't know if Mr. Banks would want us to release that information."

Mrs. Banks interrupted him. "Please, Mr. Peters. You seem like a conscientious employee. My husband and I appreciate that, but something in those lists may help Mr. Fletcher find Mr. Banks. The sooner we find him, the sooner you and the other employees get paid."

"Quite right, Mrs. Banks. Let me get those ledgers for you." He pulled some heavy books out of the drawers, all neatly hand-written with names and addresses of customers and suppliers. Peters also gave him folders of customer orders and invoices from suppliers. It was a wealth of information.

Phineas leafed through the pages. "Mrs. Banks, I should take you home, then I'll return and spend some time going through these documents."

"Don't be foolish, Mr. Fletcher. I can help. I'll look around the warehouse while you're studying the records. Two people can be twice as effective as one, don't you agree?"

A slow smile spread across Phineas' face. *This woman has more grit than most.* "Yes, I do agree. See if you can find anything that strikes you as odd. Question the employees if you like. In the meantime, I'll take these records to another desk and familiarize myself with the operations here."

Mr. Peters showed him to another desk while Mrs. Banks began to walk up and down the stacks of merchandise, introducing herself to the employees and engaging them in conversation. Phineas lost track of her as he concentrated on the books. He made notes on the names of major suppliers and customers. Almost all the customers were located in Lamar, Spencer's Mill, or the town of Wapeka to the south. The lone customer in Florissant was the general store.

Phineas walked back to Peters' desk. "Do you use a delivery service, or does one of the Banks employees make deliveries?"

"We have two delivery wagons and two employees that make the deliveries."

"What are their names?"

"There's Michael McKay and Michael Preston." He smiled. "We don't use their first names for obvious reasons."

"When could I question them?"

"I think McKay is in the warehouse right now, loading up for local delivery. You could catch him out on the dock. Preston is still out. He took a load to Florissant today, so he won't be back until late afternoon."

Phineas headed out to the dock to find McKay, who was busy hefting crates of merchandise onto his wagon. He was a young, muscular fellow with bushy red hair. "Mr. McKay, I'm here working on the disappearance of your employer. Can you answer a few questions?"

"Sure, but I don't know much."

"Maybe you know more than you realize. Tell me about your job here. What did you do Friday? What did you notice about Mr. Banks on Friday?"

McKay was happy to talk about everything he had done that day, the businesses he delivered to, what they had ordered, what route he took, and the conversation he had with Mr. Banks when he returned. Phineas wrote furiously to keep up.

"Was there anything odd about the day?"

"No, not that I can think of."

"What about Monday? Did you go through the same routine?"

McKay launched into his recollections about Monday. "The main thing is that Mr. Banks never came to work. That had never happened before. He's always the first one here."

"Did he normally come to work on horseback or in a carriage?"

"Horseback. Horse's name is Shelby. He always keeps the horse in the barn out behind the warehouse."

"Can you take me out there?"

"Give me a second. I have only two more crates to load."

After loading the cargo, McKay led him to the empty barn. Phineas walked around checking out the human and animal footprints in the earth softened by the recent snow, but there were too many over the past few days to mean anything to the case.

A few feet away, a dirty leather object caught his attention. It was filthy and stiff from being in the frozen mud. He picked it up.

"Say, that's Mr. Banks' cigarette case," said McKay. "We ought to give that to Mrs. Banks."

"We will, but I want to know why it's lying on the ground. Is Mr. Banks in the habit of dropping things?"

"I should say not. He's very particular, especially about that cigarette case. That was a Christmas gift from his employees. I'm surprised he would drop a thing like that."

Phineas nodded. "Good to know."

Back inside the warehouse, Phineas found Mrs. Banks inspecting merchandise on the shelf. "Did you get any information from the employees?"

"I did," she said. "Why don't we go back to the house, and I'll tell you what I learned as we go."

He helped Mrs. Banks back into the carriage, then hopped in and took the reins. They started with the clip-clop, clip-clop of the horse as background to their conversation. "What did you find out?" he asked.

"Most of the employees didn't know anything of value. The last they saw of my husband was Friday evening when he left the warehouse. Nothing seemed out of order to them. Then, I talked to his secretary. She said that Mr. Banks had dictated letters to some suppliers canceling orders. What does that mean, Mr. Fletcher?"

"Hm. It could mean nothing more than a change of mind about some specific orders. Or it could mean the business is in financial trouble, and he's bailing out."

"I hope that's not it. I don't know what we'd do," she said. She sat calmly as the horse trotted on. Phineas thought it impressive that the wife's reaction was so mild when he mentioned a possible financial disaster. She was very self-controlled.

He pulled the dirty cigarette case out of his pocket. "Look what I found by the barn."

She took it from him. "Why, this thing is filthy. I doubt you'll be able to clean it up enough for it to be useful to you." She tossed it down on the carriage seat as if she had never seen it before.

That, too, was a surprising reaction. He placed it behind him onto the floorboards, promising himself to inspect it more closely later.

They reached the house. "Thank you for your time today, Mrs. Banks. I'll be heading back to Spencer's Mill to get there before dark."

She nodded, climbed out of the carriage, and went into her house.

Phineas had a lot to think about on his way home. His mind raced over the information he had learned today. The most puzzling was Mrs. Banks' reaction to news of a possible financial disaster and her apparent failure to recognize her husband's prized cigarette case. Those were significant in his mind. Then he remembered that black veil she put over her face. That certainly fitted in with the pattern of

9

odd events. He would return to Lamar tomorrow; that was certain. He wished he could stay at the hotel overnight to save travel time, but Danny and Charlotte would worry if he didn't come home. He couldn't put them through that stress.

The horse headed back to Spencer's Mill over the rugged road. He arrived after dark.

"Welcome home, Pa," Charlotte said as she dished up his plate of food from the stove. "Where in the world have you been? We were worried."

"Sorry, dear. I picked up another case in Lamar today. I visited the Banks Wholesale warehouse along with Mrs. Banks. Mr. Banks disappeared a few days ago, and I've been hired to find him."

"Good luck with that."

"I'm going back to Lamar tomorrow to continue the investigation. So don't worry about me if I don't come home tomorrow night. I may be staying at the hotel."

"All right. Thanks for letting me know."

He finished his meal and then went to bed for a good night's sleep. He tossed and turned for a while, with images of the warehouse, the cigarette case, and Mrs. Banks flashing through his mind. Something wasn't right. He would figure it out tomorrow.

At first light, Phineas was out of bed and dressed earlier than anyone else, an unusual feat for him. He made oatmeal and coffee in the kitchen before anyone else was awake and left soon after.

The road was beginning to dry up, so the horse had an easier time this trip, but it was still slow going. According to his pocket watch, Phineas arrived at the town square in Lamar by 10:30 and went directly to the Banks warehouse. He entered through the front door and turned to the right, where he found Peters busy at his desk.

"Good morning once again, sir," said Peters. "Do you need more information?"

"Yes, I do, Peters. Can you direct me to Mr. Banks' secretary? I want to follow up with some questions Mrs. Banks asked her."

Peters scrunched his brow. "Sir, Mr. Banks never hired a secretary."

Phineas was taken aback. "Who takes his letters?"

It was Peters' turn to be confused. "Why, bless me, no one takes his letters. He writes out his letters by hand."

Phineas sat down heavily in the chair beside the desk. "I'm afraid there is something very wrong," he said. "The woman who was here with me yesterday — she must have lied about being Mrs. Banks. She must be involved in his disappearance." He remembered her saying that one of the employees had come to the house on Monday to check on him. "Peters, what employee went to the Banks house on Monday?"

"None, as far as I know. Everyone was in their place, doing their job. I don't think any of us know where he lives."

"Then the house where I met her might not have even been the Banks house." He sat stunned, trying to make sense of what was going on. Finally, he began writing in his notebook. He didn't want to forget the details from yesterday.

"May I see Mr. Preston?" he asked.

"He's out on the dock, loading his wagon. This is his day to deliver to Wapeka. You'll need to hurry to catch him. He's already running later than he likes."

Phineas rushed to the dock and found Preston, a tall, muscular fellow in a flat cap, striped shirt, and leather vest. He was loading the last of his crates.

"Mr. Preston," Phineas said, "may I delay you long enough to ask you a few questions? It's crucial. It's about Mr. Banks' disappearance."

Preston was eager to get on the road but paused in his business. "If it's to help find Mr. Banks, I'll make the time, sir."

"Thank you. Tell me, what is he like? Is he good to work for?"

"Yes, sir. All his employees think highly of him. Very good man to work for. He's always fair with us. We're working hard in his absence, so he'll find everything in order when he returns."

"Has there been a drop in orders going out?"

"No. Not yet, at least. You can see this load I have going to our customers in Wapeka. I go there once a week. The only problem is that if we don't get paid soon, my family won't have any way to buy food and pay the rent. It's going to get rough real quick. If the other employees or I have to get other jobs to feed our families...."

"That makes it most important that we find him immediately. Has there been anything odd or unusual lately? Anyone other than me nosing around for any reason?"

Preston grinned. "As a matter of fact, a strange man and woman were here last week talking to Mr. Banks. It was obvious he was angry when they left. I didn't think anything of it."

"What did they want, do you know?"

"He mentioned they wanted to buy the business from him, but he refused. Business is too good right now."

The light dawned in Phineas' head. "I think I know what's going on. It's possible—no, likely—that Mr. Banks has been kidnapped. The perpetrators probably plan to wait until the employees quit, then move in and take over the business."

"No, we can't let that happen," Preston said, with widened eyes. "What can we do to help?"

"First, describe the man and woman to me. Did you hear their names?"

"I don't remember any names, but I can remember faces. The man was about average height, older—about fifty years old, with graying hair that probably used to be sandy colored. He had a ruddy complexion. The lady was somewhere near forty years, taller than most women but shorter than the man. She had brown hair that she kept in a bun. And there was a mole on her face, on one cheek."

Phineas smiled, nodded his head, and wrote all that down. "That's a good description. Did you meet Mrs. Banks yesterday?"

"No. I believe she was here when I was in Florissant."

"Oh, yes, I'd forgotten. And one last question. Do you know if there is a record of employees' addresses somewhere here?"

"I wouldn't know about that. You could check with Peters."

"I will, Preston. You've been a big help. Thank you."

Phineas wound his way through the busy warehouse to Peters' desk.

"Does Mr. Banks keep a record of employees' addresses?"

"Sorry, sir, I'm unaware of any such record."

"Thank you, Peters."

Phineas thought it would be essential to find out where Banks lived. He remembered having good luck getting information from the courthouse in Florissant. So now he would try the courthouse in Lamar. He may have the same luck there.

The county courthouse was only two blocks away. Phineas climbed the steps and found the recorder's office.

"May I help you, sir?" asked the clerk, a bright young man probably not yet twenty.

"Yes, please. I need to find out if Marcolus Banks owns any property in town."

The clerk browsed through the alphabetical file and located a property. "Here it is, sir. Mr. Banks owns a property at 247 N. Pierce and a commercial property on Market Street."

Phineas made a note of that. "One more thing, do you have a way of knowing who owns the property at 321 Metcalf?"

"That will take a little longer to comb through the files. Can you come back in an hour? I should have the information then."

Reluctantly, Phineas turned and left the building. He decided to have lunch while he waited. The Tea Room was nearby, but he realized that the client who'd promised to cover his expenses probably wouldn't pay him, given that she was the most likely suspect. He'd better be more frugal. He went to the general store and bought some crackers and cheese.

Sitting in his carriage with his lunch, he considered dropping the search entirely. But, although his paying client had evaporated, so to speak, he didn't have the heart to let down the good folks at Banks Wholesale. Besides, he was naturally a nosy man—'curious' would be a kinder description—and he was eager to learn the truth of what happened.

There was still plenty of time, so he found the library and browsed the books. A fascinating volume on the history of Bledsoe County caught his attention. He took it to the librarian and asked if he could borrow it.

"Certainly, sir, if you'll have it back in two weeks." She wrote his name and address in a ledger beside the book's name. "Remember, there is a fine of one copper every day if you're late bringing it back." She gave him the impression of being one of those folks who loved rules and ensured that everyone else followed them, so he took her at her word. He was eager to read the book, but it would wait until after he found Mr. Banks and closed his case.

He headed back to the courthouse and met with the clerk again. "Did you find an answer to my question?

"Yes, sir," he said with a smile. "I cross-referenced the address with the legal description on the town map. It was easy after that. That house belongs to Mr. Clyde Warwick. Here, I wrote it down for you." He shoved a scrap of paper across the desk to Phineas. "It looks like Attorney Zedekiah Martin filed the deed."

"Clyde Warwick. Do you remember, by any chance, the date he bought the house?"

"No, but I can look it up quickly." He shuffled through the pages of the ledger and located the entry. "Look at this," he said. "He bought that house just last month. February 16, 1887."

"Interesting. Very interesting. One more thing, if you don't mind. Are there any other properties in the county owned by Mr. Warwick?"

The clerk resumed leafing through the book. "There's one other property. It doesn't even have a street address. The legal description is out east of town near the river's edge. Why, that's all uncut forest out there, and the ground is soft. There may or may not be a house on it. It may be vacant land."

"Can you show me its location on the map?"

The clerk took him to the wall where the map was hung and pointed at the property. "Right here," he said.

Phineas studied the map, and a plan formed in his mind. "I'm much obliged," he said and returned to his carriage.

His thoughts were beginning to gel. His first plan of action was to go back to the house on Metcalf Street and confront the woman who lived there. Then, he would insist on searching the house. Mr. Banks' captors may have him stashed. If not, he would have to travel to the property by the river and have a look there.

He slapped the reins, turned the horse toward Metcalf Street, and then came to his senses. What would he say when the woman opened the door? What if she wouldn't let him in to look around? That was a good possibility, and that would tip her off that he suspected her, destroying any chance of learning the truth. A better idea would be to cover himself by pretending he still thought she was Mrs. Banks. Then, he would ask if she had any new information.

It would be better yet if she weren't home. Then he would try to look through the windows to see if anyone was held captive in the house.

In just a few minutes, he reached his destination. He tied his horse to the rail, walked up the path, and knocked on the door with that brass lion's head. No answer. He knocked again. Still no answer. A young boy with a severe cowlick in his oily hair came from the house next door and walked along the side of the street, kicking a can ahead of him.

"She ain't home, mister," he said.

14

"Does she live alone here?"

"As far as I know, except for one fellow that visits a lot."

"Oh? Is he an old man or a young one?"

"Pretty old. He must be fifty."

"Do you remember the color of his hair?"

"It's gray now, but I think he used to be a redhead. He'd look better if he was still a redhead."

Phineas smiled and thanked the boy. The visitor matched the description of the man who offered to buy the warehouse from Mr. Banks.

The boy continued his zig-zag walk down the street with his hands in his coat pockets, whistling and kicking the can, so Phineas took a look around the house, peering in each window in turn. There was no sign of anyone else living there or being held captive. That meant one thing—a trip to the river property.

He pulled out his notebook for the exact location and the directions to get there. It might be slow going, with the ground being a little soft from the recent snow on the unpaved road. To make travel more uncomfortable, a stiff wind had come up. He took Market Street past the town square, past Banks Wholesale, and continued to the river. Then he found a wide trail that ran along the river, wide enough to accommodate a small carriage, so he turned left and followed it back into the woods. The treetops swayed in the wind and blocked the sun's rays.

There were fresh wagon wheel tracks on the muddy path. Someone had been there recently. He continued until the river took a bend, and there it was, a log cabin in a small clearing. It sat in the middle of a heavily wooded area of oaks, tall pines, and buckeye trees. Whoever put up that cabin didn't intend to do any entertaining. It was there to be concealed.

Phineas stopped Dancer short of the turnoff. He tied the horse loosely to a tree and took off into the woods on foot. He prayed he wouldn't be seen, but his best guess was that no one was around. He crept up to the cabin, ducking below the window just in case, then chanced a peek into the first window. It opened into a room that took up most of the floor space of the cabin. Inside the room, an old bench with a back rail, a couple of chairs, a pine table, and a bed were the only furnishings. The blackened fireplace was on the sidewall, surrounded by kitchen utensils. Phineas didn't see anyone, but there was a barred door in the wall opposite the fireplace. There must be another room.

He crept around to the side of the house. Then, slowly, carefully, he peered into the window of the second room. He gasped to see the man he was looking for, dirty and unkempt, lying on the floor with his hands bound in front of him. A plate of partially eaten beans was beside him, and his face was to the wall. Phineas' heart was thumping. What to do now? He needed to let poor Mr. Banks know that help was coming.

He tapped on the window three times and waited. Then he tapped again. He hoped the prisoner could hear him above the wind. Was the man on the floor dead or just sleeping? One more tap and the man rolled over with some effort to see who was at the window. Phineas held his finger up to his lips. The man smiled with the first ray of hope in days and nodded to acknowledge he understood.

Then the worst happened. The clip-clop of horses approached the front of the cabin, and the driver yelled, "Whoa!"

Phineas jumped at the sound. His hands shook as he tried to control his gasping breath. Luckily, he was in a concealed position at the side of the lodge, but his presence had to be known. There was no way someone had gotten this far without seeing his horse and carriage tied to a tree out by the path.

I have undoubtedly been discovered. And me without a weapon. He muttered a curse. Why hadn't he brought his revolver?

His only sensible option was to make a fast retreat into the trees behind the cabin. Whoever was on the property would surely be looking for him. He would have to conceal himself until nightfall and somehow find his way back to his carriage, feeling his way through the cold, dark woods without any lantern after the kidnappers gave up the chase. He didn't even know how many people were searching for him.

He hot-footed it to the tree line, crouching over, hoping to conceal himself in the woods before he was spotted. Unfortunately, he was at a severe disadvantage — his footprints were evident in the soft soil, and this was the time of year when the foliage hadn't yet returned to the trees. It would be dicey trying to hide behind bare tree trunks. His only hope was that he would have some protection from the underbrush.

Two voices reached his ears, that of a man and a woman. He couldn't tell what they were saying over the whooshing of the wind, but it was clear they were arguing. He assumed the woman was the same one who put the ad in the paper. The man would be her partner in crime, probably the man named Warwick who owned the property.

He ducked from tree to tree through the underbrush, trying to put distance between himself and his pursuers whenever he thought it was safe. The man and woman were outside, where he could now see them. Yes, that had to be the pretend Mrs. Banks. Very few women were that tall and thin.

They peered in every direction, trying to spot him. He didn't believe the woman would pursue him into the woods in her long dress and delicate shoes, but he was confident the man would be on his tail. He went deeper and deeper into the trees, even though that meant getting farther away from his rig.

The kidnapper entered the woods with his weapon drawn, advancing and pausing only to gaze in every direction for some sign of his prey. Phineas' heart was beating so loud he was sure it was echoing through the forest. He tripped over a tree root and nearly fell but caught himself in time to avoid landing on his hands and knees in the muck. He stopped dead still, fearing that the noise made by his stumbling had surely attracted Warwick's attention. Thankfully, the whooshing of the wind disguised it. His hands and knees shook as perspiration formed on his forehead despite the cold. Moisture leaked through his boots. He held his position, waiting. When he didn't hear anyone approaching, he righted himself and continued making his escape.

One advantage to the recent snow was that he could progress without crunching on leaves under his feet. They were all soggy. *Thank you, Lord, for wet leaves*, he prayed. *But please help me get out of here safely. I can't do this by myself.* He fought back panic.

At that moment, a feminine scream came from the front of the cabin. The man broke off the chase to find out what the problem was. Phineas circled, trying to get to his carriage, until he was in a position to see, from a distance, the pretend Mrs. Banks lying on the soggy ground, moaning. Her companion ran back to pick her up out of the mud. Maybe she twisted an ankle getting out of the carriage. Maybe her leg was broken. Phineas wouldn't have wished that on her, but God works in mysterious ways. He crept from one tree to another while the man was preoccupied, choosing the most prominent tree trunks to conceal himself. He tried to stay in the underbrush.

It occurred to him that they might take to their carriage and head back into town to get a doctor. He held his position, hiding behind a tree stump, for a few moments. Sure enough, the man lifted the woman back into their carriage, and they headed toward town. His relief was short-lived. When the couple passed Phineas' carriage, the kidnapper unhitched Dancer, yelled "Haw! Haw!" and slapped the horse on the rear. Dancer galloped down the path toward town.

Phineas was now stranded. He was shivering in the cold, and his feet were wet. He couldn't take refuge in the carriage, knowing the couple would surely be back after getting the leg treated. He had no choice but to walk back to town in the cold wind. He was in for a strenuous, miserable hike. He pictured Banks tied up in the cold cabin. He had to get to the sheriff as quickly as possible to save Banks from captivity. Now that the kidnappers knew they'd been found out, they may not need to keep him alive.

He approached his carriage, retrieving his quilt and library book. He tucked the reader inside his coat, not wanting to run afoul of that cross librarian, and then wrapped the quilt over his head and shoulders. Dreading the miserable walk, he started back to town as fast as his feet would take him. He needed to get out of the woods before the criminals returned and darkness fell.

Hunger and thirst gnawed at him. Thankfully, he found some melting icicles hanging from a tree limb and sucked on one to slake his thirst. He walked and walked. At one point, he realized what a blessing the library book was. It was large enough to cover a good part of his chest and keep the wind from penetrating his clothing.

He was almost back to Market Street when he spotted his horse grazing in the stubble. "Thank You," he said, lifting his face toward heaven. He whistled, and the horse turned toward him, chewing whatever was in her mouth, and loped in his direction. Phineas patted her neck appreciatively. "Good girl, Dancer. Good girl."

With some difficulty, Phineas used a tree stump to hoist himself up to the horse's bare back. He took off, turning away from Market Street at the first opportunity to avoid being seen by the returning criminals.

He checked his pocket watch. It was late afternoon and he was desperately tired. He yearned to get a hot meal at the Tea Room and check into the hotel, but he couldn't leave Mr. Banks tied up any longer in that cold cabin. His conscience wouldn't allow that. He rode directly to the sheriff's office.

When he finally walked in, Sheriff Beeler cursed under his breath and narrowed his eyes. "I'm about to go home to my family. Can't this wait until tomorrow?"

"Please, sir, this is an emergency," Phineas said. "There's a life at stake."

Beeler was skeptical. "We could do without the melodrama, sir. Just tell me the facts."

Phineas tried to ignore the insult and dove right in with the whole story, beginning with the ad in the paper looking for Mr. Banks, meeting with the woman who said she was Mrs. Banks, and finding her story full of lies. Then he reported interviewing the employees at the warehouse, gathering information at the courthouse, and finally finding the real Mr. Banks tied up in the cabin in the woods.

"I don't know how long they'll keep him bound," said Phineas. "He's already been their prisoner for five days. What do you think they'll do to him if he loses his usefulness?"

Beeler reluctantly strapped on his sidearm. "Are you armed?" he asked.

"No, sir, that was a foolish mistake."

Beeler handed Phineas a revolver. "I'm not going out there alone. You're my temporary deputy, sir. Be careful with the gun. It's loaded. Six rounds. Follow my lead."

"Yes, sir."

"And put these handcuffs in your pocket. Hopefully, we'll need them."

The two men headed on horseback down Market Street toward the path along the river and took the left turn. Phineas' adrenalin had given him fresh energy. They continued along the wooded trail until he spotted his carriage, still in the same spot. "Here's where we turn into the property," he said.

They rode into the clearing in front of the cabin and dismounted. Beeler motioned Phineas to go off to the side of the door while he rapped on it. When there was no answer, they tried to open the door and found it unlocked.

"That's crazy," said the sheriff, "leaving a prisoner bound in an unlocked building."

"No one said they were smart."

They crossed the main room, leaving muddy prints, boots thudding on the pine floor, and found the bar across the door to the second room. Phineas hefted the bar, and they entered to find poor Mr. Banks still on the floor, his eyes filled with fear. He had already endured more stress than he needed.

"Don't worry, Mr. Banks. I'm Sheriff Beeler, and this is Deputy Fletcher. We're here to rescue you." He untied Banks and helped him stumble to his feet, sobbing with relief. The poor man was quite weak, having been kept captive on the floor for five days with no exercise and little food.

"Thank you," he said hoarsely. "Thank you so much."

At that moment, the front door opened in the adjoining room. Someone entered, trying to creep in silently, but it was too late. Phineas and Banks glanced at each other in panic. The sheriff drew his weapon and waved the other two away from the door. Gathering his wits, Phineas drew his borrowed revolver. There was dead silence except for their guarded breathing and the careful tip-toeing of whoever was in the next room.

The footsteps came closer. A man's voice called out. "Banks, who's in there with you?"

The sheriff shook his head at Banks and held his finger to his lips. Banks took the cue and remained silent.

"Banks." the voice was more demanding, but still, Banks made no reply.

And a third time, sharply, "Banks! Answer me."

The kidnapper couldn't stand it any longer. He peered around the doorframe to see who was there and found the sheriff's gun barrel pointed right at his nose. The hammer clicked as the sheriff cocked his gun. The kidnapper held his hands up without dropping his weapon and slowly retreated from the doorframe, with the sheriff following him, step by step, into the next room. "Drop that gun right now! ... I need the cuffs, Deputy."

Phineas, still in the second room with Banks, fumbled for the handcuffs in his pocket and heard a scuffle. The sheriff had lost control of the situation. Phineas stayed in the room with Banks, wondering who was throwing the punches. The sounds coming from the other room were ominous. There was a shot fired, a metallic ping, and then silence. Phineas, in terror, realized the outcome of their predicament may be up to him and his gun now.

Relief came when the sheriff spoke. "Give me the handcuffs, Deputy." Phineas handed him the cuffs with trembling hands.

"Did anyone get shot?"

"No," said Beeler, cuffing the prisoner. "This fool tried to shoot me, but he missed and got the copper pot hanging on the wall."

Phineas took a deep breath and relaxed. "Where's your accomplice, Warwick?" he asked.

Warwick's head snapped around. "How do you know my name?"

"Good detective work. Where is she?"

"I left her with the doctor. She broke her leg."

"Phineas, let's take the prisoner to jail in your carriage. We'll have to transport Mr. Banks back to his home, too. Can we put both of them in the carriage?"

"We can tie Warwick to the back seat, and Banks can sit up on the front seat with me."

Banks intervened. "No, please, I would be very uncomfortable with that. Couldn't I ride horseback behind the sheriff?"

"That would work," said the sheriff. "First, we'll go to the jail and lock up Warwick. Then we can transfer Banks to the carriage, and you take him home, Fletcher, while I go to the doctor's office and arrest the false Mrs. Banks."

Warwick was caught off guard. "You're going to arrest Marcella?"

"Actually," said Phineas, "I'd like to know who she is. Is she Mrs. Warwick?"

"Yes, she's my wife. And she had nothing to do with this. This was all me." His lips twisted into a frown. "I planned to run Banks out of business, so I could buy the warehouse for pennies on the dollar and set myself up financially. Then I'd be set for life. He's ready to retire, anyway."

If Banks had been stronger, he would've jumped on him and given him a sound thrashing, but he was too weak. Phineas saw his hands form fists.

Phineas said, "Oh, she's quite involved. Maybe you don't know she put a missing person ad in the paper pretending to be Mrs. Banks. Maybe you didn't know she hired me to find him, then accompanied me to the warehouse under the guise of helping with the investigation."

"She what?" Warwick's eyes widened. "How stupid. Who gave her that idea?"

Beeler shoved him toward the carriage, bound his legs, and tied him securely to the back seat. Then the sheriff mounted his horse and reached down to help Banks climb up behind him. He pulled, but Banks didn't have the strength.

"Fletcher, can you give us a hand here?" asked the sheriff.

Phineas came behind Banks and gave a push while the sheriff pulled. Once, twice, three times, the struggle was great. Finally, they managed to get the weary man on the back of the horse.

"You'd better hold tight," the sheriff said. "We can't have you falling off ." And the procession headed for town.

After arriving at the jail, Beeler locked the prisoner securely in a cell. "I can't thank you enough, Fletcher. I guess here's where we part company. I'm off to arrest Mrs. Warwick."

He held out his hand, and Phineas laid the revolver in his outstretched palm. He was deeply grateful he hadn't had to use it.

"Good working with you, Sheriff. I hope I never have to do it again."

The sheriff laughed, slapped him on the back, and left. Phineas climbed into the carriage, then helped Banks climb in beside him. The man's legs were still wobbly.

Along the way, Banks had questions. "Did Mrs. Warwick really hire you to find me, knowing they had me prisoner in the woods all the time?"

"She certainly did. I couldn't figure out why she would do that until I realized she tried to make it look like your disappearance was your own doing. You had abandoned your employees and a loving wife who was looking for you. She was trying to throw up a red herring if there was ever a court case. I believe they planned to kill you and bury your body somewhere."

Banks shivered. "Thank God you found me in time. I don't even have a family. I live alone."

Phineas laughed and wagged his head. "Mrs. Warwick must not have known that. Once I realized she was one of the criminals, not your wife, I knew I wouldn't be getting paid for the job, but I couldn't quit. You have a great bunch of loyal employees, you know. They're still working hard without you, trying to keep the business in good shape so you won't have any worries when you get back. I couldn't let them down. They're working without pay this week."

Banks smacked his hand to his forehead. "Working without pay? I didn't think about that. I'll get them their pay first thing Monday. So, did someone take charge, or are they all doing their own thing without coordination?"

"Leslie Peters assumed leadership. He's doing a good job, from all appearances. The place is humming along as smoothly as a windmill in a storm. McKay and Preston are making their deliveries, your orders are still coming in, and shelves are being stocked. The paperwork, what I saw of it, is up to date. It's just that no one is getting paid — not your employees, and I assume, your suppliers, either."

Banks shook his head. "I am a blessed man. I need to reward my people, especially Peters. I didn't know he had it in him. As for you, how much did Mrs. Warwick agree to pay you?"

"She agreed to four dollars a day plus expenses, not that she'll ever pay it. I'll chalk it up to experience."

"No, I'll pay your expenses. You saved my life, man. You'll send me your itemized bill, won't you?"

"That's quite generous, sir. Yes, I'll send my bill. Say, would you like a nice, hot dinner at the Old English Tea Room before I take you home? My treat. You could probably use a good hearty meal."

Banks brightened. "Yes, sir, I would like that. Thank you. Normally I would never be seen in public looking so rough and smelling so...aromatic, but today I'm making an exception." He grinned. "You don't need to call me Mr. Banks. Call me Marc. All my friends do."

"You probably have a lot of friends."

"No, just one. You're it."

The two men arrived at the Tea Room as they were about to close for seating. When the young lady came to take their order, she gasped and stared at them open-mouthed. "Mr. Banks, is that you?"

"Yes, it is, and my appearance is a long story. I've just been rescued from a kidnapping." The girl's eyes grew as big as twenty-dollar gold pieces. She looked like she wanted to pump him for details, but he begged off. "I'm much too weary to go through it all right now. I just need some hot food and a warm, comfortable bed. I promise to give you details the next time I come in."

She took their orders and left them, but she rounded up all the other employees by the kitchen, chatting and pointing at Mr. Banks. He and Phineas grinned at each other. She brought their order, large bowls of hot Brunswick stew with crusty rolls and steaming coffee. Banks' color improved, and his strength began to return.

"So, Phineas, the sheriff said you were his deputy. You say you're a private investigator. What are you, really?" He put a spoonful of stew in his mouth.

Phineas blushed. "He only deputized me so he could let me use a weapon while we rescued you. My two-hour career as a deputy is over. And my career as an investigator has spanned only two months," he said with an embarrassed grin. "My first case started as a trespass and harassment problem, but I uncovered a murder committed in Florissant while investigating that. That got front-page headlines."

"Of course. I remember reading about that. So that was you?" Banks dunked his roll into his stew and took a bite.

Phineas picked up his coffee cup. "Yes. Then the second case involved the theft of some valuable jewels, right there in Spencer's Mill." He lifted the cup to his lips.

"You're not serious."

Phineas grinned. "I am quite serious. But that got only a second-page article."

Banks smiled. "I'll call on the newspaper editor tomorrow. You can bet this is going to get you some celebrity, too. Do you have a business card?"

"As a matter of fact, yes, I do. Fresh off the press." He reached into his pocket and passed a card across the table.

"You risked your life to save mine. I'm passing the word to everyone I know. Now, would you mind taking me home? I can't wait to crawl into my clean bed. And I'll accept your offer to pay for the meal since I have no money in my pockets. But, add it to the expenses you'll bill me for."

"Thank you, sir."

"One more thing. Will you be willing to testify in court when the Warwicks are tried?"

"You bet I will. Those rascals both need to be put away."

It had been a very long day for Phineas. He delivered Mr. Banks to his home, a lovely two-story in an upscale section of town, then retraced his route back to the town square. The hotel was on the same block as the restaurant. After that harrowing day, he wanted to settle in, maybe read his book for a while to help him relax, then get a good night's sleep.

Morning dawned brightly. Phineas slept somewhat later than usual in the hotel room, then rose, feeling energized. He checked out of the hotel and ordered a cup of coffee and a sweet roll in the Tea Room. That would hold him until he got home. He sipped the coffee leisurely at the table and thumbed through his library book.

At the dinner table that evening, Phineas regaled Danny and Charlotte with the colorful story of his adventures of the past two days. He loved being the center of attention.

When he came to the part about running for his life in the woods, crouching behind trees to hide from Warwick, and praying for God's help, he realized that the cry of distress from Mrs. Warwick was a diversion arranged by the Almighty to save his life. Tears of gratitude came to his eyes, even though he tried to be tough and not get emotional.

Charlotte rose and put her arm around her father's shoulder. "Pa, God is so good. Remember what it says in Lamentations, 'It is of the LORD's mercies that we are not consumed, because his compassions fail not. They are new every morning: great is thy faithfulness.'"

"Amen," said Phineas. He was acutely mindful that God's mercy saved him from an enemy with a revolver. It took him a few moments to get his emotions under control before he could continue with his story. Even though they had all finished eating, they lingered around the table, discussing the details of the adventure.

Later that evening, Phineas lay in his bed. He stretched out, folded his hands behind his head, and turned his face toward the window. The bright stars were scattered thickly throughout the heavens. The Milky Way was exceptionally bright in the cloudless sky. He chuckled as his mind went over the excellent ending to his investigation, even though it ended in arresting his own client.

He had certainly gotten plenty of exercise, running in a crouched position from tree to tree in the muddy woods, then walking a mile with cold, wet feet and riding his horse bareback. This new avocation of his was turning out to be absolutely wild . . . and he loved it.

THE RUNAWAYS

The living arrangements in Phineas' household hadn't seemed ideal to begin with, but for the most part, it was working out. His daughter Charlotte had been married only four months to Danny Reese. Instead of the newlyweds living with Phineas, as he'd requested, here they were, all of them, living in Danny's childhood home. Additionally, they had three of Danny's young siblings in their custody, William, Amos, and Lizbeth, who had come to stay until moving to their mother and stepfather's home at the end of the school year. Phineas pondered his plight and sighed heavily, reminding himself it wouldn't last forever.

His recent cases involved crime, missing property, and missing people. He didn't have anything going on at present, but one never knows when something might come along. He looked forward to what the day would bring.

This particular morning, Danny had left for work a little early to inventory the shipment of crates that had been delivered to the general store the day before. At breakfast, he had told the family that Mr. Link, the store owner, had been out sick all week with pneumonia, so Danny was now in charge. This was a big step. Phineas was proud that his son-in-law would be running the store alone for the first time.

Later in the morning, he went into the store to buy a newspaper and some razor blades. Activity in the store was humming as he watched Danny behind the counter laughing and joking with the customers. The cash register cha-chinged steadily. It was the kind of activity that sparked his energy.

"Ma'am," Phineas said to one of the customers, "let me help you carry your purchases out to your carriage."

She smiled at him and handed him her shopping baskets. "That's very kind of you."

After doing his good deed, he went back inside to do his

shopping.

The bell over the door tinkled, announcing the arrival of yet another customer. It was Danny's oldest sister Matilda Johnson, a harried mother of five children. She glanced toward Phineas and nodded to acknowledge his presence but went straight for her brother. She gave him a strained smile. "Hello, Danny."

"Matilda, is something wrong?" he asked as he wiped the counter.

The words came rushing out. "Danny, I'm desperate. Herbie forgot his lunch when the children left for class today, so I took it to the school. He wasn't there." Her eyes flooded with tears, and her hands shook. "He never went to school."

Danny went around the counter and put his arm around her shoulder. "I'm sure he's fine. How old is Herbie now?"

He's fourteen."

"Well, he's old enough to take care of himself, so chances are he's not in danger. He's just up to some mischief. He'll come home when he's hungry, and you can deal with his misbehavior then."

Matilda dabbed her nose with her handkerchief. "I'm sure you're right. You haven't seen him today, have you?"

"No, but I'll send him home if he comes here. Look, Matilda, you're probably expecting the worst, but I'm sure he's fine. He's a big boy, and he's always been a good son. I'm sure he'll have an explanation."

Matilda calmed somewhat. "Thank you, Danny. I'm going next door to the bakery and find out if they've seen him there."

Danny went back to his work. Phineas browsed the merchandise, working his way to the section where bags of flour and sugar, tins of food, boxes of crackers, and other supplies were kept. Something moved on the floor behind the pickle barrel. *It must be a mouse or squirrel,* he thought. Being a man who detested mice, he didn't linger there. He picked up a box of crackers and then went to the counter to pay for his purchases.

"Danny, there's a mouse or something behind the pickle barrel. You should check on it."

"Thanks for letting me know, Pop. I'll have to shoo that critter out." He took Phineas' payment, picked up a broom, and approached the barrel, only to find a red-haired boy crouched behind it.

"Herbie, is that you?" Danny asked. "What are you doing there?

27

Your Ma is worried sick."

Herbie got to his feet. "Uncle Danny, please. I have a serious problem. Could you loan me fifty cents? I promise to pay you back."

Danny stood with his hands on his hips, gazing at the boy. "That's a lot of money. What do you need fifty cents for? Have you done something illegal?"

"No, no, cross my heart. I haven't done nothing. I need the money for an emergency, that's all."

Phineas decided to butt in. "You need to go home, Herbie."

"I'd like to, sir, but Ma would want to know what's going on, and I promised not to tell. Please. It's an emergency. If I told you what it was, you'd want to help, but I can't tell."

Danny took a moment to say a silent prayer, asking for wisdom. Finally, he reached into his pocket and pulled out the coins. "I'm trusting you, Herb. Please don't disappoint me. Really, your Ma is worried sick. Go home as soon as you take care of this."

"I'll fix it as soon as I can. Thanks for the loan. Now, I'd like to use it to buy bread and cheese. And an apple."

Danny stood there for a moment, wondering, with his hands on his hips, brow furrowed, and lips pressed together. Then he gathered the requested items for Herbie and gave him the change for his payment. The boy shoved the coins into his pocket with dirty hands and left quickly. He turned to the left, scampering down the street with his bag in his hand.

Danny ran to the door to see where his nephew went, but Herbie had ducked down an alley out of sight. Puzzled, Danny strolled inside and leaned on the counter with both hands, shaking his head. "Was I a fool to loan that boy the money?" he asked Phineas.

"Only time will tell."

Danny couldn't get his encounter with Herbie off his mind. At six o'clock, he locked the store and rode to Matilda's house. She was in the kitchen cooking dinner. Her other children were milling about, but Herbie was still not home.

"Matilda, I may have made a big mistake today."

She wiped her hands on a kitchen towel. "What happened?"

"Pop and I found Herbie hiding in the general store," he said. "I told him you were worried about him, and he needed to go home. He said he had an emergency but couldn't tell me what was happening because he promised someone he wouldn't. He assured me he wasn't up to anything illegal. He wanted to borrow fifty cents, and I loaned it to him."

"You did what? How do you know what he was going to use it for? Maybe he was gambling with those older boys or something else foolish. He'll use that money to finance his misbehavior."

"Well, no, Matilda. He used it to buy bread, cheese, and fruit. Then he took off down the street."

She slowly tilted her head to one side and furrowed her brow. "If he was hungry, why didn't he just come home?"

"Just a guess, but he might be feeding someone else."

"I hope he comes home soon. It's going to be cold tonight." She chewed her lip and paced the kitchen.

"I hope he does, too. I'm heading home now so Charlotte doesn't worry. Why don't I ask my father-in-law to look into this? He's good at finding people."

"I'd thank you for doing that. Pray for my boy, will you, Danny?"

"Of course."

Charlotte prepared a fine supper, and the family sat down with Danny at the head of the table. They were all there, including the three children. Danny led the family in grace and, as a footnote, prayed for Herbie.

"What's going on with Herbie?" asked Charlotte. "He wasn't at school today. Not like him at all. I'm concerned that he might be sick."

"No, he's left home for some reason. He was in the general store asking to borrow money and refused to explain why he needed it. I don't know why I did it, but I loaned him the money. He used it to buy food."

"That's worrisome," said Charlotte. "He wasn't the only one who missed class. So did Lottie Mae Skinner. She's probably just sick, though. There's a lot of illness going around right now."

Phineas was enjoying his meal, but something twigged in his mind.

"The two absences might be connected," he said.

"That's unlikely, Pa," Charlotte said. "Why would a boy Herbie's age and a girl barely thirteen years old stay out of school together on the same day? What would they have in common?"

Phineas took a sideways glance at her and raised one eyebrow.

"And you call yourself a teacher?"

Charlotte blushed. "Please, Pa, not in front of the children."

The oldest of Danny's siblings, William, was fifteen years old and sweet on Lottie Mae. "I can't believe she would run off with Herbie, of all people," he said. "I think she's a lot smarter than he is."

"Let's not jump to conclusions. She probably didn't," said Danny. "As Charlotte said, she most likely has a cold." That soothed William's ruffled sensibilities.

"If Herbie is still missing tomorrow, I could look into this for you." Phineas was eager to try to solve a problem that would challenge him.

"Matilda would appreciate that," Danny said. "She already said so."

The following day Phineas stayed in bed later than the rest of the family. His morning solitude was the most enjoyable time of day to him, and he protected it with jealous zeal. But today, after slurping down his coffee, he was curious to find out if the missing boy had been found. He dressed in business attire, shaved, mounted his horse, and took off for the school where Charlotte was teaching.

Opening the schoolhouse door, he waited at the back of the class while Charlotte finished a reading lesson with some of her younger students. She spotted her father and said, "It looks like we have a new student, class."

The children turned their heads around to view the older man and giggled.

"This is my father," Charlotte said. "What do you need, Pa?"

"Just a word, please." He walked to her desk to talk to her quietly. "Did Herbie come to school today?"

"No, he's not here."

"What about Lottie Mae?"

"She's not here, either."

"Can you give me her address? I want to talk to her Ma."

"Pa, I don't think that's proper. She's probably just in bed with a cold or some such. I don't think her mother would appreciate a stranger asking after her daughter."

"If you won't give it to me, I'll get it somehow."

"Sorry, Papa. I can't do it."

"Then at least remind me of her last name. Appease me."

"All right, Pa. That's common knowledge. It's Skinner."

"Thanks." Phineas slipped out of the classroom quietly.

Phineas had a plan. He decided to visit his friend, Sheriff Lane of Spencer's Mill, who had worked with him before. He mounted Dancer and rode to the jail, where he found the sheriff tacking a new 'Wanted' poster on the wall.

Lane grinned when Phineas came in. "You're getting to be a regular here, Phineas."

"I guess I am. I need a bit of information. There's a family in town named Skinner. They have a daughter Lottie Mae who hasn't been in school for the past two days. My son-in-law has a nephew about the same age, and he's also missed school for the last two days. In fact, Herbie didn't even go home last night. I thought I would check with the Skinner family to see if Lottie Mae is home, sick in bed, or if those two youngsters are in cahoots. Can you give me an address for the Skinners?"

"The name Skinner is familiar to me for some reason. Let me see if I can find it." He flipped through his record of complaints. As he searched, he asked, "How old are these children?"

"Herbie is fourteen, and Lottie Mae is thirteen."

"Hm. Just the right age to be dangerous. Oh, here it is. This doesn't sound good. There was an incident at their house last month. Yes, now I remember going there. Mr. Skinner was found unconscious on the floor. I didn't arrest anyone because I wasn't sure who did it. It might have been either the wife or the daughter. They both claimed he passed out drunk, but there was a gash on his head. The address is 901 Hope Street."

"That's a new one on me," Phineas said. "Where's Hope Street?"

Lane scrounged around his desk and found a blank piece of paper. He sketched out a rough village map. "It's on the west edge of town. I think there are only two houses on the street out there." He traced his finger along the streets. "Lottie Mae has quite a long walk to school."

"Well, I'll go check on her. I want to be assured she's where she belongs. Then I could clear my mind and concentrate on finding Herbie."

"Good luck with that, Phineas. Keep me informed."

"Will do."

On the way to the Skinner house, Phineas considered different approaches he might take with Lottie Mae's mother. Should he tell her he was a truant officer checking on the school's absentees? Maybe he should say he's working on behalf of the school teacher. Or he could get to the point and ask if Lottie Mae was sick. He decided that the direct approach would be best. There would be no need to scramble for explanations if he were caught in a fib.

He found Hope Street at last. It was a short street, and just as the sheriff said, there were only two houses. Phineas knocked on the door with the number 901 painted on the letterbox.

A short, timid woman answered the door, opening it no more than she had to. "Who are you?" she asked.

"We noted that Lottie Mae has missed school two days this week, ma'am. Is she ill?"

The woman's eyes grew as big as twenty-dollar gold pieces, and her fingers gripped the edge of the door until her knuckles were white. "Yes, she is. . . ill. I hope she'll be well enough to be there tomorrow."

Phineas hesitated. Something was off, but he didn't know what else to do until he analyzed the situation. He asked, "May I tell Mrs. Reese what her ailment is? She's worried about her."

A male voice bellowed from the other room. "Who's at that door?"

Mrs. Skinner flinched. "It's only the truant officer, dear, asking about Lottie Mae. I told him she's sick."

She turned back to Phineas. "You should go now." The door began to close slowly but steadily until the only visible parts of Mrs. Skinner were her fingertips on the edge of the door and one eye.

"Thank you, ma'am." He tipped his hat and walked back through the fence gate to his waiting horse. He had the uncomfortable impression that he was under someone's stern gaze. He mounted up and started back to town, keeping his horse at a walk, giving himself time to think.

Maybe she's sick, but maybe not. Maybe she's home, or maybe her mother is lying. If she ran off, the parents didn't want me to know for some reason. Why would parents try to hide that their child is a runaway?

He pictured the terrified face of Mrs. Skinner in his mind. *The Skinners are hiding something.*

He thought that if he could find Herbie, he might also find Lottie

Mae, so he urged his horse to pick up the pace back to town and went to Matilda's house.

Phineas knocked on Matilda's door, hoping she would be home. When she opened the door, it was clear she was still worried. Her eyes were red-rimmed, and she twisted her apron in her hands.

"Mr. Fletcher, please come in. Do you have any news for me?" she asked.

"No, I'm sorry, Matilda. I need more information."

She motioned for him to sit on the Chesterfield and took the chair nearest him.

"Does Herbie have any friends he would confide in?"

"Sometimes he talks about that Jackson boy—I think his name is Walter. I'm not sure where he lives, but Herbie talks about him a lot."

Phineas jotted the name in his notebook. "Does he like to go anywhere and play? To the park, maybe, or somewhere else?"

"Sometimes he stays late at school and kicks a ball around with some of his schoolmates."

Phineas' eyes lit up. "That's good. I'll go over to the school when class is over. Maybe I'll find Walter there. I may be able to question some of the other boys, too."

"I hope you find him soon. It gets bitter cold at night, and I'm afraid he'll freeze if he doesn't starve."

Phineas' heart went out to her. "I promise, Matilda, I'll do everything I can."

She wiped her eyes with her apron and let Phineas out the front door.

He checked his pocket watch. It was nearly lunchtime, but he didn't want to go home yet. He decided to stop in at the bakery and satisfy his sweet tooth.

Phineas opened the door of the Crust & Crumb Bakery and walked in to the heady aromas of sourdough bread, chocolate cake, and sweet cinnamon desserts. The clerk recognized him. "Welcome, Mr. Fletcher. What can we do for you today?"

Phineas had a guilty grin on his face. "Let me have that apple pie there, will you, George?"

"Ah, yes. That will make a lovely dessert for your family." George wrapped it in a sheet of paper and tied it with a string. "Anything else?"

"No, thanks." Phineas paid for the pie and carried it outside. He stared at his horse, realizing that he hadn't thought things through very well. He needed to mount up in the saddle while balancing a warm pie without spilling it. He carefully put the dessert on the saddle and held it level with his right hand while he slid his left foot into the stirrup. With some difficulty, he managed to hike his right leg over the horse without sitting on the pie, then hoisted it up into one arm. He clucked at the horse and urged him toward home . . .very carefully.

He arrived at the house with the pie intact, much to his relief, and carried it into the kitchen. Counting out six household members, he cut the pie into seven pieces. He ate one of them slowly, savoring the warm sweetness, and washed it down with a glass of milk. He still had one piece for each member of the family for dinner. He patted his belly with a grin—a very satisfying lunch.

After a short nap, it was time to head to the school to talk to the young students. His primary purpose was to speak to the boy named Walter, but he would question as many of the children as he could. He pulled his horse in front of the school just as class was dismissed. Several boys had a ball and formed a kickball game in the side yard.

Charlotte came out of the school last and locked the door behind her. "Pa, what are you doing here?"

"I'm looking for Herbie. Can you point out which of the boys is Walter Jackson?"

"Sure. The tall, curly-haired boy over there in the brown jacket. That's Walter. Why do you want to talk to him?"

"He's a special friend of Herbie, according to his mother. Say, I'll be here for a while. If I'm not home in time for supper, go ahead without me. And save me a piece of that apple pie."

"I didn't make any."

"I know. . . Walter! Walter, could I speak to you for a minute?"

Charlotte shook her head and started the walk home.

Phineas approached the boy with wild curls. "Is your name Walter?"

"Yes, sir." The boy gazed at the man with questioning eyes.

"I'd like to find out if you know anything about Herbie. Do you know where he is?"

"No, sir."

Phineas couldn't read him. He didn't know if he was telling the truth. "Do you know if he's with Lottie Mae?"

The boy shifted from one foot to another with his eyes averted. "I'm not sure."

"Walter, those two are in a lot of danger. You know how cold it gets at night, and they don't have much food. They're probably hungry."

"I don't think they're hungry, sir."

"Why is that?"

"Well...yesterday Herbie met me on the way home from school and asked me to put some food by the big rock over by the stream. My Ma wasn't home when I got there, so I found some food and took it to the rock."

"I see. Do you know if he came and got it?"

"No, sir."

"Do you know anything about Lottie Mae? What's going on with her?"

"I don't know. She wasn't with Herbie when I talked to him. I didn't ask about her."

"Have you noticed whether she was nervous lately, or upset?"

"I don't know. I don't pay any attention to girls."

Phineas smiled. Give him a couple of years. "Thank you, Walter. Do you know if any of the other boys might know anything?"

"Well, you might talk to Joey. He's one of Herbie's friends." Walter called Joey over to join the conversation.

"Hi, Joey. I'm a friend of Herbie's mother, and she's worried because Herbie hasn't been home since yesterday morning. She's afraid he'll freeze at night without any place to go. She's afraid he'll go hungry, and he'll be lonely because he's running around all by himself for some reason."

"Oh, no, sir, he's not all by himself." Joey shifted his eyes away and gritted his teeth. Phineas' remark about Herbie's being alone had done its job.

"Who is he with, Joey?"

Joey scraped his toe over the ground a few times.

"It's important, Joey. Herbie and his friend are in danger."

"What kind of danger?"

"An angry man is looking for them." That was an assumption, but he would have risked a heavy wager on it.

"Don't I know it," Joey said.

Phineas pressed the question. "Who is he with?"

"He's with Lottie Mae. He's trying to take care of her."

Now he was getting somewhere.

"Don't her Ma and Pa take care of her?"

"I don't know. Herbie just said he needs to."

Phineas pressed his lips together and pondered the situation. Taking care of a girl was a big job for a fourteen-year-old boy.

"Do you know where they are, Joey?"

"No. He wouldn't tell me. I hope you find them before Lottie Mae's pa, mister."

"I do, too, son," Phineas said. "If one of you boys learns anything else, or if you see Herbie, would you tell your teacher, Mrs. Reese? She'll get the information to me."

"Yes, sir."

"Let me ask one more question. If one of you wanted to hide from your parents somewhere, where are some places you might go?"

The boys stared at each other and shrugged their shoulders. "Maybe the woods?"

"Hmm. I don't think that's where Herbie went. It's too cold. Give it some thought, will you, boys? If you think of some other hiding place where you could stay warm, figure out a way to tell me, all right? You can tell Mrs. Reese, and she'll tell me."

"Yes, sir."

Phineas was out of ideas. He decided to go home and retreat to his bedroom to think about everything he had learned. Sometimes something clicks in a body's mind when they sit and think.

The family gathered for supper and discussed the day's events that evening. Phineas was mindful of the three youngsters at the table. They were cousins of Herbie and friends of Lottie Mae, so he waited to talk about his search. As soon as the young folks left the table and went upstairs to their rooms, Phineas asked Danny and Charlotte to sit with him to discuss the Herbie problem.

"I visited Lottie Mae's parents today," he said. "It was an unpleasant experience, and I left still not knowing whether she was there. After school, I talked with Herbie's friends and learned that he was with Lottie Mae. He's making sure they have enough food. I just don't know where they are."

"I wonder why Lottie Mae has run away from her parents," Charlotte said.

"I'd love to find that out. I can tell you her Pa has a mean streak, and her Ma is afraid of him."

"Maybe he's too strict with her," Danny said. "Maybe she's trying to get out from under his thumb."

"Or fist. Just thinking out loud," Phineas said. "I don't have any evidence to back that up."

"I hope they have a warm place to stay," Charlotte said. "We need to pray for them."

It was a sad and shocking situation. Even if there was a good reason for them to be hiding, gossip could destroy both children's reputations after this was over. That could affect the rest of their lives in a village like Spencer's Mill.

In the morning, Phineas arose after a restless sleep. His brain had been working all night, trying to put the puzzle together, even though it was impossible when some pieces were missing. He needed to find those pieces.

The rest of the family had left for the day, so he was free to pursue his search. The first thing he wanted was a hot cup of coffee, so he put it on to brew. He decided to visit the spot where Walter left the food for Herbie. He was curious to find out if it had been picked up.

Phineas saddled his horse and headed to the stream. He was familiar with the big rock Walter spoke of. It was a favorite gathering place for children, not too far from Phineas' home. He found the wooded area beside the stream, and there was the rock. He searched around it, but Herbie--or squirrels—had picked up whatever food was there.

He reasoned that the boy was probably on foot, so he and Lottie Mae must be staying within walking distance of this spot. He had no other clues to pursue. He might as well take a circular ride, starting with the rock. He would circle a block away, then two blocks away, and so on, looking for a likely place for youngsters to hide.

He set off at a trot, passing cozy houses with smoke rising from chimneys, then heavily wooded areas. He rejected the wooded areas as likely hiding places. He wondered if the children were sheltering in a barn somewhere. Phineas considered what he would do if he were fourteen years old. He figured he would want to stay in a familiar place. Of course! They may be in the shed at Herbie's house. He went to the Johnson home and told Matilda he would check the hayshed.

The two of them walked out back and opened the door. "Look, Phineas, I believe Herbie's been here. Look at how the hay has been arranged as a place to sit, and look here. There's blood in the dirt." Matilda's tears flowed. "What could he be thinking? What kind of trouble is he in?"

Phineas placed an arm around her shoulder. "I don't know, Matilda, but I'll keep looking. He can't have gone far."

Matilda went back into her house, crying and wiping her eyes. Phineas went to look for a place that could provide more warmth than a drafty barn. He passed the park, a public area with a picnic table, but there were no hiding places — not a shed or even a cave. He kept going.

He eventually came to the business district, but that didn't seem promising. Two kids wouldn't be able to find overnight shelter in a store without being discovered. He went to the general store and walked inside to ask Danny if he had any new information about Herbie. Danny was busy with a customer, telling her that he and his wife were looking forward to moving to Illinois as soon as school was out. The customer loved chatting. She was a lady of ample girth, well into her senior years, and lonely.

"I see I have another customer, Mrs. Golding," Danny said. "Let me take your payment so I can help him."

She paid what she owed, then turned to take her heavy bag. "Mr. Reese," she said to Danny, "could you help me get my bag in the carriage? It's getting more difficult for me every time I go shopping."

Phineas stood nearby. His heart was moved to sympathy for her plight. He saw himself in her situation in a few years, so he intervened. "I'll be glad to help." He took her bag, and escorted her out the door."

Mrs. Golding tried to step up into her carriage but couldn't make it after three tries. She gasped for air. Her bosom heaved with the effort.

"You need to carry a little step stool when you travel, don't you?" asked Phineas.

"I tried that, but once I was in my carriage, I couldn't retrieve the stool from the ground."

Phineas' hand went over his chin as he thought. "I'll get a stool from the store and help you, but then I'll have to follow you home and help you down."

Her hand fluttered over her chest. "Oh, you are so kind. That would be a huge help."

Phineas rushed back into the store and asked Danny to borrow a stool. "I need to escort Mrs. Golding home, and then I'll bring the stool back."

Danny got the stool from the back room. He laughed as he handed it to Phineas. "Plan to be a while. Mrs. Golding can talk a lot longer than you can listen."

Phineas smiled and took the stool. Outside, he placed it next to the lady's carriage, helped her step up, and then put the stool in beside her. "I'll follow you there," he said, and the two of them went down the road toward Potter's Lane, one behind the other.

When they reached the house, the procedure with the stool was done in reverse. "Would you be kind enough to carry my bag inside?" she asked.

Phineas picked up the heavy bag and held his arm out to steady Mrs. Golding while she toddled into the house.

"Look at that house over there." She pointed to the home in the woods next to hers. "Something funny is going on over there. It's been empty for a couple of years now, and suddenly there's smoke coming out of the chimney. I don't see any horse or carriage about, just smoke. I went over and knocked on the door—I have a right to know who's living right next to me, don't you agree?—but they didn't answer. I knew somebody was in there, but they wouldn't answer the door. Funny goings-on, wouldn't you say?"

Phineas would, but he didn't take her seriously. They walked to her door, and Phineas deposited her bag on her kitchen counter.

"Wait, young man; I'll get you a cup of coffee." She opened a cupboard door and reached in. "Normally my son comes once a week, but he didn't come today."

"Thank you, ma'am, but I don't have time for coffee. I'm on an important errand and need to get back to it. First, I need to return the stool to the general store. Take care of yourself, Mrs. Golding. Goodbye." He walked out the door as he finished his sentence, hoping to cut off whatever she wanted to say next.

As he left, she raised her right hand and pointed at him, saying, "But...."

He rushed to his horse and pulled out of Mrs. Golding's yard to return the stool. As much as he sympathized with her plight, he needed to find Herbie.

It took a few minutes to reach the store, just enough time for him to come to his senses. That could be Herbie and Lottie Mae in that house next door. He urged the horse on that much faster. He dropped off the stool and told Danny he might have a lead on Herbie. He would fill him in later.

He was off to the sheriff's office as fast as he could, and luck was with him. Sheriff Lane was behind his desk, filling out a report to file.

"Phineas. You're back." Sheriff Lane stood up from his chair. "How are you getting on with your search?"

"I may have good news, but first I hope you'll keep this confidential for two reasons, which I will explain. The situation is this: I'm certain the two young people I told you about have run away from their homes together. The boy told one of his friends that he needed to take care of the girl. I believe the girl is being abused at home somehow, but I have no proof. I've done everything I can think to do, but I can't find them."

"Isn't that the girl that I thought attacked her Pa recently?"

"Yes, but I doubt if she did. If so, it was to protect herself or her mother."

"What are the reasons for the secrecy? You don't want me to mention this to anyone?"

"Quite right. Well, the boy comes from a family with a good name. They probably don't want other people to find out about this due to the delicate nature of the situation. Boy and girl together, hiding out unchaperoned, and so forth. You understand."

"Yes, I can understand that. You mentioned a second reason?"

"Frankly, I don't know what the girl's father will do to her or the boy when he finds them. The girl's mother is afraid of him. I'm not certain why. I can only guess. And Herbie hasn't put on enough muscle yet to be able to fight off an angry father."

"I see. It would be good to find them before the father does. Then we could assess the situation and decide what to do."

"Exactly, and I have a possible lead. I just helped an elderly lady take her groceries home. She lives on Potter's Lane. Do you know the street?"

"Yes, I do."

"She told me that the house next to hers, which has been vacant for a couple of years, now has smoke coming out the chimney, even though she hasn't seen anyone around, and no one answers the door." Phineas raised his eyebrows in an unspoken question.

"We'll check it right now," said Lane. "I'll follow you." Lane hung a sign on the door with the scribbled message: BE BACK SOON.

Phineas' adrenalin was pumping now. This was a promising lead. He recognized the timing of this information as a gift of providence, an answer to last night's prayer around the kitchen table. He and Lane both mounted their horses and headed to Potter's Lane.

They planned their strategy as they rode.

"At least one of them is probably there right now... maybe both," Phineas said. "So, how do we approach them?"

"First, we need to find out how many doors the cabin has. If there's a back door, you cover it while I knock on the front. There's a good chance they might try to run out the back when they figure out they've been discovered."

"No guns, right, Lane?"

"Right. There's no need to threaten youngsters with a revolver. But I have some rope hanging from my belt. We might need to restrain them. I'm prepared if we do."

They rode on, busily analyzing the situation in their own minds until they approached the cabin. They left their horses by the road and carefully crept toward the cabin on foot, trying to stay hidden behind trees and underbrush. They scouted the property and discovered a back door, so Phineas took his position behind the cabin while Sheriff Lane rapped on the front door.

There was no answer, so he rapped again. Suddenly the back door burst open, and Herbie shot out like a red-haired streak, right into the arms of Phineas Fletcher. Phineas held the boy while he thrashed about, trying to escape. "Lane! He's back here," he called, struggling to maintain his hold. The boy was almost too strong for him.

Lane came running around the side of the cabin with a rope at the ready and bound the boy's hands behind him. "Let's go back to the cabin," he said.

The boy was in tears. "Don't send her back, please, sir. You've got to protect her. Please don't send her back. I tried to take care of her."

Herbie stumbled into the cabin ahead of the sheriff and Phineas. The men's eyes took a few seconds to adjust to the dark interior. There was plenty of evidence the children were taking care of themselves—a pile of fresh firewood, hot coals in the fireplace, scraps of food on the table, and a basket of eggs on the floor, ready to be cooked. It was apparent the two weren't starving.

Phineas fastened his gaze on the girl. She sat with her elbow on

41

the table, her right hand covering the side of her face.

Lane addressed the girl. "Lottie Mae Skinner?"

"Yes," she said.

"Why are you holding your face like that?"

"I don't know. No reason."

"Move your hand, Lottie Mae," Herbie said. "They need to know what happened."

Lottie Mae's hand moved slowly to her lap. Phineas sucked in his breath. The right side of her face was battered and bruised. The area around her eye was purple and green, and her eye was swollen shut. Her left arm was in a makeshift bandage stained with dried blood.

Phineas' hand went to his mouth, and his stomach turned at what he saw. "Lane, look at this girl," he said. "What can we do about this?"

Lane sat in the other chair to speak to her at her eye level. "How did this happen?" His voice was gentle.

"I fell."

"No, she didn't," Herbie said. "Tell the truth, Lottie Mae, or they'll send you back home. Her Pa did that."

She leaned over the table and put her head on her arm, crying.

"Did your Pa do it?"

She said nothing.

Lane spoke gently but firmly. "What did you do to deserve punishment?"

That did it. Her head snapped up, and she stared at Lane with her one good eye. "I didn't deserve this. He gets mean when he drinks too much." Her voice was sharp. "He does this to Ma, too, but she don't do nothing about it. She says a Christian woman submits to her husband." She raised her volume. "If that's the way it is, I don't want to be a Christian woman." She began to sob. "He wasn't always this way. He used to be a good pa until he lost his job two months ago. Then he started to drink. Oh, this is awful." Her body shuddered with sobs, and her voice quivered. "The next morning, he says he's sorry and treats us nice all day, then it starts all over again after supper." She wiped her nose with the back of her hand.

"That's why we came here, to hide," Herbie said. "I couldn't let her go back home and get more of the same. I had to take care of her."

"That's admirable of you, Herbie, quite brave," said Phineas, "but I don't think you went about it the best way. Your family is sick with worry over you. And what do you think folks will say when they find out you and a girl have spent days and nights together without being chaperoned?"

"I'm sorry about all that, but this was a desperate situation. We didn't do nothing sinful. She's been sleeping in the bed, and I slept on the floor."

Phineas' heart went out to him. What a brave, honorable kid, even though his planning was flawed.

Herbie continued, "Would you please untie me, mister? I promise I won't run."

Sheriff Lane took the ropes off the boy's hands. "I trust you, son. Prove me right."

"Yes, sir. I want to stoke the fire. It's getting cold in here again."

"Fine, go ahead and do that."

Herbie stirred the coals with a stick, then picked up two small pieces of wood and laid them over the top. The burning wood snapped and popped, then came to life. A warming fire began to glow.

Lane turned to Phineas and lowered his voice. "Phineas, I need to figure out how to handle this situation. If the parents find out we know where Lottie Mae is, they'll demand her return. We can't arrest the father without proof. He would just say she fell. We'll have to be very careful. Here's what I think we should do." He laid out a plan. "I'd like to take her to the jail where she'll be safe overnight. I won't lock the cell. She'll be free to move about. We need to find a discreet woman willing to stay with her so she won't be alone."

"My daughter Charlotte is the school teacher, and she already knows these two ran away together. She's as discreet as they come. You can trust her. I'll get her to stay at the jail overnight."

"Good. So here's how we'll do this. You ride home and hitch up your carriage. I'll stay here to protect these two, should the father somehow find out where they are. Bring the carriage back here with Charlotte. We'll put Herbie and Lottie Mae in the back on the floor so they won't be seen moving out of here. We'll take Lottie Mae and Charlotte to the jail, and I'll stay to protect them. You take Herbie home. He needs to get a good meal and a good night's sleep. And tomorrow, he needs to go to school like normal."

"What will we do tomorrow, then?"

"You'll pick up Charlotte at the jail and take her to school so nothing will look unusual to the other children or the parents. Then come back to the jail. You and I will take Lottie Mae to a lawyer in

Lamar and show her injuries to him. He'll tell us what to do next."

"That sounds like a good plan. I'm on my way to get Charlotte. I'll be back soon."

On his short walk back to his horse, Mrs. Golding was on her front lawn and spotted Phineas. She waved at him to come over. "Woohoo, mister, over here," she shouted. He tried to avoid her by mounting his horse and riding past her. She hailed him again. "Did you find the squatters?"

He didn't slow his horse. As he passed, he said, "Yes, ma'am, and we got them." He hoped she wouldn't go over there to indulge her curiosity.

But she did.

The sheriff was still at the table with Lottie Mae, and Herbie had found a place to sit on the bed when there was rapping at the door. Lane drew his pistol and motioned the youngsters to get over in the corner behind the door. He opened it up and discovered Mrs. Golding.

"Sheriff, that man went past and told me you found squatters here. He said you got them."

"Yes, we did. I'm just now cleaning up the crime scene, so I can't allow you to come in. I wouldn't want you to disturb the evidence."

"Were they dangerous people, then?"

"Oh, yes, ma'am. We're taking them to jail. They won't bother you any longer. You run along now so I can continue with my work."

She leaned to the left to better peer into the cabin, but the sheriff blocked her view by shifting his position. She turned slowly. "Glad you caught them," she said and shuffled home on her cane.

An hour later, Phineas was back with Charlotte. She ran into the cabin and threw her arms around Lottie Mae. "Let me look at you," she said. "Lottie Mae, this is heartbreaking. I'm so sorry this happened."

"It's not so bad," the girl said.

"Yes, it is. Fathers should not be allowed to do this."

She turned to Herbie. "Herbie, I wish you had handled this differently, but thank you for taking care of Lottie Mae. You have a good heart."

The boy lowered his head, looking down at the floor. "I wish you'd call me Herbert now, Mrs. Reese."

Charlotte smiled. "Of course, Herbert. I think you deserve a man's name." Herbert grinned.

"It's getting dark outside," said the sheriff. "This is a good time to get these two out to the carriage so no one will see them. Herbert and Lottie Mae, I want you to wrap quilts around yourselves. Cover your heads to disguise who you are, and slip out to the carriage as fast as you can. Each of you, huddle down on the floor, covered up like baggage."

They both smiled, beginning to enjoy the adventure. They took the quilts they had been using, covered their heads, and ducked out to the carriage without being spotted.

They reached the jail in the dark of night, where the sheriff dismounted and helped Charlotte out of the carriage first, then Lottie Mae.

"Herbie...Herbert," said Lottie Mae, turning to her friend. "I can't thank you enough for saving me from my Pa. I'll always remember what you did for me." Her voice was thick with emotion, and her lower lip quivered as she gave him a shy hug, then turned to go into the jailhouse.

"Good luck, Lottie Mae," Herbert said, blushing. Then he clambered up onto the seat with Phineas, and the two drove off.

Phineas thought this would be an excellent time to give the boy some words of advice.

"Herbert," he said, "we need to talk about the best way for you to handle this at school. Some of the boys will ask about this, and you'll want to tell them. But you can't. You can't, Herbert, or you will ruin Lottie Mae's reputation along with your own."

"I wouldn't want to do that," he said.

"We need to stop as much gossip as possible, so here's what you need to do. After Lottie Mae heals and she comes back to school, you can't pay her special attention in front of the other boys. You can't sit by her in class. You have to pretend she's just another girl."

"That'll be hard since I know her so well now."

"I know that, Herbert, but this is important. Very important. Treat her just like any other girl. That's the only way to protect her. Remember, her reputation depends on what you do and say. I'll explain to Lottie Mae why you're going to seem distant to her so she won't be offended."

"I understand. But what do I say to the other boys when they ask about what happened?"

"Tell them everything worked out fine. You made sure she had enough to eat for a couple of days. And she went to Lamar for help, so you don't know what happened after that. There is no need to tell anyone you stayed together for two nights. No need at all. That would damage her reputation and yours, even though nothing bad happened."

"I understand."

"Now, when we get you home, I'll try to smooth this over with your Ma. She's been distraught. I hope you can understand that."

"Yes, sir. Can I tell her what happened?"

"Yes, that would be a good idea if none of your brothers and sisters overhear. They can't be allowed to know."

"Yes, sir."

Arriving at Herbert's house, they tied the horse to the rail and went inside. At the sight of her son, Matilda ran toward him with outstretched arms. "Herbie, Herbie, where have you been?" She was still angry but greatly relieved. Phineas stood by, choking back his emotion.

"I'd appreciate it if you'd call me Herbert, Ma," he said. "I'd like to tell you the whole story, but we need to do it in private."

Matilda stepped back and stared at her son as if Phineas had brought her someone else in the boy's skin. Slowly she transferred her gaze to Phineas. He could almost see question marks in her eyes.

He grinned. "He deserves to be called Herbert now, Matilda. He's done a lot of growing up in the last two days. He'll explain everything to you privately. I believe you'll be proud of him."

"I'm really sorry I made you worry, Ma," said Herbert. "That won't happen again."

Matilda was still speechless. She recovered enough to say, "Thank you for finding him, Mr. Fletcher. We're forever grateful."

Phineas gave her a nod. "You're welcome. I'll be off now so you can have a conversation with your son. And Herbert, if you need to talk to me about anything, tell Mrs. Reese, and she'll get the message to me."

"Yes, sir, and thank you."

Phineas walked out the door, wishing he could be a bug on the young man's cap tomorrow to listen to the conversations between him and his pals. Would Herbert keep his word and not say too much? Only time would tell.

Phineas left his bed much earlier than usual in the morning, eager to start the day. He didn't even bother with breakfast. He downed a left-over cup of coffee from last night's supper — yecch! — then took off in his carriage to get to the jail.

"'Morning, Sheriff," he said. "How did your guests do overnight?"

"I think they slept well."

Charlotte was all ready to go. "We did fine, didn't we, Lottie Mae?"

The girl smiled. Her demeanor was more relaxed than yesterday. "Yes, we did . . . Mr. Fletcher, will you be back after you drop off Mrs. Reese?"

"Sure will. You and the sheriff will need to be ready. I'll probably be back in twenty minutes or so."

Phineas dropped Charlotte off at school, reversed his route, and returned to the jail. Sheriff Lane and Lottie Mae were ready as promised.

Lane said, "Since there are a lot of children out on the streets on their way to school this morning, I told Lottie Mae to ride on the carriage floor covered up like cargo until we're out of town."

Lottie Mae put a quilt over her head and crawled onto the carriage floor behind the driver. Phineas and the sheriff took the driver's seat. Phineas slapped the reins, and they were on their way.

It was a long ride to Lamar, bouncing over the rough road. The wheels squeaked and rattled as the horses kept up their pace. Once they were out in the countryside, Lottie Mae was free to sit on the seat and enjoy the view.

Her bruises and swelling had improved slightly overnight, so the lawyer needed to see her quickly. They drove directly to the office of Christian Wolf, Attorney. Phineas recommended him because he was well acquainted with his legal talent — and he was Danny's new stepfather, having married Danny's widowed mother in December.

The sheriff and Phineas entered Wolf's office with the girl. The clerk greeted them and ushered them into the attorney's private consultation room.

"Mr. Fletcher," said Mr. Wolf. "How are you?" He stood to shake his hand.

"Fine, thank you, Mr. Wolf. I'd like you to meet Sheriff Lane from

47

Spencer's Mill, and this is Miss Lottie Mae Skinner."

Wolf shook hands with Lane, then focused his attention on the girl. One eyebrow arched at the sight of her colorful injuries.

"Please have a seat. What happened to you, young lady?"

Lottie Mae blushed.

Phineas spoke up. "Her Pa hit her."

Wolf held up his hand to interrupt. "I'd like to hear her tell it. Lottie Mae?"

"He's right. Pa did it. He lost his job a while back, and since then, he's been drinking every night. A lot. When he gets drunk, he hits Ma and me." Tears formed in her eyes. "He used to be good to us."

Sheriff Lane spoke. "We brought her to show you her injuries. We don't want her to get sent back home. This seems to be an ongoing problem."

Christian locked eyes with Phineas and sighed. "I see. This is a difficult situation. First, we'll need proof acceptable to the court that it's her Pa doing this, then we'll need a place for Lottie Mae, and maybe her mother, to stay until Mr. Skinner goes to trial. We'll need to file a restraining order to keep him away from his family. The judge will be going to his next post in just a few days. There's hardly enough time. Let me think. . ."

Lottie Mae teared up and began to cry. "I don't want nothing bad to happen to Pa. Please. He just needs a job. I just want him to be the way he was before." Having no handkerchief available, she wiped her nose on her sleeve.

The room went silent, except for Lottie Mae's whimpering.

"Lottie Mae, what kind of work does your Pa do?" Wolf asked.

"He's a carpenter."

"Why did he lose his job? Do you know?"

She sniffed. "He was working for a man named Mr. Hardin. Mr. Hardin bought some properties between Lamar and Spencer's Mill. He hired Papa to build a barn on one of them, and on the other, he needed an extra room built onto the house. Pa did some painting and roofing for him, too, I think. Whatever odd jobs he needed."

"Did he finish the work?"

"Yes, and Mr. Hardin don't have nothing else for him to do."

Wolf turned to the men. "There may be a different way to handle this. We may be able to avoid getting a restraining order if we can just put the man to work. We still need to find a temporary place to house

Lottie Mae for a few days while we work this out, preferably not in Spencer's Mill."

"I don't know anyone who lives in Lamar," said Lane.

"I don't either," said Phineas.

Wolf sighed. "We have an extra bedroom at our house. We could keep Lottie Mae there if my wife doesn't mind. I'm almost sure she would be happy to have her for a while. . . All right, here's what we'll do. First, we'll take Lottie Mae to the courthouse and try to see the judge today. He needs to see her injuries first-hand, just in case this has to come up for trial later. We'll hope it doesn't. Then, you two will deliver Lottie Mae to my house and explain the situation to my wife. If Susannah can't take her in for some reason, you'll bring her back here, and we'll figure out something else."

"Yes, sir. That sounds good," said Lane.

"While you're getting Lottie Mae situated, I'll be looking for Oliver Hardin."

Lane nodded his understanding.

Wolf told his clerk where he would be, and the three men escorted Lottie Mae to the carriage.

At the courthouse, Wolf told the other men to find seats in the lobby while he and the girl tried to see the judge.

Half an hour later, Wolf and Lottie Mae emerged smiling from the judge's chambers.

"It went well, did it?" asked the sheriff.

"Yes, it did. The judge made some notes on her injuries. It's too bad we don't have any way to keep a picture of her in the file, isn't it? Anyway, he approved our plan to find work for her Pa. The court is sending Mr. Skinner a summons to appear before the judge, who will tell him the consequences if he continues this behavior. He'll lay out a plan where Sheriff Lane will drop in on the Skinner home twice a week at first, at unannounced hours, to see if everything is going well. If not, Mr. Skinner will have to be jailed, but we hope that won't happen."

"What did he say about Lottie Mae and her Ma?"

"Lottie Mae will stay at my house until things settle at home. Her Ma may come and stay with her if she likes, or she can stay with Mr. Skinner. That will be up to her. Lottie Mae probably won't be at our house for more than a week or two."

"One more thing," he continued, "the judge also wants Lottie Mae to be seen by a doctor and the report put in her file, so please go by Dr.

Yarwood's and ask him to stop by my house at his earliest convenience. Time is important."

"We'll do that. We'll be on our way now, Mr. Wolf," said the sheriff. "Thank you for everything... Phineas, do you know where Mr. Wolf lives?"

"Yes. We passed it on the way here."

Phineas and Lane took Lottie Mae to the carriage and started to the Wolf house to follow their instructions. As the carriage rolled down the bumpy road, Phineas developed a queasy feeling in his stomach. It was mere months ago that he had tried to court Mrs. Wolf when she was still a widow. He rolled her name around in his mind: Susannah Reese. Beautiful Susannah Reese. She had rebuffed him, then married Wolf. He had let go of his feelings for her and had already met another charming lady — but memories of that experience made him feel foolish and resentful. This meeting may be awkward for him.

The horse clip-clopped along the road to the Wolf house. Phineas was unusually quiet.

"Is something bothering you, Phineas?" asked Lane.

"It's nothing. I was just thinking about Mrs. Wolf. My daughter married her son, you know."

"Really?"

"Yes. And the Wolfs just married three months ago."

The sheriff turned his head to stare at Phineas. "You don't say. I didn't know you were that familiar with the Wolfs."

Phineas nodded and turned away from Lane, pretending to view the passing scenery. He had said enough about it.

Reaching the Wolf home, Phineas turned the carriage up the long driveway. Mature trees lined each side of the drive. They were bare of leaves now, but they would be a breathtaking sight once they filled out next month. The three passengers disembarked, walked up the wide steps, and knocked on the double doors. Sometimes the housekeeper would answer a knock, but it was Mrs. Wolf herself this time. Her eyes widened, and her mouth dropped open.

"Mr. Fletcher," she said, "I am certainly surprised to see you. And Sheriff Lane. "

"Hello, Susannah. I'm rather surprised to be here," he said. "Your husband sent us. This this young lady is Lottie Mae Skinner."

Mrs. Wolf stared at Lottie Mae. "What happened to you, Lottie

Mae? Oh, forgive my manners. Please come in."

The trio trooped into the house and found themselves welcomed. Susannah asked, "Could I get you a cup of tea while you tell me the story? I know it's been a cold ride from Lamar."

Susannah asked the housekeeper to bring tea, and Sheriff Lane launched into the story, telling her how the girl was abused by a drunken father and rescued by a boy named Herbert Johnson.

Susannah's mouth flew open. "Herbie Johnson? My grandson?"

It was Lottie Mae's turn to be astonished. She leaned forward with widened eyes. "You're Herbert's grandmother?"

"Yes, and now I remember who you are. My children — William, Amos, and Lizbeth Reese — went to your birthday party a few months ago."

Phineas' heart warmed to see Lottie's shoulders relax for the first time since he laid eyes on her. She clearly felt much safer now that she knew the connections between them.

"Well, let me explain why Mr. Wolf sent us here," said the sheriff, and told her that Lottie Mae needed a place of refuge while her father was being helped. "Mr. Wolf will try to find work to help him get his life back on the right path. Lottie Mae said he was a good father until he lost his job."

"Being out of work causes emotional and financial problems for a man. Yes, our family has experience with that," said Susannah.

Once she understood the situation, she was pleased to have Lottie Mae stay for a while. "We have a bedroom for you upstairs," she said. "When the gentlemen leave, I'll show you where you can sleep. And we may have to go into Lamar and get you another dress. That one could use laundering."

The sheriff stood. "We need to be going now, ma'am. Thank you for sheltering Lottie Mae. Your husband asked us to send the doctor to your house to check the girl over and make a record for the court file, so we'll head over to his office now. I don't know exactly when he'll be here."

"Well, thank you for bringing her. We won't go anywhere until the doctor comes. Maybe after she gets some rest, she and I will go into the kitchen and make cookies together."

Lottie Mae's eyes sparkled, and a broad smile crossed her face at the idea of making cookies with Herbert's grandmother.

The men left the house and headed back toward Spencer's Mill.

Several days later, Mr. Skinner arrived at the courthouse for his hearing. He was newly employed and sincerely apologetic. He took his seat, stared at the floor, and wiped his face with the back of his hand. Phineas sat in the courtroom, curious to learn the outcome.

The judge gazed at the wayward family man and told him to stand. "I'm not going to fine you, Mr. Skinner, since lack of income has played a major part in your problem. However, I will put you on probation to ensure you don't injure your wife or daughter again. Here's what will happen. At least twice a week for the next four weeks, Sheriff Lane will drop in at your house unannounced to see that everything is in order. If he finds you've been abusing either of the women, you will be arrested and imprisoned. Do you understand?"

"Yes, sir."

"At the end of the four weeks, you and Sheriff Lane will appear here together, and I will get a report on how you're doing. At that time, we'll figure out what happens next."

"When can I have my daughter back?" he asked.

"Mr. Fletcher has agreed to pick her up today and return her to you. You make very sure she is treated properly."

"I will, sir."

"Good luck, Mr. Skinner. Dismissed." The judge rose from his chair, and it was all over.

Phineas slipped out of the courtroom to pick up Lottie Mae at Susannah's house.

As Mr. Wolf predicted, Susannah and Lottie Mae had grown fond of each other. Susannah had taken her into Lamar to her favorite thrift shop and bought her two lovely dresses to add to her wardrobe, so Lottie Mae was leaving there well-outfitted. It was a sad parting for both of them.

Susannah reached toward Lottie Mae and hugged her like one of her own. "Lottie Mae, promise me you'll stay in touch."

"I will, Mrs. Wolf. Thank you for letting me stay with you and for everything you did for me."

"I'll pray for you. And Herbert will bring me news about you. I hope you get to visit me once in a while."

Phineas helped Lottie Mae into the carriage. She waved as the horse pulled them down the long drive. "'Bye, Mrs. Wolf," she shouted as they turned onto the road.

On Friday after school, Herbert went to Danny's house while the family ate supper. Charlotte answered the door.

"Come on into the kitchen, Herbert. Would you like to join us? We have plenty of stew."

"No, ma'am. I'm not hungry. I'd like to talk to Uncle Danny."

She led him into the kitchen and asked him to have a seat.

"Hello, Mr. Fletcher. Hi, William, Amos…Lizbeth."

"What can we do for you, Herbert?" Danny asked.

"I need to talk to you about the fifty cents. I'm sorry, Uncle Danny. I'm still trying to figure out where I can get fifty cents to pay you back. Can I have a little longer?"

Danny smiled. "How about working it off, Herbert? I need someone to sweep the store."

The boy's eyes lit up. "Can I start tomorrow?"

"Yes, sir, you can," said Danny. "You show up first thing in the morning, and I'll give you an apron and a broom."

Herbert beamed while his cousins stared at him with new respect.

Phineas grinned at the expressions on the faces around the table. He remembered William saying that Herbie wasn't as bright as Lottie Mae. That may be true, or it may not be. In any case, Herbert had dignity, integrity, and a heart of gold. That's often worth more in life than being smarter than someone else.

THE SINGING BLACKMAILER

The morning sun spread golden rays over the earth, warming the little Ohio village on the Lord's Day. Buggies filled the streets and headed for worship services.

That morning in late March, Phineas climbed into the carriage with Charlotte, Danny, and Danny's three younger siblings. They rolled down the bumpy road to the church, laughing and chatting. The weather had taken a sudden warm snap on the cusp of spring. Precisely according to schedule, maples and oaks were beginning to leaf out. The world was glorious.

After the service, as the family climbed back into the carriage, one of the men of the church approached and asked to speak privately with Phineas. It was Cyrus Blackburn, a man he knew only by name. Mr. Blackburn was a distinguished-looking man with a Roman nose, thirty-five years old, and neatly dressed. He wore a worried look on his face.

"Mr. Fletcher, may I have a word?"

"Certainly, friend," said Phineas.

"This is confidential," said Blackburn. "I wonder if I might meet with you privately this afternoon. I was told you were experienced at solving problems."

"You could come by the house. It's a beautiful day. We would have privacy on the front porch, away from the family's ears."

"Thank you. Shall I be there around two o'clock?"

"That's fine. I'll see you then."

Mr. Blackburn arrived at the appointed hour. Phineas spotted his approach through the window.

"Charlotte, our guest is here. Would you brew a pot of tea?"

"Sure, Pa." Charlotte busied herself in the kitchen.

Phineas stepped onto the porch to greet Blackburn. "Welcome! It's a beautiful day. Let's talk in these rocking chairs on the porch."

Blackburn took a seat. "Thanks for seeing me."

"Now, what did you want to talk about?"

"It's rather embarrassing." He sat with his head down, wringing his hands, unable to continue speaking.

"It's just between the two of us," said Phineas. "Whatever you say here is confidential."

Blackburn fidgeted in his seat and wrung his hands for another minute while his host waited patiently.

To break the silence, Phineas offered his sympathy. "This must be a serious problem."

Blackburn gathered his courage. "Here's the situation. I want to open a wheelwright and carpentry shop here in Spencer's Mill. The closest one is in Lamar, fifteen miles away, but folks around here need someone closer they can go to."

"You're right. That would be a good service here in town."

"Here's the problem. There's a woman who accused me of making improper advances. But I didn't do it. She knows it, and I know it, but she says if I don't give her fifty dollars by Thursday, she will make a complaint against me with the sheriff. I'd give her fifty dollars to get rid of her if I had it, but I don't have it. I need every penny I have to get the business going. But if she brings charges publicly, no one will want to do business with me anyway. Worse, my wife might believe it. I've never been in deeper trouble in my life, Fletcher. What am I going to do?"

Phineas' heart went out to him if his story was accurate. His investigation would reveal the truth, one way or the other, but in the meantime, it would be good business to sympathize with him until he learned more. "I can't imagine a more devastating trick to play on a man than to make false accusations. What would you like me to do?"

"I want to hire you to set some trap for this woman. Can you figure out a way to prove she's lying and expose her for what she is?"

"I'll see what I can do," said Phineas. "Let me go in the house for my notebook and pencil, and we'll talk over the details."

He ducked into the house and came back outside with his notebook and favorite pencil, the new one with the eraser attached. Charlotte followed him out with the tea and put two cups on the table between them before returning to the kitchen.

"Let's start with the basics," said Phineas. "What is this woman's name?"

"Her name is Comfort Gillespie. I met her at a pub in Florissant. You see, I was there on a sales trip for my former employer. I confess I was at the pub having more drinks than I should have, and she sat beside me at the bar. I bought her some drinks, we talked, and then I left. I swear nothing happened."

"Hm. I'm familiar with Florissant, and the sheriff is a friend of mine. What was the name of this pub?"

"I believe it was just called The Taproom." Blackburn took a sip of his tea.

"Was she a customer, or was she working there?"

"It was a Saturday night, and she was singing there. I don't think they have singers during the week, but on Saturdays, they have special entertainment."

"So she might have worked other pubs, too. Can you describe this woman to me?" His pencil was poised to begin writing.

"She's about average height, a little skinny, red hair. It was the red hair that caught my attention at first. I was pretty stupid, wasn't I?"

"Well, I don't know about that. It sounds like you were suckered. Where is Miss Gillespie right now?" Phineas tried to put his teacup down without looking at the table and spilled a few drops. He muttered an oath and blotted it up with his handkerchief.

"I think she's staying at the hotel in Lamar. Who knows? She might be working somewhere in one of the taverns over there."

"She might be. Let's get to the specifics of the threat. Exactly what did she say?"

"She said if I don't pay her fifty dollars by this Thursday night, she will go to the sheriff on Friday and file charges against me for personally assaulting me."

"Did she mention any particular type of personal assault? That could mean different things."

"I took it to mean she'll accuse me of fondling her in some way or making improper suggestions." Blackburn almost choked on his words.

"But she could have meant something else, couldn't she? What day did this supposed assault occur?"

"It was last month. I remember it was the 12th of February, the same day I met with my employer's customer."

"What kind of products were you selling?"

Blackburn's face reddened. "Ladies' unmentionables. Bloomers and corsets and such. Now you know why I quit my job to start another business myself."

Phineas' face broke into a broad grin, then he leaned back and chuckled. "I'm sorry, Blackburn. I didn't mean to be rude, but . . ."

Blackburn had a sheepish grin on his face. "I guess it is funny."

Phineas wagged his head slowly. "All right, back to business. Did Miss Comfort mention anywhere else that she had worked?"

"I don't think so."

"Does she have a family? A husband? Children?"

"That never came up."

"We have four days before her deadline. If you agree to my fee of three dollars per day plus expenses, I think my first move should be going to The Taproom in Florissant to learn more about this woman. I'll stop in Lamar first, in case she's there."

"That's good. You do whatever you think is necessary. I just want her out of my life."

The men shook hands, and Blackburn went to his own home. Truth be told, Phineas was excited to go to Florissant again. He had a friend there—Adelaide Courtney, and he was eager to see her. That would be a bonus.

He went inside to talk with Charlotte and tell her he was on another case. "I'll be leaving early in the morning for Florissant. I might not be home for two or three days."

"Be careful, Pa," said Charlotte. "I'm proud of you, but be careful. You're not a young man anymore."

Phineas packed a valise and included his revolver and ammunition. He learned that lesson while being chased through the woods unarmed in the Banks case.

Florissant was a full day's ride away, so he was ready to leave by seven o'clock in the morning. The air was crisp, and the sun was bright. He hoped to have dinner at The Taproom that evening. With a bit of luck, Adelaide would accompany him.

As the horse trotted ahead of him, he mulled over the details of the case, but he also spent some time thinking about Adelaide. She was the widowed owner of Mrs. Courtney's Rooming House in Florissant, a bed and breakfast establishment where he had stayed before. She was a lovely lady whose company he very much enjoyed.

It was a long drive, taking Phineas east through Lamar. A quick stop at the hotel confirmed that Comfort Gillespie was not registered. Phineas continued northeast for several hours, occasionally stopping to rest the horse and have a snack from the stash in his pockets. The route took him through miles of pleasant farmland. Farmers were in the fields, turning the soil behind teams of draft horses, mending their fences, and doing other chores they had been prevented from doing during the harsh winter months. It was as if the world had come out of hibernation.

Occasionally, Phineas passed another carriage traveling in the opposite direction and greeted the passengers with the tip of his hat.

Finally, at about five o'clock in the evening, he approached Florissant and went directly to Mrs. Courtney's Rooming House. He had been a guest there very recently. When he took his bag inside the lobby, no one was at check-in. He tapped on the bell, and a sharp, silvery "ding" filled the air. Adelaide came from the back room. When she recognized Phineas, her eyes lit up, and she hurried around the front desk to grasp his hand. "Phineas, you're here again. Welcome back, my friend."

He grinned, overjoyed to see her. "I came to stay for a couple of nights, Adelaide. I'm on another case."

"You're just in time. I have one room left."

"Am I in time to take you to dinner?"

She giggled. "I can be ready by six. Do you want to go to the pub again?"

"Actually, I want to go to The Taproom tonight."

Adelaide's left eyebrow arched, and she took a step backward. "The Taproom? Are you serious?"

"Quite. I'm on another case. Are you up for an adventure?"

"At The Taproom? Well…"

Phineas was a little alarmed at her reaction. "Let me ask you this, since I've never been there before. Is it safe for a lady?"

"I've never been there before, either. I've only heard rumors. Things happen there."

Phineas' stomach took a turn. "I'm obligated to go there to work my case. Maybe I should go alone."

Adelaide rallied. "Not on your life. I'm going with you. I'll be ready at six." She turned and started back to her quarters to dress for the occasion. As she disappeared into her private parlor, Phineas called after her.

"Adelaide, which room is mine?"

"Oh. Take the key to room 5. I always rent that room last, hoping you'll come." And she kept walking.

Phineas chuckled. He walked behind the desk, lifted the appropriate key off the hook, and took his bag upstairs.

At six o'clock, he was refreshed and downstairs in the lobby. Adelaide wore a colorful outfit with a string of cheap beads rather than her typical tasteful dress. "Phineas, you take off that bowler and vest. They make you look like a lawyer. You don't want to show up at The Taproom dressed like that. You'll get laughed out."

"What kind of place is it? Have I taken on more than I can handle?"

"I doubt it. You caught a murderer last month, didn't you? Here, give me that hat and vest, and I'll put them behind the desk until we get back." She handed him one of her late husband's flat caps, and he slapped it on his head.

"How do I look now?"

"Perfect." She grinned, took his arm, and went out to the carriage.

Phineas guided the horse in whichever direction Adelaide told him to go. Along the way, he filled her in on the details of his case. "Did you ever hear of a red-haired singer named Comfort Gillespie?"

Adelaide's lips parted and broke into a crooked grin. "That's not her real name, is it?"

"I don't know. Maybe not, but it's the only name I know her by."

They soon arrived at The Taproom. The parking area was jammed with horses, but they found enough room on the side road for the carriage and tied the horse to the rail.

"Take a deep breath, my dear. Here we go," he said, and together they crossed the threshold of the rowdy establishment. They found a table away from the bar where a dozen men and women of a certain type—the type favoring bright red lips and ostrich feathers—were drinking the evening away, laughing raucously, and telling bawdy jokes. There was so much noise that they could barely hear each other speak.

Phineas cringed. "I'm sorry to bring you here," he said into her ear. "Let's order something to drink. I'll ask the questions I need to ask, and then we'll go to that other pub where we know we can get a good dinner in a more suitable atmosphere."

She put on a brave smile and nodded, trying to ignore the conversation around her that was shockingly inappropriate. A young woman dressed in red silk and lace, showing an abundance of bosom and leg, came to take their order. She flirted shamelessly with Phineas. "What can I get for you, honey?" She gave him a wink.

Phineas said, "We just want to start with a pint, miss."

"You got it, sweetie." She turned to get the ale, but Phineas stopped her with a question.

"Wait a minute, please. You had a singer here named Comfort Gillespie. Is she going to be here again this week?"

"I'll find out for you." Miss Red Silk went to the bar to get the ale. In a moment, she was back again.

"The boss says Comfort ain't coming back." She set the mugs of ale down a bit too hard, spilling a few drops. "Sorry," she said, wiping most of the spilled ale off the table with the side of her hand. "Do you know her?"

"She was recommended to us as a good singer," lied Phineas. "We were hoping to hear her."

"She was a good egg," said Red Silk, "but she had a bad patch. Her rotten husband stole her little girl and said she'd never see her again unless she paid him fifty dollars by Monday. Now I ask you, where will a girl get that kind of money? That man ought to be swung from a tree."

Adelaide's eyebrows raised. "Phineas, that girl needs help. What can we do for her?"

With this new information, Phineas realized that if he could solve her problem, he would also solve Blackburn's. "We have to find her before we can help her. Miss, do you know her husband's name?"

"Something Gillespie is all I know. Wait, I think she might have called him Sam. Yes, I believe that was it. Sam."

Phineas scratched the name in his notebook. "Would you know where he lives?"

"No. I think he lives in town, but I couldn't tell you where."

"Thank you. I'd like to pay for our ale now. We need to go."

"You ain't even drunk it yet."

"I know, but if you get my bill quickly, I'll add a nice tip."

Miss Red Silk scurried off to get the bill and brought it back.

Phineas paid her and pocketed the receipt. He and Adelaide left their ale on the table. As they exited, Phineas glanced behind him. Red Silk was serving their ale to other customers. He shook his head. *Waste not, want not,* he thought.

Adelaide was doubled over with laughter by the time they reached the carriage. "I've never been in such a disgraceful place. I swear, Phineas, I have more adventure with you than I ever had with anyone else."

Her laughter was contagious, and Phineas joined in. They laughed until their stomachs hurt. "Did you hear that joke going around the bar?" he asked.

"Yes. Absolutely shocking." She laughed again. "I hope I can forget it. I'm surprised my ears didn't burst into flame."

Once their laughing subsided, they climbed into the carriage and headed for their familiar pub. They enjoyed the privacy of a table in the back, lingering over a well-prepared meal with a candle glowing between them. It was reminiscent of their first evening together. They ordered roasted chicken, talked in low tones about everything they could think of, and touched fingertips. When it became embarrassingly late, they left the pub and drove back to the rooming house by moonlight.

Phineas shed the flat cap and collected his bowler and vest. "Good night, my dear. I'll see you at breakfast."

He longed to wrap his arms around her and kiss her but wasn't sure if she would be willing. He settled for kissing her hand, then went upstairs to his room, settling into a peaceful slumber.

Early in the morning, Phineas planned to see the sheriff as soon as possible. He went downstairs and joined the other guests in the dining room for Adelaide's exceptional breakfast. She gave him heartier servings than the other guests. He grinned and winked at her by way of thanks. She grinned back.

"Adelaide, I'm going to visit the sheriff today and see what I can learn about Sam Gillespie. I'll be back by dinner time, if not sooner. Would you go out to dinner with me again this evening?"

"Yes, of course. I'll be ready by six. If you're not back then, I'll wait for you."

He put on his bowler and adjusted his collar. "I'll see you then."

The sheriff's office was within a ten-minute ride. Sheriff Milligan was surprised to see him again. "Fletcher, so good to see you. What brings you to Florissant?"

"I'm on another case. Say, whatever happened to that murderer we brought here last month?"

"He's due in court in two weeks for the trial. You may be called to testify, by the way. But tell me about this new case. Can I help?"

"I don't know. I'm looking for a lowlife named Sam Gillespie. I don't know if he even lives here in town. Here's the story. He took his daughter away from her mother and demanded that she pay him fifty dollars to get the child back. In desperation, the mother is trying to blackmail my client in Spencer's Mill for fifty dollars, or she'll claim he assaulted her privately, which he didn't. The charge would probably come to nothing, but my client is trying to start a business, and she could ruin his reputation. It's an evil mess."

"I'd say it is. But the name Sam Gillespie doesn't ring a bell. I wish I could help you."

"Well, if you hear anything, I'm staying at Mrs. Courtney's Rooming House until tomorrow morning. I think I'll stop at the courthouse and see if the man owns any property around here."

"Good luck, Fletcher. It was good to see you again."

"Same to you."

Phineas had been to the courthouse before on his first case and found the recorder's office with no trouble.

"Good morning, sir," he said to the clerk. "I'm looking for a fellow named Sam Gillespie. Can you tell me if he owns any property in this county?"

The clerk pulled out the heavy record books and searched the entries under "G." "I don't see anything for a Gillespie here. Do you think he might appear in the court case records somehow?"

Phineas' mouth formed an 'O' as he realized there was a second way to search for someone. "I think it quite likely," he said. "I don't think he's a reputable gentleman."

The clerk lowered his head and chuckled. "Just a moment," he said and went to another record book. "This could take some time to search because the entries are in date order, not alphabetical. I'm under a deadline to get some other work done. Would you like to search this record yourself?"

"I would be happy to do that," Phineas said.

The clerk invited him around to the other side of the counter and put the book on a table.

"You can sit here. Take your time."

Phineas adjusted his spectacles and started with the latest entries, slowly and carefully, so as not to miss anything. This was a record of complaints against perpetrators, with addresses and notes of victims' names. Phineas realized it was a gold mine of information. He started backward through the cases in March, then February. Still nothing in January. But back in December, there was a complaint against Sam Gillespie by Comfort Gillespie for kidnapping a child. There was a note that the case was dropped because Mr. Gillespie was the child's father.

Phineas scribbled the details in his notebook. Mr. Gillespie's address was listed as 651 Rosedale Avenue, Florissant. *So, he rents a place. I'll see if I can talk to him.*

He asked the clerk where Rosedale Avenue was. Fortunately, the clerk passed it every day on his way to work. He gave Phineas accurate directions.

After nodding his thanks, Phineas went to his carriage and drove a half-mile to Rosedale. Several houses lined the street, but none of them was numbered 651. There was a 675 and a 751. He drove slowly along the road, trying to size up the homes. Where would a disreputable man with a little girl rent a home? He decided to try at 751. That address was a large, wooded parcel of land with a one-room log cabin, slightly seedy-looking. Gray smoke curled out of the chimney. That was an encouraging sign.

He parked his rig and walked the short path up to the door. When he knocked, a small girl answered, opening the door wide enough to stick out her dirty little face with a button nose.

"Hi, honey. Is your daddy home?" Phineas put on his best non-threatening smile.

"He's sleeping."

Phineas squinted and peered through the narrow opening. In the dim indoor light, he could just make out a bed with someone in it.

"Oh, I'm so disappointed. I wanted to talk to him about your mama."

The girl's eyes lit up. "Do you know my Ma?"

"No, but I have a friend who does. Say, I'll bet you got your red hair from her."

The girl grinned and nodded.

The voice from the bed said, "Nan, who's at the door? I'm trying to sleep."

Phineas decided to interrupt. "My name is Phineas Fletcher, sir. I'm looking for your wife. Do you have a minute to talk to me?"

There was silence, then grumbling. "Come on in. I'd like to know where she is, myself. She's not much of a mother."

Phineas stepped inside with some uneasiness. Gillespie threw his quilt off the bed, then sat up fully dressed in his street clothes, except for his boots.

"I work nights," he said to explain his late hours in bed.

"I sometimes do, too. What kind of work do you do?"

"I work in the back room at The Taproom. It's a living."

Phineas nodded. *He gambles for a living,* he thought.

Gillespie continued. "So what do you want with my wife? Does she owe you money? Oh, you can sit in that chair over there."

Phineas lowered himself into the straight-backed chair. The uneven legs rocked slightly. "No, your wife doesn't owe me money. Do you think we could talk privately?"

Gillespie's interest was piqued. "Nan, take that bucket and go get some water."

Nan put on a coat and walked outside with the bucket. As soon as the door closed, Phineas spoke quickly, not knowing how long before the child would be back.

"I think she's in trouble financially. She's trying to blackmail a man for fifty dollars. Do you know anything about that?"

Gillespie studied his feet with his head down, trying to conceal his delight, but he wasn't successful. "No, I don't know anything about that."

"Does she have friends around here I could talk to?"

"I wouldn't know of any."

"Does she have people somewhere?"

"Her family comes from Lamar. You might find her there. I'm trying to get her to send me money to help raise Nan, but she won't send nothing. She owes me for all the money I'm putting out to feed the girl. She eats like a pig."

Phineas doubted that. The child was skinny, like she didn't get fed often.

Just then, Nan came in with a bucket. It had a little water sloshing in it.

"Put that bucket down by the fireplace, then go back outside and play," said Gillespie. "I need more sleep."

"I'll be leaving," Phineas said, rising. "Thanks for your help." He let himself out and walked to his carriage. Nan came outside and waved at him. He remembered an apple that Charlotte had given him to eat along the way.

"Nan," he called. "I think I have something for you."

The little girl came running. "What is it?"

He dug the apple out of his bag and handed it to her. Her eyes lit up. "Can I eat this all by myself?"

"Yes, you can eat it right now," Phineas said. She took a juicy bite of the apple and turned around, skipping away. Phineas hoped she would get the whole apple eaten before her father found out about it. He climbed into the carriage and headed back to the sheriff's office. Maybe Milligan could help him think out loud.

Milligan was still in his office.

"Fletcher, come on in and sit down. Did you get any information today?" he asked.

"I did. I found Sam Gillespie. He's living on Rosedale Avenue, and he says he works nights in the back room at The Taproom. I'd say that translates to gambling, don't you agree?"

"More than likely. Did you find his wife with him?"

"No, he gave me a story about not knowing where she is. But the daughter is living with him. Poor little thing looks hungry. I gave her an apple. I wish I could have bought her a chicken dinner. Sam claims the girl's mother should pay him back for the food he gives her. Can you believe that? That's why she's trying to blackmail poor Mr. Blackburn for enough money to ransom her daughter."

"Unbelievable. So what's your next step?"

"I haven't thought that far yet. Is there any law on the books that you could arrest Sam for? If he were in jail, the girl would go back to her mother, and the mother wouldn't need to blackmail my client. It seems like putting Sam in jail would solve everyone's problems."

"I'll think on it. I might come up with something."

"What about illegal gambling?"

Milligan sighed and crossed his legs, resting one elbow on his desk. "I can't tell you how many times I've tried to bust up that game in the back room. They seem to find out every time I go over there and break it up before I get in. I don't know how they do it."

"So you've given up?"

"Not entirely."

"Maybe there's another way to get at them. What about arresting Gillespie for having no visible means of support? Can you get bank records to confirm he can't legally support himself?"

"There's an angle I hadn't thought of. I'll go to the bank this afternoon and see what I can learn."

"Would you let me know? I'll be at the rooming house."

"You bet. I'm going to the bank right now."

Phineas left ahead of the sheriff and returned to his room for a good think.

In forty-five minutes, the sheriff came to see Phineas and climbed the stairs to room 5.

"Did you find out anything useful?" asked Phineas.

"I learned the man has no bank account. Everything he does is with cash or barter, and since he has no regular employment, no visible assets, and no crops growing out back, I'd say it's illegal gain."

"The only problem with that," Phineas said, "is that he says he works at The Taproom. The owner would probably swear that he employs Sam to cover up the illegal gambling in his back room. But if you had the names of the other gamblers, the Taproom owner would have to claim he employs them all. Then you could look at the financial records of The Taproom to see if it takes in enough money to cover that large a payroll."

"There's the problem. I don't know who the other gamblers are."

"And we're coming up to a deadline. If I don't get this mess solved by Thursday night, my client's reputation will be destroyed on Friday. That gives me a little over forty-eight hours."

Milligan pursed his lips. "I don't know how to get anything done that fast."

"I don't either."

The two men sat there for a minute or two, thinking, without results.

"I might as well head back to the office," said the sheriff. "I'm sorry I couldn't help. Good luck with your case, Phineas."

"Thank you." Phineas remained seated as the sheriff left and closed the door behind him. Then he bowed his head and asked for divine help. He was out of options. *Why do I ask for God's help as a last resort? Why didn't I do that first?*

He couldn't think of anything else he could do in Florissant right then, but there was no point leaving for Lamar this late in the day. He might as well take a nap.

An hour later, he was awakened by a knock on the door. He sat up, groggy, and went to find out who it was. He opened the door to an excited sheriff. "Phineas, I think I might have a plan."

Phineas smiled. "Come on in, Milligan. You're an answer to prayer."

"I don't know about that, but listen to what I came up with." Milligan took the chair, and Phineas sat on the edge of the bed. Milligan's voice dropped to a whisper. "You and I could raid the card game together tonight. It would be an entirely different situation with someone guarding the back door. Did you bring your pistol?"

"I have a revolver."

"Good. You could hide behind The Taproom, behind that stone wall in the alley, and watch who comes and goes. After dark — after the card game starts — I'll charge in the front door. Everyone will run out the back, and you'll stand there with your revolver drawn. Then I'll come around back and arrest them."

"That's a tall order, Milligan. I might get overwhelmed if there are many of them."

"You might, but if we could get two or three of them, I could probably talk them into snitching on their friends. Are you in?"

"I'll take a chance on your plan since it's all we have. Let me go downstairs and tell Adelaide I'll be out for a few hours. Then I'll head over to The Taproom and hide."

"Good man. Take your weapon."

Phineas reluctantly loaded his weapon, slid it under his belt, and made sure he was appropriately dressed. He fervently hoped he wouldn't need to fire the revolver. Then he went downstairs to ask Adelaide to borrow the flat cap again. He explained the plan and asked if they could have dinner after the prisoners were in custody.

"Phineas, it might be too late to go out after that. I'll cook a special dinner, and we can eat together here when you get back, even if it's midnight. Wait, let me give you a bag of cookies to take with you. It may be a long evening."

"You're a good woman, Adelaide. I'll see you later tonight." He took off in the carriage, parking about two blocks from the Taproom. He did his best to look casual as he wandered aimlessly to his position, glancing around to see if he had been spotted. He hoped he would be taken for nothing more than a no-account with a thirsty throat if someone happened to see him. Satisfied that he was alone, he hid behind the stone wall and waited.

In about half an hour, the hopeful gamblers started coming down the alley, peering to the right and left to make sure they weren't seen before ducking into the back door of the Taproom. One of them nearly spotted Phineas, but just in time, he was distracted by one of his friends entering the alley.

Darkness was falling quickly. Phineas contented himself to sit on a rock and wait.

An hour passed, and there was no activity. He wondered how long Milligan would stall before he raided the game. He stamped his feet to keep awake. Inside, loud talking and bawdy laughter grew louder and rougher as time passed, and the liquor flowed.

Finally, angry shouting reverberated clear into the alley. Phineas grinned nervously and fingered his weapon. Milligan was executing his plan.

He drew his revolver with a trembling hand and stepped into the alley. Hopefully, he would get one of the gamblers. Two or three would be better, but this wasn't his area of expertise. He would happily settle for one.

The door flew open, and angry, startled men burst out, feet pounding on bricks as they scattered in both directions. Phineas' heart thumped hard. He stepped forward and stuck his foot in front of one of the men, who went sprawling in front of another man, who fell over him. Two men down. As the gamblers tried to scramble to their feet, Phineas fired his weapon into the air and shouted, "Hold it!" The gun blast was almost deafening, echoing off the surrounding buildings. The two on the ground didn't move.

Phineas' attention was diverted for just a second by the men who fled down the alley — what if one of them was Skinner? — and one of the men on the ground leaped up. He grabbed for Phineas' revolver, and the struggle was on. Phineas fought bravely, but his assailant was younger and stronger. Phineas' heart was beating so wildly that he thought his chest would explode. He wondered if he would come out of this fight alive. Just as the second man jumped up to join the melee, Milligan bolted out the door and fired his revolver into the air.

The action stopped immediately, and there was dead silence as Milligan bound the assailants' hands behind their backs.

"Now get going, both of you. You're under arrest for illegal gambling...and attacking an old man." The sheriff grinned apologetically at Phineas for calling him an old man and took charge of the prisoners. He loaded them into his carriage. "Great job, Phineas. We got two. I'll see what information I can squeeze out of them."

Phineas' heart was still pounding with the exertion and the excitement. His breath came in heavy puffs. "I'll follow you back as far as the jailhouse," he said, "then I'll keep going. I have a date with Adelaide."

Sheriff Milligan nodded.

Phineas continued. "I'll come by early in the morning and find out if you have enough to arrest Gillespie; then I'll know how to proceed with my case."

"That'll be fine. I'll be there early."

Phineas followed Milligan as far as the jail, then continued to the rooming house. It was about eight o'clock, and Adelaide was ready with a roast beef dinner. She invited him into her living quarters, where they could enjoy dinner quietly in private.

"Phineas, I want to hear all about it. I participated, you know, by showing you how to dress yesterday and providing cookies for your stakeout and now dinner. I feel like I'm a part of it all."

"You are, Adelaide. I'm sure it would have turned out very differently if you hadn't given me wardrobe pointers yesterday, and I'm serious about that. That was a valuable contribution. And so is all the food you provided for me today. I owe you a lot."

"No, all you owe me is details. So let's hear it." Her eyes were dancing.

He chuckled as he took his chair and scooted up to the table. Adelaide placed a beautiful plate of food before him, and he admitted to being famished. The two said grace and thanked God for the day's success.

"Now, my dear," he said. "here are the details." He recited the whole evening, how he hid behind the wall, observed everyone entering the back door of The Taproom, and waited for the sheriff to raid the game. He was especially proud of firing his revolver and shouting, "Hold it," while the two men tripped over his foot.

Adelaide had a great laugh over that. "I wish I had been there."

Phineas' heart was thrilled that she was excited over his success. She was getting into his head and his heart.

"I'm very sorry I have to leave in the morning," he said. "I'll be leaving right after breakfast." The room became quiet, and he reached for her hand as the smiles slipped from their faces. They sat with their fingers interlaced on the table for a long minute.

"I can't thank you enough for everything, Adelaide."

"You're more than welcome. I hope you come again very soon."

"I can't make any promises. I was able to come this time only because I was hired to do a job."

"Then my prayers will be for you to get other Florissant jobs."

"He smiled and nodded. "Let me help you clean up the dishes. You wash, and I'll dry."

"There's an offer I can't refuse," she said, and stood to begin clearing the table.

The bell at the front desk dinged. "I can't imagine who that is." As soon as she reached the lobby, she called, "Oh, Phineas. It's Sheriff Milligan."

Phineas wiped his mouth on his napkin and rose from the table. "I'm surprised to see you this late."

"I apologize for intruding on your evening, but we have a problem," said Milligan.

"We do? What kind of problem?"

"One of the men we arrested is Sam Gillespie himself. That leaves his five-year-old daughter at home alone while he's in jail, and that could be a very long time. Do you have any ideas?"

Phineas thought. "Yes, I do. I'll drive out to the cabin and pick her up. Adelaide, would you allow her to sleep in your quarters tonight? I'll take her to Lamar tomorrow and try to find her mother. If I can't locate the mother or any of her people, I'll take her home with me. We can find room for her until we figure out a more permanent solution."

"That would be very helpful. I'll tell her father we have her situated with caring people, but I won't tell him where she is until the court forces me. The judge will frown on withholding that information from her father, but I'll explain. Maybe he won't be too hard on me."

"I'll let you handle that end of things. We can communicate by telegram, right? If you get critical information that changes anything on my end, please let me know."

"I'll do it, Fletcher, and thanks for your help. I have a feeling we've broken up that card game for a long time. The owner of The Taproom is quite upset, I'm sure. He was getting a cut of it."

"Hm. Serves him right. Well, I must beg off drying the dishes, Adelaide. I'm going to go pick up a little girl in distress."

"Not without me, you're not. The little girl will need a woman around. I'll go with you, and we'll bring her back here for the night. We can take care of the dishes when we get back."

Phineas grinned at her. "Thank you, Adelaide. That will make the trip so much more pleasant. Now please get your cloak. The temperature has taken a dip."

The sheriff left, and Phineas and Adelaide climbed into the carriage together.

"Where does this little waif live?" asked Adelaide.

"Out on Rosedale Avenue. It's a bit of a drive. I need to light the gaslights on the carriage so we can find our way." The stars in the sky were some of the brightest they had ever seen. The air was crisp, and Adelaide snuggled against Phineas for warmth. Their breath made clouds in the air. It was a perfectly wonderful ride.

After twenty minutes or so, they reached the cabin on Rosedale Avenue. No light came through the windows, and there was no evidence of fire in the fireplace. The child must be cold and frightened.

Phineas knocked on the door, but there was no answer. He knocked again. "Nan!" he called. "Nan, it's me, the man who gave you the apple today." There was still no answer.

"Adelaide, I'm going to have to get in there somehow. I need to find out if she's there. If she's not, we have another problem on our hands." He pushed on the door, and it opened just a crack.

"Nan?" No answer. "Nan, answer me, honey."

A wee voice in the darkness of the cabin asked, "Where's my Pa?"

Phineas let out a long breath in relief. The girl was safe. "Your Pa is talking to Sheriff Milligan. Would you like to go see him?"

"Yes."

"Get your coat, honey. It's cold out." Phineas didn't have any way to light the lamp. They could only feel their way around in the dark. "Do you have your shoes and socks?"

"Yes, sir."

The little thing stepped out into the moonlight and was startled to see Adelaide.

"Who's this lady?" she asked.

"This is Mrs. Courtney. She's my friend, and she's going to help us."

"All right."

Nan took Phineas' hand and walked to the carriage with Adelaide.

"We're going to see my Pa," Nan said.

Adelaide threw a glance at Phineas. "How are we going to do that?"

"Sam doesn't know you. When we get to the sheriff's office, I would like you to take Nan inside to see her Pa for a minute. Then we'll take her to the rooming house and make sure she's safe and warm."

Adelaide nodded. "All right. I can help Nan see her Pa — can't I, Nan?"

The child sat primly with her hands in her lap and nodded.

Shortly they reached the jail. "I'll wait here," Phineas said.

Adelaide stepped out of the carriage and lifted Nan down. The two held hands and walked into the building. The sheriff wasn't at his desk, so Adelaide called out for him.

"Sheriff Milligan?"

In a moment, the sheriff came in from the other side of the door. "I'm busy with a prisoner —" He spotted Nan, and his eyes widened.

Adelaide interrupted. "This is Nan Gillespie. She would feel better if she could see her Pa. Phineas is waiting in the carriage."

"I see." He thought for a moment. "All right. Let me take her back to the cell. This might be a good idea after all. You wait here, Mrs. Courtney." He led Nan back to the cell where her father sat on the edge of a cot.

"Pa!" she said, then stopped, confused. "Why are you in there?"

Gillespie stood and came close to the bars with his hands shoved in his pockets. "I need to stay here for a while," he said. Turning to the sheriff, his voice took an angry tone. "Why did you bring her in here?"

"To give the child some reassurance. She's been tossed about between different family members, so she wanted to see you before she goes into the care of someone we have appointed for her until the court makes some decisions."

"You'll see she's cared for until I get out of here?"

"Yes, we will."

Gillespie turned to his daughter. "Nan, you be a good girl, all right?"

"Yes, Pa. But I want to hug you before I go."

"You can't. I'm in here, and you're out there."

The little thing turned her head sharply to the right and carefully slid right through the bars sideways, shoulder first.

The sheriff gasped with widened eyes. "I would never have believed it if I hadn't seen it myself."

Sam Gillespie hugged his daughter. "You go on, now. I'll see you later."

"No, Pa, I want to stay with you." She clung to his leg and began to cry.

He tried to pry her off his leg, but she held tight, crying louder. "Nan, let go. I have to stay here, and you can't. You have to go." She continued to cry and cling to him until he picked her up. "Nannie, you must be a big girl for me, all right?" He wiped the tears from her face in an unusually tender gesture for him.

She hung on.

"How did you get here, Nan? Who brought you?"

"I don't know. A lady and the man who gave me an apple."

"She'll be well cared for, Gillespie," said the sheriff. "We have her placed with good people."

He gave his daughter one last hug and set her down. "You go now, Nan, and I'll see you as soon as I can."

Without replying, she slid out of the cell as easily as she had gone in. The sheriff took her small hand and led her out of the jail into his office. There she rejoined Adelaide.

"You don't need to worry about him," the sheriff whispered to Adelaide. "He won't ever be a threat to you, looking for the girl. He didn't see your face."

"Sheriff, thank you," she said. "Let's go, honey."

The two of them went back to the carriage.

"That was a brief encounter," said Phineas. "What happened?"

"I saw my Pa," said Nan. "He said he'll see me as soon as he can.

Where are we going now?"

"We're going to Mrs. Courtney's home, where there's food and a nice warm bed for you tonight."

Phineas and Adelaide took Nan into the rooming house, walking her behind the front desk and into Adelaide's private quarters. When Nan spotted the leftover food on the table, she stopped short.

"Can I have something to eat?" she asked.

Adelaide brought a plate for her and filled it with cold roast beef, roasted potatoes, and green beans. The child ate like it would be her last meal. Adelaide and Phineas, fascinated, watched her eat.

"We'd better get you to bed, honey," Adelaide said. "Phineas, I'll get her tucked in on the sofa, then tackle these dishes. I have to clean them up before cooking breakfast for the guests in the morning."

Guilt stabbed Phineas. He was responsible for her having to work so late at night, so when she took Nan to get her ready for bed, Phineas cleared the dishes and heated some water to wash them. *I'll not tell anyone at home that I washed dishes. They'll have me doing women's work.* He smiled to himself. Then he and Adelaide teamed up and made quick work of the kitchen duties.

"This wasn't the evening I had in mind for us, my dear," said Phineas, "but I'm forever grateful for your help. Now I'm afraid we must both get to our beds. Tomorrow is going to start early."

They held hands briefly, then Phineas headed upstairs to room 5.

Before falling asleep, he took the time to review his case. It was now Tuesday night. It would take him until tomorrow afternoon to return to Lamar with Nan and try to find her people. Then he would either leave her with her mother or take her home to Spencer's Mill with him. That would leave all day Thursday to resolve the problem between Comfort Gillespie and his client before Comfort's deadline. He smiled to himself. Even if Comfort couldn't be deterred from carrying out her threat and filing charges, Phineas had the facts, and Sheriff Milligan would back him up. He would contact the newspaper and give the editor the actual story. That should cancel any damage to Blackburn's reputation.

He went into a sound sleep.

Phineas woke early in the morning. He was still tired, so Adelaide must be worn out. She was probably downstairs cooking breakfast for a whole house of guests. His heart ached for her.

Down in the dining room, he spotted Nan seated at a table with a full plate of eggs and bacon in front of her. Her eyes were brighter today, and she was eating with enthusiasm.

"Good morning, Phineas," Adelaide called. "Would you like to sit with Nan?"

"Yes, I would, thank you. And how are you doing today, little lady?"

Nan gave him a shy smile and kept eating.

"How are you doing, Adelaide?"

She smiled at him, but her eyes were weary. "I plan to get a good nap today before I start cleaning rooms."

Guests seated themselves at the breakfast tables, and Adelaide was filled plates, bringing them to the dining room.

Phineas hesitated. "I'll help you serve the guests."

She chuckled, thinking it was a joke, but he was true to his word. He put on an apron and went to the kitchen to help. Adelaide filled the plates, and he served the guests. They chatted and laughed together as they worked.

"You know," said Adelaide, "I could use some permanent help around here."

Phineas smiled and gave her a sideways look.

The guests were served, then Phineas and Adelaide had a quick breakfast together. It was time for Phineas to leave. "I've already delayed too long, Adelaide. Once I get to Lamar, I need time to find Nan's people, and I don't even know where to start."

"I know, Phineas. I must tell you that this has been an exciting two days. You'll come again, won't you?"

"I fervently hope so. Until then, we can stay in touch by letter."

"And I'll keep reading the newspaper for any word of you."

He smiled sadly and paid his bill. Then he gave Adelaide a quick hug, collected Nan, and left, but part of his heart stayed behind.

Phineas' carriage rolled down the road with Nan beside him, passing pleasant farms and fields of cattle.

Nan finally spoke. "Where are we going now?"

"We're going to try to find your mama. Would you like that?"

"Yes. I haven't seen her for a while."

"Do you know where we might start looking for her?"

"I don't know. Maybe she's at Grandma's house."

"Where is that?"

"I don't remember."

Phineas wrinkled his brow. If he had Grandma's name, maybe there would be a property record at the courthouse.

"Do you know your Grandma's last name?"

"Do you mean Grandma Gillespie or Grandma McGinnis?"

"I mean Grandma McGinnis. Do you have a Grandpa?"

"Yes. Grandpa McGinnis."

"Do you know where he works?"

"I think he works at the doctor's office."

"What does he do there?"

"I think he's the doctor."

That was a comforting bit of information. That would make Grandpa McGinnis easier to find.

"What about your Ma? Do you know where she works?"

"She works in lots of places. She's a singer."

"It must be nice to have a mama who sings pretty songs."

"Yes."

"Does she sing in places where people eat?"

"I think so, but I was never there."

There were hours left on the trip. Phineas decided to give the questions a rest.

They stopped twice to give the horse a break and refresh themselves with snacks from the bag.

Back on the road, Nan began to get drowsy, so Phineas got his extra quilt out of the back and wrapped it around her. She soon curled up on the passenger seat, asleep.

The trip to Lamar lasted until two o'clock in the afternoon. Both travelers were weary. Phineas' first stop was the courthouse. He took Nan inside with him and inquired about property owned by anyone named McGinnis.

The clerk smiled. "You must mean Dr. McGinnis. Let me get you the addresses."

"More than one property?"

"Oh, yes. I think he has four or five." He searched his records under "M" and came up with addresses he wrote on a piece of paper. "Here you are," he said and slid the paper toward Phineas.

"Would you happen to know where he lives or where he has his office?"

The clerk made a check mark beside one of the addresses. "That's his office. You'll probably find him there this time of day."

"I'm very grateful. I have his granddaughter with me. We need to find her people. Oh, that's another question. Does the name Comfort Gillespie sound familiar to you?"

"She used to be Comfort McGinnis. We went to school together. Yes, she was quite a girl." He smiled as if his mind had traveled back to old times. "I've lost track of her now, but her Pa should be able to tell you where she is."

"Thank you again, sir. You've been a tremendous help."

The address of Dr. McGinnis' office wasn't too far away.

Phineas turned a critical eye toward his small traveling companion. "Is that the only dress you have?"

"Yes."

"Let's see what we can do about that." He drove to the used clothing store Danny's little sister mentioned. Phineas picked out two dresses in Nan's size.

"Can I keep these dresses when we find Grandma?" she asked.

"Of course, you can. They're yours." Phineas had a feeling that new dresses were a rare experience for the child, even if they were someone else's castoffs.

They were only a few minutes from the doctor's office. Phineas tied the horse to the rail, and they went inside.

A tall, gray-haired man in a white coat greeted them. "How can I help you today?" he asked.

"Grandpa!" Nan went running to the man and grabbed him around the legs.

He stared down at her in amazement. "Nancy?" He picked her up, held her tight, and spun her around. Then his brow creased as his attention went back to Phineas. "What are you doing with Nancy?"

"We're looking for her mother," Phineas said. "I'm working a case for a gentleman in Spencer's Mill and found Nan while working that case. Her Pa is in the hoosegow in Florissant. We need to find her Ma."

"Sadly, we don't know where her mother is. She's been out of contact with us for about a year. But please, leave Nancy with us until she's found. She's our blood, and we want her."

"I have two new dresses, Grandpa."

"That's good, honey. Where are they?"

"In the carriage."

"Would you go out and get your things? You're going to stay with Grandma and me for a while."

As soon as Nan was out the door, the doctor asked to hear the whole story. Phineas fished in his pocket for a business card and gave him a brief overview before the child returned. "It's important I find Comfort by tomorrow. She's given my client a deadline of Thursday night to come up with fifty dollars, or she has threatened to file false charges against him, ruining his reputation."

The doctor reached for his chair. "Oh, she's sunk to a new low." He closed his eyes and shook his head as if that would somehow make that knowledge disappear.

"In her defense, sir, she's desperate," Phineas said. "Her husband took Nan away from her and said Comfort would never see her again if she didn't come up with fifty dollars by Monday. Since he's in jail for illegal gambling, I suspect he's trying to get money to cover a gambling debt."

"We told her not to marry that worthless scoundrel, but she didn't listen. Well, leave the child with me. We are deeply grateful."

"Do you know where I could start looking for Comfort?" Phineas asked.

"I don't know if she's even in Lamar, but you could start looking in taverns that hire singers."

"I'll do that. Thank you, sir."

Nan came in from the carriage with her dresses and a bag of leftover rolls Adelaide had given them. "Can I keep these rolls, mister?"

Phineas smiled. "You bet you can. I have to leave now, little lady. It has been a real pleasure getting to know you."

She smiled shyly but said nothing.

"Goodbye, Doctor."

"Thanks again, Mr. Fletcher."

Phineas made his exit. He was sure that Nan's little face and charming personality would be on his mind for a long time, but solitude had its advantages, too. He stopped at the Old English Tea Room for an early supper. He longed to go home and relax in his bed, but the strain on his conscience told him he was obligated to look for Comfort. He lingered over his meal until his strength was revived, then prepared to make the round of the taverns. There were three of them nearby.

The Two Roosters Tavern had few patrons that early in the evening. Two large painted roosters faced each other at either end of the sign over the door. Phineas stepped inside and inquired about Comfort.

"We don't have singers here," said the bartender. "We have a piano player but no singers. You might try down the street. Maybe they have a singer."

Next on his list was the Golden Lamb Tavern. The bartender's eyebrows raised at the name of Comfort Gillespie.

"Yes, she sings here once in a while. In fact, she'll be singing here Saturday night if you'd like to hear her."

"Actually," said Phineas, "I'd like to speak to her earlier than that. It's about her daughter. The little girl is here in town and wants to see her mama. Do you know where I could find Comfort this afternoon? I think she'd like to hear the news."

The bartender leaned over the bar. "Confidentially, sir, I wouldn't normally give out her whereabouts, but she lives right upstairs over the bar." He pointed at the ceiling. "She's been living there for about three weeks. I'm sure she'll be glad to see you if you want to go up."

"Thank you, sir."

"Just take the stairs outside, right beside the tavern door."

Phineas tipped his hat and left, heading up the flight of steep, cheerless steps to the apartment. He rapped on the door at the head of the stairs.

The door opened, and a slender, weary-looking redhead stood before him. "What do you want?" she asked.

Phineas handed her a business card. "May I come in? I have some news about your daughter."

Comfort's eyes flashed, and a scowl formed on her lips. "About Nan? Did my husband send you to make another threat?"

"No, ma'am. He's in jail in Florissant, arrested yesterday for illegal gambling."

"That's no surprise. Please come in and give me the details. Where is my daughter?"

Phineas stepped inside, and Comfort waved at a chair for him to sit in. Phineas said, "I just dropped her off at your father's office. She's safe. Since last night she's been well-fed, and I bought her a couple of dresses. Her clothes were in rags."

Her eyes flooded with tears. "Poor Nan. I thank you for that, but why my father's office? Why didn't you bring her to me? I haven't spoken to my father in over a year."

"You're hard to find, Mrs. Gillespie. Nan told me her grandfather's name, and I was able to find him through the courthouse records."

She lowered her head.

"Now, we have a matter to discuss. I was hired by a man in Spencer's Mill named Cyrus Blackburn."

Comfort pressed her lips together. "Why did he hire you?"

"To solve his problem. It seems you're trying to blackmail him for fifty dollars. I've been working hard for the past two days to figure out how to stop you from carrying out your threat. I believe you wanted the fifty dollars to ransom your daughter from Sam. Is that right?"

"Yes. The man made me crazy." Her eyes flooded with tears. "He said I'd never see Nan again if I didn't pay him fifty dollars by Monday. I was desperate. Where was I to get that much money? I can't earn that much in a month. He probably wanted it to pay off somebody threatening to hurt him."

"Yes, that's what I thought. But you know that blackmail is illegal."

The pitch of her voice raised. "I was desperate. How can I make you understand that? I was desperate." She began to cry.

"Yes, I know you were desperate. But now you don't need the fifty dollars since Nan has been rescued. Can I tell Mr. Blackburn that you will not file any charges?"

"If you are who you say you are, and if my daughter is really at Pa's house, I promise not to file charges."

"That's fine, Comfort. Let me tell you what will happen if you change your mind. Since I know the whole story about your threat and why you made it, and since your husband is now in jail and the sheriff from Florissant will back up my story — if you file charges anyway, I'm going straight to the newspaper and tell them the whole of it. They love to publish juicy stories like this."

"I understand what you're saying."

Phineas rose and prepared to go. "I honestly wish you the best of luck, Mrs. Gillespie." He went back down the dark, treacherous stairs, holding tightly to the rail.

The following day, Phineas met with his client in Spencer's Mill. "Mr. Blackburn, I have excellent news. I met with Comfort Gillespie, and she has agreed to drop her blackmail scheme."

Blackburn choked back a sob and coughed to mask his emotion. "How did you get her to do that? You've saved my whole future."

Phineas explained the entire story, how they broke up a gambling ring in Florissant and restored a child to her mother, all while trying to solve Blackburn's dilemma.

Phineas still had the delicious privilege of sharing the details with his family at home. He anticipated that with relish. The best part of success was seeing the looks of admiration from his family.

He also wanted to write a letter.

It would begin, "Dear Adelaide . . ."

DELIGHTFUL SENILITY

Usually, Phineas cherished solitude in the morning after the rest of the family went about their daily routine, but today the weather was lovely. He decided to stretch his legs and walk to the business district. He was still on the crest of his energy high after finishing his last case. Breaking up an illegal gambling ring and reuniting a small girl with her mother had been so rewarding. He needed someone to talk to.

The April temperature was cool, perfect for taking some exercise. He decided to stretch his legs and walk to the business district. He stepped along smartly until he got to the main street, where he came to the bakery owned by Danny's brother. On a whim, he opened the door and walked in. The heady aromas of yeast bread and cinnamon made his mouth water.

"Good morning, George," he said to the clerk. "I'd like one of those sweet rolls for breakfast. Do you think Mrs. Reese would make a cup of coffee for a presumptuous old man?"

Katie Reese, the cheerful wife of the bakery owner, came in from the kitchen. "Good morning, Mr. Fletcher. I recognized your voice. We don't sell coffee here, but for you, of course, I'll make some coffee." She had made it clear that she'd have done anything for him since he'd rescued her family from a deadly threat in February.

She turned to the clerk. "George, you can charge him for the roll, but the coffee is on the house."

"Yes, ma'am."

"Mr. Fletcher, why don't you come back to the kitchen and have your roll and coffee? We can talk while I knead the bread."

Phineas smiled, paid for his roll, and followed Katie to the kitchen like a puppy. He liked kitchens. There was something homey and welcoming about them.

"Do you want to talk about anything in particular?" he asked her.

"Not really. Someone said you had some success with that blackmailing case recently. Do you want to tell me about it?"

Phineas did. Grateful for someone with willing ears, he supplied her with every detail. She smiled and nodded as he spoke, folding and pushing her dough as she listened. Occasionally, she slapped it against the countertop.

"Is there anything new with you, Katie?" he asked, taking a bite of the sweet roll. He waved it at her with his mouth full. "This is good."

"Well, a friend from church came by yesterday afternoon. She's having a strange problem with her elderly mother. The old lady sees and hears scary things that aren't there, but she's very consistent about it. To my friend Mamie, it sounds so real. Mamie wonders if there's a genuine threat, and her mother can't explain it clearly. I suggested that she talk to you about her mother's problem. She said the next time I saw you, I should ask you to visit her."

"That's not my usual sort of problem, but I'll be glad to listen. Where does she live?"

"The address is 522 Mulberry. Do you know where that is?"

"Yes, I do. I'll go back to get my notepad and pen before seeing if she's home."

"Thanks, Mr. Fletcher."

Back at the house, Phineas dressed in his business jacket and bowler, mounted up with his notepad in his pocket, and gave his horse a good run to 522 Mulberry. Was this the beginning of another adventure, or would it fizzle into a family problem?

He rapped on the door. As he stood on the porch waiting for someone to answer, a petite, white-haired lady in the window to the right pulled the curtain aside just a wee bit and peeked out. He smiled at her, and she ducked back out of sight. He chuckled to himself. That must be the mother of his prospective client.

The woman who answered the door was a gentle, cautious lady with brown hair and blue eyes. She opened the door just a few inches. Phineas guessed her to be in her thirties.

"Hello, madam, I'm Phineas Fletcher. I came at the request of Katie Reese. May I come in?"

"So you're Mr. Fletcher. Yes, do come in." She opened the door wider, and he made his entrance. Her parlor was comfortably furnished, although small and cozy. "Please have a seat."

Phineas found a chair while the lady of the house settled on the sofa.

"What can I do for you?" he asked.

"My name is Mrs. Richard Fleet — Mamie Fleet," she said as she twisted her handkerchief absentmindedly. "Katie said you may be able to help my mother."

"I'd like to hear what the problem is."

"I'm not sure how to explain it," she said. "You see, she's been declining somewhat lately — mentally. She says strange things and complains about someone following her or staring at her through the windows. I don't know what's real and what she's imagining. She talks to people who aren't there, but she seems so *earnest*."

Phineas began to think this wouldn't turn out to be a good case for him, but as long as he was there, it wouldn't hurt to chat. He pulled out his notebook and pencil.

"Mrs. Fleet, I like to start with the basics. What is your mother's name?"

"Her name is Clementine Hensley."

Phineas jotted the name in his notebook. "Would she mind if I asked her age?"

"A woman of her age almost brags about it," she said, smiling. "She's sixty-eight."

"You say she talks to people who aren't there. Do these people have names? Have you formed any idea of what they mean to her?"

"Well, she does mention a name now and then. She talks to an imaginary man she calls Mason."

Phineas smiled patiently as he made a note of that. "What kinds of conversations does she have with Mason?"

Mrs. Fleet giggled self-consciously. "She urges him to hide in the wardrobe. Sometimes she asks how long he'll be gone. Sometimes she warns him that Charles is looking for him."

Phineas' brow wrinkled, and he gazed up toward the ceiling. "What do you suppose is going on in her head?" He didn't expect an answer.

Mrs. Fleet shook her head slowly. "I wish I knew."

"May I speak with her?"

"That's probably a good idea. I'll bring her in. Just a moment." She went into the next room to fetch her mother. She returned with the

84

frail, tiny woman who had peeked at him earlier. "Mama, this is Mr. Fletcher. He'd like to talk to you about Mason and Charles."

Mrs. Hensley's face lit up. "Do you know Mason?"

"No, ma'am, I never had the pleasure. Would you tell me about him? Who is he?"

"Oh," she said and blushed. "I thought everyone knew. He's my husband, the best husband a girl could ask for."

"When was the last time you saw him?"

"This morning. He's back now."

"Where did you see him?"

"In my bedroom. He's in such a dilemma, you see."

"Oh, my. What is his dilemma?"

"Charles is trying to get him. He's trying to get me, too, you know."

"That sounds serious. Are you in danger?"

"Of course I am, and so is Mason. Charles has a pistol. We're afraid of him."

Phineas stared at her. He tilted his head and locked eyes with Mrs. Fleet, his eyes full of questions. He didn't even know where to begin. The daughter sat wide-eyed, with her mouth open.

"May I ask you some more questions, Mrs. Hensley? What is Mason's last name?"

"Oh, you can call me Clementine," she said. "Mason's last name is Hayes, the same as mine."

Tears ran down her daughter's cheeks. Phineas' heart went out to her. She must have wondered why her mother was inventing a whole new life.

"That's very nice, Miss Clementine," Phineas said. "Who is Charles? What is his last name?"

"His last name is Hayes, too. He's Mason's brother. He's a bad man."

Phineas and Mrs. Fleet stared at each other in amazement. There may be a real story behind her fantasizing. Maybe she wasn't just a raving old woman. If the men she imagined were a part of her early life, it would all make perfect sense to her. There was only one problem. If it happened, it must have occurred decades ago, back in the mists of her memory, and she was only reliving it now, filling in forgotten parts with invented details.

This probably wouldn't be a paying job, but Phineas was more than a little intrigued. He wanted to follow this strange tale and see where it ended. Besides, he had no other cases to take his time.

"Mrs. Fleet, I am quite interested in your mother's story. I believe it may have some truth, and if you don't mind, I'd like to follow it to the end to find out when this happened and why. I'm a man of deep curiosity."

"I'd like you to do that, Mr. Fletcher, but I can't afford your fee. We're in difficult straits temporarily. You may want to wait until our situation is better."

Phineas grinned. "I'm not asking for a fee. You couldn't stop me from looking into this case. This is the most interesting puzzle I've come across."

"That's very gracious, but I promise to pay you when our situation changes. I must say, you've already drawn more information out of my mother in fifteen minutes than I've been able to do in months . . . and please, you may call me Mamie."

Clementine's eyes were glazing over. Her attention was beginning to wane, and Phineas wanted to draw her back.

"Miss Clementine, do you like tea?" he asked.

"Oh, yes, with sugar, please," she said with a cherubic smile.

Phineas glanced over at Mamie, who took the cue. She grinned. "Coming right up. How do you like your tea, Mr. Fletcher?"

"With a teaspoon of sugar, thank you."

When she went to the kitchen, he continued with his interview. It was like wandering into the depths of a maze. After a few general questions, Phineas got to the point.

"Miss Clementine, can you tell me why Charles is after you and Mason?"

She leaned toward him as if to tell him a secret. "He thinks Mason stole his inheritance, and he thinks I helped him."

"He must be furious about that."

"Oh, yes. But it's not true. Charles was always a no-account scoundrel. He got into money trouble and asked his father for a big loan. He never paid it back, so when his father died, the will said everything would go to Mason."

"That seems fair, doesn't it?" asked Phineas.

Mamie came in with a pot of tea and three cups. She served tea all around but poured only a half cup for her mother. "Be careful, Mother, that you don't jiggle your cup and spill the tea."

"Thank you, dear," said Miss Clementine. "Yes, Mr. Fletcher. It seems fair to everyone except Charles."

"Where did they live when their father died? Did they live in Spencer's Mill?"

"Oh, I should say not," she said. "They preferred a big city. They lived in Lamar."

Phineas smiled. Lamar was a town of a few thousand people, but calling it a big city was quite a stretch. He took a sip of his tea.

"When was the last time you saw Charles?"

"I saw him last night. He was looking in my window."

"That must have been very frightening."

"It was no problem. I stuck my tongue out at him, and he went away."

Phineas and Mamie both stifled a laugh. Miss Clementine was busy blowing on her tea and didn't notice.

Phineas downed his tea to the bottom of the cup. "Well, ladies, I must be going. Mamie, I'll do some research at the courthouse in Lamar and let you know what I find out."

Mamie rose to go to the door with him. "I'm much obliged, Mr. Fletcher. Good luck with your research."

Phineas tipped his hat to the ladies, returned to his horse, and rode home. Tomorrow he would go to Lamar and begin his research.

This promised to be a fascinating puzzle.

Morning dawned, and Phineas was eager to take the fifteen-mile ride east to Lamar. It would take up to four hours if he went by carriage, so he would go on horseback to save time. He found his daughter still in the kitchen.

"Charlotte, I'll be in Lamar today doing some research. I have no idea where it will lead me, so if I don't come home tonight, please don't worry."

"All right, Pa," she said. "We'll see you when we see you." She busily buttoned her shoes before leaving to teach her class.

As soon as Phineas was alone in the house, he stopped to ask for divine help in his search. "Father, I know you're a God of the little things as well as the big, so I ask your help in untangling this little mystery. And thank you."

During the last adventure, he learned that the results are better if you ask for God's help first, not after you have wasted time beating your head against a problem on your own.

Phineas traveled directly to the Bledsoe County courthouse north of Lamar's town square and found the recorder's office. He searched the property records for the name Hayes, especially Mason or Charles.

He found the record of a parcel of land transferred to Mason Hayes from Jacob Hayes in 1852. Jacob may have been the father of Mason and Charles. He wrote all the details in his notebook, then asked to look at the court records for 1852. He wanted to find out as much as he could about the probate of Jacob Hayes' estate.

"The court records that far back were never indexed," the clerk said. "You'll just have to look through the old files."

"That will be fine," Phineas said. He preferred to look through them independently, pausing to study a detail that caught his attention, then skimming over irrelevant information. The clerk pointed to an old wooden filing cabinet in the corner at the back of the room. The top drawer sagged and had scratches in the varnish. It must have been standing there for decades.

The clerk said, "There's an extra desk at the back. You can sit there and work."

The drawer in the cabinet was stuck from disuse, but Phineas struggled to work it open. It creaked and squealed with the effort. The clerk cast a watchful eye at him occasionally but said nothing.

He began to look through the folders. A. B. C. D, and on to H — Hayes. He found the file he was searching for, the probate of Jacob Hayes, deceased.

He pulled out the dusty, discolored folder and laid it across the desk, reading each page in turn. Jacob's will was in the file, where Phineas got his first shock. The list of heirs named only two sons and the family of one of them. The family of Charles was listed as Charles and Clementine Hayes and their only daughter, Mamie.

What?

Phineas thought his head would explode. Clementine used to be married to Charles, in her opinion, a 'no-account scoundrel,' and those two were the parents of Mamie Fleet. Now he was faced with the dilemma of how to break this news to Mamie. This was sure to be a shock for her. He forced himself to continue. He could think about that later.

He made notes in his notebook and continued looking through the file. Clementine was right, that the entire estate was willed to the younger brother, Mason. The reason was spelled out in the will. Charles had borrowed a large amount of money from his father and never paid it back. Jacob's bequest to Charles was forgiveness of the loan. It was a logical way to handle things, but Phineas guessed that Charles disagreed.

He made more notes in his notebook, slid his pencil into his pocket, and prepared to drop the file into its correct slot when he spotted another file under 'Hayes.' It was a divorce file, nearly unheard of at the time. In amazement, he wiggled that file out of the drawer.

He opened the divorce file on the desk and studied the formal complaint. It was Clementine Hayes v. Charles Hayes. She accused him of infidelity with a barmaid. There was no request for a money settlement. Charles had no means to pay it, and there was no reason to look for coins in an empty piggy bank.

Phineas sighed. He put the folder back in the drawer and talked to the clerk. "Pardon me, sir," he said. "Where could I find the marriage records for Bledsoe County?"

"They're all listed in one register, back to the beginning of record-keeping." The clerk pulled out a bound book with rows and rows of precise script written with a quill pen.

"Here you are. Enjoy yourself."

Phineas returned to the spare desk, planning to search until he found a record of Clementine Hayes marrying someone named Hensley. He found the date of the divorce, June 1851, then began moving forward. He didn't need to go far. He found a record of Clementine Hayes' marriage six months later, but here was the second shock. She married Mason Hayes. Phineas was stunned. Clementine was right—Mason was her husband. He hurried back to the filing cabinet to look for another Hayes divorce, but there wasn't any. Back to the marriage records. He started at the date of the marriage of Clementine Hayes to Mason Hayes and worked his way forward. Three years later, in 1854, there was a record of a marriage between Elias Hensley and Clementine Hayes.

Either Clementine is a bigamist, or Mason Hayes died. Phineas nearly ran back to the filing cabinet. Nothing there. He asked the clerk, "Are there separate records of death?"

"Oh, yes. We keep them in another book." He went to another drawer and pulled out a blue book similar to the green marriage records.

"Thank you," said Phineas, taking that volume to the desk with the other files. The deaths were in date order, so he started working forward at the date of Mason and Clementine's marriage. It turned out that Mason and Clementine had been married for just over a year when Mason died, and the cause of death was . . . homicide.

One shock after another. I wonder if the newspaper keeps old copies.

He returned the marriage and death records to the clerk. "Do you remember the murder of a fellow named Mason Hayes thirty-four years ago?"

The clerk smiled. "No, sir, I wasn't born yet. But you might check with my grandpa. He's a walking history book, and he's always looking for someone to talk to."

Phineas smiled. *He may be able to make a new friend.* "Would you tell me your grandfather's name and where I could find him?"

"I'm embarrassed to say I don't know his first name. I only know him as Grandpa Jaffee. He lives on a farm. You go west until you come to that road halfway to Spencer's Mill, the one that goes south. Do you know the road?"

"Yes."

"Then you go about two miles. The farmhouse is on the left. It's a white two-story house with a big red barn out back. And you should see cattle in the field. Please tell Grandpa I miss him."

"Much obliged. I'll pass on your message." Phineas tipped his hat, tucked his notebook in his pocket, and went outside to his horse.

While I'm already in Lamar, I'll check with one of the newspapers. The office of the Lamar Daily Democrat wasn't very far. In five minutes, he was there. The newspaper had only a small staff. Unfortunately, the owner-reporter was out, possibly chasing a story. Phineas would have to return later.

He mounted up once more and took off toward the west. Reaching the road that went off to the south, he turned left and followed it for about two miles, checking on every farmhouse on the left side of the road. There weren't many, so when he came to the Jaffee farm, it was easily identified.

Phineas guided the horse up the drive where the forsythia was in fresh bloom, a long row of vibrant yellow bushes clamoring for his attention with their showy color. He tied the horse to the rail, walked up to the wide porch across the front of the house, and knocked on the door. "Just a minute!" called a voice from inside the house.

The door opened, and the farmer's wife eyed Phineas with a suspicious frown.

"What are you selling?" she asked impatiently.

Phineas grinned. "I apologize for not having a thing to sell. I was sent here by your grandson, the clerk at the courthouse. I'm here to talk to your husband."

A sheepish grin crossed the woman's face. "Sorry for my rudeness. How is Johnny?"

"He's very well. Doing a fine job at the courthouse, from what I can see. He's a very polite and helpful young man. You should be proud."

She beamed. "Good to hear. You'll find my husband in the barn."

Phineas tipped his hat and turned to go to the barn as she closed the door. His boots crunched through the gravel to the barn, where he stuck his head inside. "Mr. Jaffee?"

The farmer was milking the cows. "Whatcha need, mister?" He kept milking.

Phineas stepped inside. The earthy aromas of hay and cattle met his nostrils. "Your grandson Johnny suggested I come to see you. I'm here to find out if you know anything about a murder committed in the spring of 1853. A fellow by the name of Mason Hayes. Do you remember that?"

Jaffee twisted on his stool to get a good look at Fletcher's face. "Who are you?"

"Sorry, Mr. Jaffee." He laid a business card on the busy farmer's knee. "I'm an investigator. A young woman asked me to find out why her elderly mother thinks she has been talking to Mason Hayes."

"That would be a miracle, wouldn't it?" The farmer chuckled but kept milking with his back to Phineas. "I do remember that. Pull up a stool, mister. Let's have a chat."

Phineas was delighted. He may have met a kindred spirit and a good source of information. He spotted an extra stool nearby and pulled it closer to the farmer.

"I'd shake your hand, friend, but my hands are busy."

"Yes, I can see that. You must have been around in 1853, right?"

"Oh, yes. Mother and I have been living here since '48. Raised our family here."

"That's quite a luxury, living in the same home all that time. So you remember that murder?"

"It was all the talk back then. A fella named Mason was murdered by his brother, who accused him of stealing his inheritance…and his wife, if I remember right. There was a child involved…It's starting to come back to me now."

"Would you mind telling me everything you can remember?"

The farmer let out a long sigh and rubbed his chin with the back of his wrist. "Well, let me see. The brother got cut out of his Pa's will for some reason; then his wife left him. We were led to believe it was because she expected her husband to get a share of the considerable estate, and when he didn't get it, she married the brother that did. It was quite a scandal."

Phineas squirmed uncomfortably on his stool, realizing that Clementine had probably endured the scorn of her neighbors years ago. He rushed to defend her. "I just read the courthouse records, and that may not have been the whole story. She filed for divorce, claiming the first husband committed infidelity."

"Hmm. That may be true, too. Anyway, she married the second brother, Mason. A year or so later, their cabin caught fire with the whole family inside. The husband and wife ran out but realized the child was still there. Mason ran back inside to get the little girl. As he came out the door carrying her, someone fired a pistol at him, and the bullet found its mark."

Phineas gasped. "That's a horrible story," he said. "Can you imagine anyone doing a thing like that? It would take a special kind of snake."

"Everyone said it was Charles, but naturally, they never caught him. Never saw him again."

"Seriously? Never found him?"

"No. Evidently, he left the area. It was like he had evaporated into thin air. So, the lady who asked you to look into this—what's her relationship to the story?"

"She was the little girl in Mason's arms when he was killed."

The farmer's hands went still, and he stared at Phineas. "You don't say. So they're still around, are they?"

"Yes, living in Spencer's Mill . . . Do you remember where that burning house was?"

"Oh, yes. It was just down the road from here. It burned clean to the ground and was never rebuilt. If you're curious, you could go down and look. The fireplace is still standing."

"I am curious. I was already curious when I was in nappies."

The farmer chuckled. "Me too. If you can wait for me to finish my milking, I'll ride down there with you."

"Thanks, Jaffee. I'll wait."

The two men changed the subject and chatted about other things while Jaffee finished with his cows and dumped all the milk into a metal can. After he carried the milk safely into the kitchen, they clambered into his buckboard and traveled about ten minutes down the road to a wooded area grown up in underbrush. The only structure on the property was an old, blackened chimney rising from a stone fireplace.

"I'd like to walk the property," Phineas said. The two men stepped out of the wagon and waded through the high weeds toward the cabin's site. Whatever was left of the charred wood had rotted and suffered the ravages of many Ohio winters. The only evidence of a family ever living there was a row of decomposed logs hinting at the location of the walls, and a rusty iron pot near the fireplace.

"Imagine someone living here with a little girl," said Phineas. "Odd, isn't it, that someone who had recently acquired a sizeable inheritance would live in such a small cabin? Wouldn't there have been enough money to live much better than this?"

"I never thought of that," said Jaffee. "That gives the lie to the theory that the wife was a gold digger, doesn't it?"

"I wonder whatever happened to the money. According to the probate file, there was just over four thousand dollars."

"Amazing! That's enough money to fill a hay wagon."

"Yes, it is. I wonder if the wife, in her feeble state of mind, could tell me what happened to it."

The two men wandered around the area of the burned-out cabin for a few more minutes, not finding much after all those years, but trying to understand the events of that awful day. They talked about the family inside, going through an ordinary day. Maybe Mason had just come in from feeding the chickens, and Clementine may have been doing something routine like knitting a sock. Maybe Mamie was playing with a rag doll. Then suddenly, their lives changed forever.

They must have smelled smoke first, then realized their walls were in flames. Clementine and Mason probably panicked, running outside, maybe in different directions, each thinking the other had Mamie...then, realizing, to their horror, that the two-year-old child was still inside, terrified and unable to escape on her own. Mason, the brave heart, risked his own life to save his brother's child and carried her out successfully, only to be shot and killed in his tracks, possibly by that same brother. It was tragedy compounded upon tragedy that could barely be fathomed. Phineas' hand covered his mouth as his eyes closed in horror.

As his thoughts continued, he considered the odds of shooting a man carrying a child, yet missing the child. The girl was saved only by the hand of God.

The two men stood silently on the spot where a family's home had been destroyed and a heroic man had died. They were standing on holy ground.

After a few moments of reflection, they climbed into the carriage and drove back to the farm.

The two men shook hands. "I'm much obliged, Jaffee. Thanks for the information and the tour."

The farmer nodded. "You're welcome back here any time, Fletcher. Come back for a cup of coffee and a game of checkers."

"You can count on it!" said Phineas. He mounted his horse and headed back toward Spencer's Mill.

Phineas was home in time for dinner and sat down with the family. They said grace at the table, then began to dig into the pork and vegetables that Charlotte had prepared.

"Are you working on anything interesting, Pop?" asked Danny.

"I should say I am," Phineas said. "Pass me the salt, will you? Well, a friend of Katie's has a mother who is suffering from dementia. . . Actually, suffering may not be the correct word. She seems to be enjoying it." He chuckled.

"So, what do they want you to do?"

"The imaginings of this lady are quite vivid and involve two men she thinks she sees. The only problem is, the one has been dead for almost thirty-five years, and the other one, well, no one around here has seen him since then. He may be dead, or he may have just moved away somewhere. So the daughter wanted to know why those men are significant to her mother."

"Did you find out anything yet?" asked Charlotte.

Phineas relayed his findings, how the mother had been married to both brothers at different times, and the daughter was raised by the third husband, thinking he was her father.

"That's confusing," said William. "Lizzy, pass me the brussels sprouts, please." William was fifteen years old and trying to work out his ideas of life. "I'm not going to let my life get that confusing. I'm going to school to be a doctor, and when I marry, she will be the only one for the rest of my life."

"Good man," said Danny. 'I just hope you won't feel like a failure if something unforeseen happens, and your nice, tidy plans get upset."

"They won't."

Phineas and Danny glanced at each other and smiled. The boy had so much to learn.

"Well, I talked to a farmer named Jaffee," Phineas said. "He remembers the murder."

"Murder?" said Charlotte. "You didn't say anything about a murder."

Phineas elaborated on the fire and the shooting, his voice growing softer toward the end.

"That's shocking," said Charlotte, with her hand on her chest.

"Whoever did it must have been confident of his aim," said Danny. "It wouldn't be easy to shoot someone like that without hitting the child."

"I thought of that," said Phineas. "I'll have to chew on that for a while. What if the child was the target, and he missed? That's too horrible to consider. In the meantime, I'm going to revisit Mamie tomorrow."

Phineas slept fitfully that night, his mind going over the details of the puzzle he was working on. He had agreed to research the ravings of an old woman, thinking at the time that it was just a frivolous way to pass his time, but now he wasn't so sure. Now there were multiple marriages, the questionable paternity of his client, a fire, possibly a missing fortune, and an unsolved murder with a missing suspect. He tossed and turned until morning.

The following day, Phineas stayed in his room until the rest of the family left the house. Over breakfast, he studied the scriptures and then spent time in prayer.

He loved his solitude when the house was empty. He stood by the window sipping his morning coffee while the occasional carriage drove by. The hot brew tasted good and energized him. It was time to pay another visit to Mamie.

He returned to Mulberry Avenue, still wondering how much he should tell her. As he walked to the door, he whispered, "Father, you promised wisdom if I would ask, and I'm asking now." He raised his hand and knocked. Just as before, Clementine peered out of her bedroom window and ducked back when he spotted her.

Mamie opened the door.

"Mr. Fletcher," she said, "come in. Do you have any news for me?"

His heart was heavy. "Yes, I do, as well as some new questions."

"I can hardly wait to hear. Please have a seat. Would you like some tea?"

"No, ma'am, thank you. I just want to give you a brief overview of what I found. Mamie, some of this may be difficult for you to hear." He clasped his hands and lowered his head.

Her eyebrows raised. "That sounds mysterious. I don't know what to expect."

Phineas took his notebook from his pocket and gave her the chronological order of events as gently as he could, as they were recorded in the county records. As he expected, she was in shock. "I believe that Charles was your father," he concluded. He swallowed hard and waited for her response.

Her hand went to her forehead and slowly raked her hair back. "So the man I believed was my father—he raised me as his own, knowing I was someone else's child? No, that's impossible. Mother would have told me." Tears ran down her face. She crossed her arms and squeezed them to herself, shuddering.

He gave her a minute to process that information. "Mr. Hensley must have loved you very much."

She leaned forward with her elbows on her knees and hands on her forehead. "So my real name was Mamie Hayes. For as long as I remember, I've always thought my maiden name was Mamie Hensley."

After a few moments passed, Phineas said gently, "I have some questions I'd like to ask your mother. May I talk with her?"

Mamie was still confused, running her hand over her head in a fog. "Mother? Oh, yes. Wait, I'll get her."

She brought her mother into the room as if she were leading a stranger.

"Please have a seat, Mother. Mr. Fletcher would like to ask you some questions."

"Have you seen Charles or Mason again, Clementine?"

She leaned forward to tell him a secret. "I have Mason in the closet. And Charles was on the porch just a few minutes ago. I closed my curtains so he wouldn't see us."

He smiled at her. "That's fine, Clementine. Say, I found out some things about you yesterday."

"You did?" She smoothed her skirt and folded her hands. Her eyes were sparkling and fixed on Phineas.

"Yes. I found out you used to be married to Charles."

"Well, Mr. Fletcher, I hope you don't spread that information around. He was a nasty man. He took up with a barmaid, and I caught them doing something shameful. You know what that was, don't you, Mr. Fletcher?"

"Yes, I think I know what that was. But he was Mamie's Pa, wasn't he?

"That was supposed to be a secret. You won't tell Mamie, will you?"

Mamie paled and closed her reddened eyes as if that would erase the pain of hearing her mother admit it.

"I promise I'll never mention it to her again," said Phineas. "But then you married Mason."

A bright smile lit up Clementine's face. "Yes, Mason is my husband. He's my very heart. But I have to hide him in the closet, so Charles doesn't hurt him."

"Did you know that Mason's Pa left him a lot of money?"

"He did? That's wonderful. How much?"

"It was close to four thousand dollars."

Childlike, she giggled with delight. "I didn't know that. Does

Mason know?"

"I don't know if anyone told him."

The older lady's attention drifted to some unseen place out the window. She retreated into her own mind. Phineas needed her attention.

"Clementine, do you know where Mason is buried?"

"Yes, he's buried out behind the cabin. It burned down, you know. We buried him there and put up a nice marker." Her mind was flipping from past to present and back again.

Phineas frowned. He hadn't seen any monument when he was there with Farmer Jaffee.

"And then you married Mr. Hensley."

"Yes."

"Do you know who shot Mason?"

"The sheriff asked me that. He asked if I saw Charles do it. I said no, I didn't, but it had to be Charles. He hated Mason. He hates me, too. He thinks Mason and I took his money." She giggled. "You can't take someone's money if he doesn't have any. Charles is a big drinker, you know."

"So he drank all his money away?"

"He sure did. Every time he got money, he would go over to the Two Roosters and drink it as fast as he could. That's where he met Lila."

"Lila?"

"Yes, the barmaid he did those icky things with."

"Oh, that Lila," said Phineas, hoping for more information. Lila might have had the money.

He continued. "Clementine, would you mind if I checked your room?" There was a chance she could have stashed the money and forgotten it.

"That's a strange request, young man, but if Mamie doesn't mind, I don't either."

He turned to Mamie, and she nodded.

"Mamie doesn't mind," he said. "Let's go look."

It didn't take long to search her room; it had so little in it. There was a large, free-standing wardrobe. Phineas opened the doors, half expecting to see Mason huddling inside. The bureau drawers were filled with dainties and various souvenirs she had collected through the years, but no money. He knelt and peered under the bed. There was nothing there but dust balls. He slid his hand under the mattress. Then, as long as he was there, he lifted both windows to find out if there was a place outside for someone to hide and scare the poor woman, but there wasn't. The search of the room revealed nothing useful.

They went back to the parlor. "Clementine, do you remember Lila's last name?"

"I'll never forget it. It's Beech. Lila Beech. She's quite a little strumpet, you know. I wonder if Charles is still dallying with her. Maybe she got tired of him." She laughed, a light, amused laugh.

Phineas made a note of the name. "Thank you for your help, Clementine."

She stood. "You're welcome, Mr. Fletcher. Now I'd like to finish my nap."

She left the room, leaving Phineas alone with Mamie, who had been waiting impatiently to talk with him.

"Mr. Fletcher, are you sure my father wasn't Mr. Hensley?" She was still in shock. The man she had loved and called 'Pa' all those years—he wasn't her father?

"I am quite sure, and I apologize for making you aware of it as abruptly as I did. There was probably a better way to handle that. You see, you were born when your mother was married to Charles, but she divorced him on the grounds of infidelity, then she married Mason, who was shot and killed about a year later with you in his arms, then she married Mr. Hensley."

"It will take me a while to come to terms with that."

"Think of it this way, my dear. Charles Hayes was your father, but Mr. Hensley was your Pa."

Her face slowly lit up. "That helps. Yes, you're right. My Pa was Elias Hensley."

"I'll be leaving now, Mamie, but I still want to track down that inheritance money. It's probably been spent by this time, but my curiosity won't rest until I know what happened to it."

She finally relaxed enough to smile. "Good luck with that. You'll let me know, won't you? I have an active curiosity, too."

He promised to let her know what he found out, then left.

There was still time to go to Lamar and be home by dinner. Phineas stopped at Link's General Store where Danny worked and bought an apple for lunch. "I plan to be home by supper time, Danny, but don't wait for me if I'm not. I'm doing more research in Lamar."

"All right, Pop. Good luck."

Phineas made his exit to the jingle of the brass bell over the door. He mounted up and headed for Lamar once again. He chuckled, thinking the horse could probably get there without guidance since he had been there so many times lately. He made quick work of his apple, tossed the core to the side of the road, and continued.

Mile after mile went by as the horse's hooves pounded rhythmically on the dirt road. Finally, he reached Lamar. At the courthouse, he went in to speak to the clerk.

"Good afternoon, Mr. Fletcher," said the clerk. "You're getting to be quite a regular here."

"Yes, I am, Johnny, and thank you for sending me to your grandfather. I learned quite a lot. Now I need to track down an old inheritance and find out what happened to it. Could I see the old records of court hearings and trials?"

"You bet." Johnny pulled out the appropriate record book, and Phineas took it back to the spare desk to read at his leisure. But first, he wanted to review the probate file for Jacob Hayes. He went to the old filing cabinet and found the folder. Sure enough, the bequest to Mason Hayes was $4,010.28. He made sure his note about that was accurate. He searched the file but saw no receipts signed by anyone who might have received the funds. There must be documents missing...or this could have been the result of more casual record-keeping thirty-five years ago.

He searched for another probate file for Mason Hayes. He found a thin folder with an order deeding the property with the burned-down cabin to Clementine Hayes. The attorney who had handled both probate cases was deceased, so there would be no interviewing him. Clementine probably didn't even know she owned the property.

He jotted down the vital information in his notebook, then returned to the criminal records on the desk. He looked for anything about Charles, Mason, Jacob Hayes, or Lila Beech. He started his search with the 1850 entries. He had been reading for about fifteen minutes when he came across the arrest record of Lila Beech for being a "woman of easy virtue," to quote the court file. She had been jailed for three days and reportedly left town. This was after the death of Mason.

100

Perhaps Charles had gone with her. There was no later mention of Charles in the records anywhere that Phineas could find.

He folded up the file and closed the record book.

"Thank you for your help, Johnny. Maybe I'll see you again soon." Johnny smiled and nodded.

Phineas thought to stop by the newspaper office again. This time he found the editor in the office, redlining an article. Phineas dropped his card on the desk and said, "Excuse me, sir, could I ask you some questions about an old murder?"

The writer lifted his eyes. "And you are...."

"Phineas Fletcher, sir. I'm an investigator looking into an 1853 murder. Do you think you could help me?"

"First, let me introduce myself. I'm Geoffrey Hamilton, owner of the Lamar Daily Democrat. Would you like to have a seat?"

"Thank you." Phineas pulled the chair over to the desk.

Mr. Hamilton fingered his business card. "I know who you are. I've been writing articles about you lately. I'm very pleased to meet you."

Phineas smiled. "Thank you for your publicity, Mr. Hamilton. Your readers have been keeping me busy. Now, let me ask you, do you remember the murder of Mason Hayes?"

Mr. Hamilton's eyes squinted and slanted toward the ceiling. "Oh, yes . . . I believe I do. I was quite young, but it was such a spectacular murder. It was on everyone's lips for miles around. Wasn't that the murder where the cabin was burning, and Mr. Hayes was shot carrying a child out of the fire?"

"Yes, it is."

"I don't have any archived papers going back that far, but I can tell you what I remember."

"Was there any evidence to make anyone believe the shooter was his brother Charles?"

"No, if I remember right, it was only speculation. But the speculation had plenty of basis in Charles' behavior."

"That was the same conclusion I came to, myself," said Phineas. "My other question pertains to the probate of the estate of Jacob Hayes, Charles and Mason's father. If you remember, the entire estate went to Mason since Charles had defaulted on some loans from his Pa."

"Oh, yes. I do remember that."

101

"I haven't been able to track down what happened to that money."

"Well, if Mr. Hayes didn't spend it, it would have passed to his widow."

"You would think so, but here I reached a dead end. The widow didn't even know Mason had been bequeathed that money."

"You don't say. Well, it's been a while. Maybe her memory is faulty."

Phineas laughed. "You don't know how true that is." He stood and thrust out his hand. "Thank you for your time, Mr. Hamilton. It was very nice meeting you. Maybe we'll have a chance to get better acquainted another time."

Hamilton shook his hand and opened the door for him.

The next errand on Phineas' list was a stop at the Two Roosters, where Charles drank his resources away, enraptured by the charms of Lila Beech. As he entered, the bar owner was cleaning the tables, getting ready for his evening clientele.

"Can I help you, sir? We're not open yet."

"I'm here only for information if you have any," Phineas said. "Have you been working here long?"

"I started out as a young'un when my Daddy owned the bar. I've been around for a pretty long time. What do you need?"

"Maybe you're old enough to remember a fellow named Charles Hayes or a girl named Lila Beech. Years ago, they used to spend some time and money in here."

The bartender stared in the distance for a moment, stroking his chin. "Oh, yes. It's coming back." He chuckled. "Those two had a thing going, didn't they? If I remember right, Lila used to sing here on Saturday nights, but she had a side business she got arrested for, if you know what I mean. While she was sitting in jail, Charles left town. Word was he hightailed it to Chicago over rumors of that murder. Soon as Lila got out of jail, she went up there to find him."

"Did they seem to come into money?"

The bartender swore. "Not a chance. If they had, I would have taken it to pay their bill. No, they just left, both of them. I heard years later that Charles got killed in a bar fight. Probably shot his mouth off once too often. I never heard what happened to Lila."

"I appreciate the information, sir. I'll be off to see a client." He waved his arm and left the barroom.

Standing on the brick sidewalk in the sunlight, Phineas suddenly thought of going to the bank and seeing if his friend McDonald, the bank manager, could help him. That possibility was slim, but the bank was only a block away. He had nothing to lose.

Phineas entered the First Ohio Bank and spotted McDonald at his desk in front of the large, ornate safe.

"Phineas," said McDonald, reaching out to shake his hand. "So good to see you."

Phineas took a chair in front of his desk.

"I have a favor to ask you. Can you search your records and see if you have any accounts under the names of Jacob Hayes, Charles Hayes, Mason Hayes, or Lila Beech? And check Lila Hayes and Clementine Hayes while you're at it."

"Hm. You're on one of your cases again, aren't you?"

"Yes. This one is unique. Most of the subjects are dead."

"Let me write those names down and get them to the teller. It won't take him long to get the information you need."

In a few minutes, they had their results. McDonald scanned the sheet given to him by the teller. "This says there is an account in the name of Clementine Hayes. It's an old account—been drawing interest for thirty years, but no one has claimed it."

Phineas' chin dropped. "Can you tell me the balance?"

"It's up to $5,688.87 with interest at one percent. Quite a healthy balance, if I do say so. I wonder where the owner is."

"I know where she is. She's in Spencer's Mill, widowed by her third husband. Her name is Clementine Hensley."

McDonald's eyes popped in amazement. "Why doesn't she come to get her money?"

"She never knew she had it. It started as an inheritance bequeathed to her husband Mason, who was shot and killed, presumably by his jealous brother. The funny thing, though, is that the probate file for Mason Hayes says nothing about the cash distribution. It only has information about the transfer of real property."

"I imagine a lot of those old files are incomplete. Things get lost over the years, you know."

"What will Mrs. Hensley need to do to prove she is Mrs. Hayes?"

"I'd get a lawyer involved if I were you. She'll need a marriage record, at the very least. The lawyer can help you. She's going to be a wealthy lady."

Phineas stood and shook McDonald's hand. "Thank you, friend. We'll have another lunch at the Old English Tea Room, you and I."

As he turned to leave, McDonald called after him, "Just say the time, Phineas."

Phineas was so excited to give the news to Mamie that he rode directly to her house, even though that would make him a little late for dinner. He urged the horse on as fast as he dared.

When he knocked on her door, he didn't even wait for her to speak. He blurted out his news. "Mamie, I've found the four-thousand-dollar inheritance, and it's been collecting interest all these years."

"No," she said. "Can that be?" She grabbed the arm of the nearest chair to stop herself from fainting. "I believe I need to sit down. Mr. Fletcher, you don't know what this means. We were going to have to either sell the house or take out a bank loan to cover my husband's recent business losses and continue to support Mother."

Phineas helped her into her chair. "Then this is divine timing," he said, smiling. "Let me give you the details. The money was bequeathed to Mason by his father. When Mason died, his attorney filed probate, and the money went to your mother as his next of kin. It was deposited into the bank under the name of Clementine Hayes. The bank manager said they didn't know who Clementine Hayes was, so it's been there ever since. The attorney never told your mother about it. Well, anyway, there you are. With interest, the money has grown to exactly" — he checked his notes — "$5,688.87."

Mamie gasped as her eyes grew wide. "That's a lot of money."

"Yes, it is. Your mother also owns the property where the cabin burned down. I'll take you there tomorrow to look it over if you like."

"I would love to go. We'll take Mama, too, but it might be a painful experience for her."

"It may, but it could also be what she needs to jolt her out of her flights of fancy."

Mamie hesitated. "Perhaps I'd rather get a neighbor to stay with Mother while you and I go, if you don't mind. She so enjoys her time with Mason; I'd hate to take that away from her."

His heart filled with sympathy for this thoughtful daughter. "If that's what you want to do, you and I will go. Now, there's a small problem with getting that money. Since your mother's name isn't Hayes anymore, she'll need to hire an attorney and provide proof of her marriage to Mr. Hensley. If you don't have an attorney, I recommend Christian Wolf in Lamar."

"I know Mr. Wolf. He's a fine man. I'll take Mother to see him on Monday. Oh, Mr. Fletcher, this is wonderful news. I can't thank you enough. Would you accompany us to Mr. Wolf's office on Monday? He may ask some questions that I don't have answers to. I'll pay your regular fee."

He nodded. "I could pick both of you up on Monday morning. We'll go in my carriage. Right now, I'm going home, where my daughter has dinner waiting. I just couldn't wait to tell you about your good fortune. I'll see you tomorrow for our property tour, Mamie."

He mounted his horse and rode home in a joyous mood.

In the morning, Phineas threw his bedroom window open, breathed deeply of the fresh air, and thanked God for his success in finding Clementine's money.

He found Miss Clementine chatting with the neighbor who would be staying with her for a few hours, giving Mamie some time for uninterrupted conversation with Phineas on their journey.

The two of them headed east for a few miles and conversed about unimportant things along the way, then took a right turn, going past the Jaffee farm and continuing for perhaps ten minutes. Phineas tied the horse to a tree and helped Mamie out of the carriage.

"Is this it, Mr. Fletcher? Is this where the fire was? Where my step-father died?"

"This is it, Mamie. Come over here by the fireplace." She took Phineas' arm and struggled through the underbrush, lifting her long dress and slipping a little as she walked in her delicate shoes. The creek bubbled over rocks a few yards away from the cabin, and birds chirped happily in contrast to the gruesome events of the past.

"Mother would have cooked our meals in this fireplace," said Mamie. She gazed around, trying to find something familiar about her old homestead.

"I wonder if there was a garden out back."

"Your mother said Mason was buried behind the house with a

nice marker, but I didn't see it when I was here." He wandered back and forth where the back of the cabin would have been and pushed weeds aside. "Mamie, I think I found it." He leaned toward the ground and found a piece of a broken monument. She stooped over and touched the stone with her hand, gently and reverently. She had tears in her eyes.

"He sacrificed his life for me, didn't he?"

"Yes, he did."

She lingered there with the stone for a long minute.

"Where do you think he was shot?" she asked.

"It was in front of the cabin, so it may have been over here." They walked to a likely spot.

Mamie inspected the trees all around. "That big oak over there. Do you see the one I mean, Mr. Fletcher? Don't you think that would have been a good spot for a man to hide with a pistol?"

"Yes, it would have."

She walked to the tree and stood behind it, looking at the spot they had chosen as the likely place for the murder. "Pure evil," she whispered hoarsely.

Phineas remained silent for a few moments, giving her privacy with her thoughts.

"I'm ready to go back home now," Mamie said after wandering the property with a deep frown.

He helped her back into the carriage but hesitated before leaving the scene. "Take a look around with fresh eyes, Mamie. This is an appealing property. Didn't you hear the little stream at the back? If you and your mother don't want to build anything on it for yourselves, she might get a good price for it."

"Yes. Well . . . we'll think about that another time."

Phineas slapped the reins, and they traveled back to Spencer's Mill in contemplative silence.

Monday morning, true to his word, Phineas picked up Mamie and Clementine and transported them to Lamar. The trio traveled in the cool spring air, chatting amiably. Clementine drew her shawl around her arms. She prattled on about putting Mason in the closet and chasing Charles away with various methods, including shaking her fist at him through the window. It was an interesting trip.

They arrived at Wolf's law office and waited for a few minutes in the reception area while he finished up with another client, then they were ushered into his private office.

"Good morning, Mr. Wolf," said Phineas. "I'd like you to meet my client, Mamie Fleet, and her mother, Clementine Hensley."

"Please have a seat, ladies. Fletcher, you can sit over here. Now, what can I do for you?"

Phineas outlined the situation for Mr. Wolf and showed him the notes he had taken from the court records. He gave him the bank balance in Clementine's account and asked what would be needed to access the money and to get a clear deed for the property she had inherited.

"Well, Miss Clementine," Wolf said, beaming. "You are to be congratulated on this bit of good luck."

"Thank you, sir. Mason will be pleased, too."

Wolf furrowed his brow and glanced back at Phineas with questioning eyes. "Isn't Mason—"

"Yes, he is. Mama has frequent flights of fancy," said her daughter.

Wolf nodded his understanding and smiled. "It may be a good idea, then, to appoint you as her Power of Attorney, giving you the right to make decisions concerning her assets. We'll need proof of her marriage to Mason, which should be easily acquired from the courthouse. I'll look up the marriage document, then write up a certification to take to the bank. I'll also draw up a Power of Attorney. I could have that ready within the hour if you want to come back and have your mother sign it."

He turned to her mother. "Miss Clementine, would you sign a document for me after lunch?"

She nodded with a cherubic smile. "Whatever you want, Mr. Wolf, as long as Mamie says it's fine."

"I'll treat you ladies to lunch at the Old English Tea Room," said Phineas. "Then we can come back and take care of the paperwork."

Lunch at the Tea Room with both ladies was delightful. Miss Clementine reacted to the experience with child-like joy.

"Mamie, did you see these prices?" she asked, peering at the menu through crooked spectacles. She spoke in a stage whisper. "It's a good thing Mr. Fletcher is paying the bill. We could never afford anything like this."

Mamie and Mr. Fletcher locked eyes for a moment, smiling. Miss Clementine had already forgotten she was a wealthy lady.

A week later, Phineas received a letter written in a feminine hand.

'My Dear Mr. Fletcher,

There are not enough words to thank you for what you have done for Mother and me. I've decided not to disturb Mother's enjoyment of Mason, and I have come to terms with having both a father and a Pa. I can see now that Elias Hensley loved me because he wanted to, not because he had to. That's not a bad thing to know.

Even though you took on our job without asking for pay, I enclose a check for a finder's fee. If you hadn't pursued all the clues to the end, we would still be without Mother's money. So may the Lord bless you richly. We are telling everyone we know what kind of investigator you are.

Yours most truly,
Mamie Fleet'

Phineas stared at the check in his hand. $150.00. A smile lit his face. That was far better than his usual three or four dollars a day.

But there were still questions to be answered. What caused the cabin fire? Did Charles commit arson? Did Charles kill his brother, or did someone else do the deed? Did the shooter have training as a marksman, or did he pull off a lucky shot? Why did no one tell Mason he had inherited thousands of dollars?

Phineas sighed. He may never know. Or perhaps – someday, when he had nothing else to do – perhaps he would dig into those questions and finally come up with answers.

TURKEY IN THE CROSSHAIRS

It was the sort of relaxing evening that brought folks out to their porches to sit in their rockers and reminisce about the good old days. The air had been misty with soft rain all day, rinsing dust off the trees, but now the clouds were gone. Buds broke through the soil all over town. The air was cool, as it often was in Ohio in late April. Danny, Charlotte, and Phineas rocked at a lazy pace on the front porch, drank their lemonade, and chatted about nothing in particular. The sun dropped low, and shadows lengthened.

As the darkness deepened, Charlotte rose. "I should call the children in," she said. "They still have to go to school tomorrow."

"I'll go get them," Phineas said. "You worked all day, and I didn't. I could at least do that much for you."

Charlotte sat back into the rocker, grateful for the rest. "Thanks, Pa."

Phineas lumbered out toward the creek, calling, "William, Amos, Lizbeth!"

William, age fifteen, and Lizbeth, the ten-year-old, came out of the shadows of the trees at the creekside, but the awkward middle child, Amos, was not with them. Amos was twelve years old and small for his age.

"Where's Amos?" Phineas asked.

"He took a walk down the road," William said. "He'll be back in a few minutes."

Shortly Amos came up the road, swinging his yo-yo and whistling a tune.

"It's time for you three to go to bed," Charlotte said.

William's bedtime habits were well-established. The boy sat up every night, reading books by the light of his oil lamp, but Phineas decided not to tell Charlotte. The three children would be living with them for only another month, and there was no sense spoiling William's routine now. The children had stayed with Danny and

Charlotte only to finish school with their class. In the summer, the children would rejoin their mother and new stepfather in a home several miles away.

In the morning, while Phineas enjoyed his blissful solitude, Charlotte was at school settling her class in for the day.

There were students of every age in her class of twenty-eight children, crowded into one room with a potbelly stove. There were fifteen desks, enough for every two students to share and one for the teacher. She had grouped the children into learning levels as far as possible. At the moment, most of her students were doing lessons in their readers, while she had a group of more advanced students learning math in one corner of the room.

The doors burst open, shattering the tranquility and order. Charlotte immediately knew there was danger, and her stomach turned in anticipation. An angry farmer barged into the school, brandishing a stick. His voice, contrasted with the general quiet of the classroom, sounded like thunder. It was Farmer Ragsdill.

"Where is Amos Reese?" he bellowed. His face was red, and the veins of his neck were bulging. He brought the stick down on the nearest desk, causing the girls to scream and cry. It was happening so fast that Charlotte didn't have time to think. She jumped up and positioned herself between the angry man and the students, who were staring wide-eyed and open-mouthed.

"What do you want with Amos?"

"He shot one of my turkeys. I'm going to skin his hide." He waved the stick in a slow circle.

"You'll do no such thing," Charlotte shouted back. Her pulse was pounding like a racehorse, and her hands shook. She grabbed one of the desks to steady herself and glared at the farmer. She pointed at the door and shouted again. "You get out of here right now. You're interrupting my class."

"I'm not leaving without young Reese."

"You're leaving now," she said. She stared at him with steel in her eyes, knowing that backing down was not an option.

"Get out of my way," he said, and pushed her aside, heading toward Amos. Charlotte stumbled into a student desk and knocked it askew before she could right herself.

Lizbeth leaped out of her chair and jumped in front of Ragsdill, screaming like a banshee. "You get away from my brother. He did not shoot your stupid turkey, and you know it."

William stood and walked toward the farmer calmly but purposefully. "You're not going to touch my brother or my sister, either one," he said, glaring and defiant. "If you think you are, you'll have to go through me first."

Ragsdill sized him up. He thought he could overcome William with his stick, even though the boy had put on some muscle in the past year, but he thought better of taking on three children and their teacher. Amos was meek enough, but Lizbeth was a little spitfire, and William was muscular. It was William's calm determination that seemed to give him pause.

He prepared to make his retreat, but he wanted the last word. He turned, pointed at Amos, and said, "I'll get you later."

As Ragsdill stomped out the door, Amos' face was drained of color, and he had tears running down his face.

Charlotte slumped into one of the desks. The room began to spin as the noise in the classroom seemed to fade and recede into the distance.

William took her wrist and gently slapped the back of her hand. "Someone get some water," he said. One of the girls went to the pump and brought water back in a dipper. Charlotte took a few sips. It revived her enough to gather her wits.

"Children, I want you all to go home for the rest of the day. I'll try to find out what's going on so Mr. Ragsdill won't threaten us again."

The children picked up their books and filed out, talking in low tones, wondering if it could be true. Would Amos have shot a farmer's turkey?

Charlotte and the three siblings in her care walked home, surprising Phineas, who was enjoying his morning coffee and reading a book.

"What are you all doing home so early?" he asked.

"I sent the children home from school today. A terrible thing happened this morning, Pa," Charlotte said. She sank into a chair and recounted the traumatic tale. "It was a horrifying experience. I never in my life...." She turned to William and Lizbeth. "But I'm so proud of the two of you for standing up to that threat."

Phineas took on a dark expression. "I can't let a man push my daughter around and threaten a child. I'll teach him a lesson he won't forget."

She paused, shaking her head at the memory. "Pa, would you mind bringing me a cup of tea?"

She had never before asked her father to bring her tea. He went to the kitchen to get it for her.

"So what's the whole story?" he asked when he returned with her teacup. "I want everyone in the parlor, and we'll talk this out."

The five of them tried to figure out what to make of the situation. It had just come up without warning, without reason.

Phineas took charge. "Amos, let me ask you first, did you shoot a turkey?"

"No, sir."

"Do you know anything about someone else shooting a turkey?"

"No, sir."

"You better be telling me the truth."

"I am."

"I believe you." He couldn't imagine shy Amos behaving like that. The very idea was ludicrous.

"All right. Here's what we'll do. First, I'll go to Ragsdill's farm and ask him why he thinks Amos did it. Then, I'll find out when this event was supposed to have occurred and try to find out who the real culprit is. Once we come up with the truth, Ragsdill will have to leave Amos alone."

"Pa, I'm not so sure that's a good idea. That man was raving mad. He's dangerous."

"I'll take my revolver and hope I don't need it. Maybe if he sees it, he'll behave himself."

Phineas picked up his notebook and pencil out of habit, tucked his revolver in his belt, then went out to the barn and saddled his horse. Ragsdill lived on the farm a half-mile north of town where all those turkeys gobbled and squawked from sunup to sundown. Phineas turned his horse north and went at a trot.

He was not looking forward to this interview.

He arrived at the Ragsdill farm to the din of gobbling, cackling, and squawking turkeys. The racket from all those birds would make anybody edgy. The front door had a metal knocker shaped like a rooster — tap, tap, tap.

The lady of the house opened the door. "What can I do for you, mister?" she asked.

"I'm looking for Mr. Ragsdill. My name is Phineas Fletcher, and I understand that Mr. Ragsdill had an issue with one of the students at the school this morning. I want to help him find out who stole his turkey." He flashed his most charming smile.

That was a diplomatic way to introduce myself. He thought he deserved a pat on the back.

Mrs. Ragsdill invited him in. "Please have a seat here in the parlor. I'll go get my husband," she said. "Would you like a cup of tea?"

"Thank you for offering, ma'am, but I just had a cup of coffee, so I'll pass on that tea."

She nodded and went out to the barnyard to get her husband. When the two of them came back in, the farmer was belligerent.

"What's your interest in my affairs?" he asked.

Phineas stood and put his hand out to shake the farmer's hand, and the farmer reciprocated without thinking. Then, the two of them sat down. "For one thing," he said, "the schoolteacher whose class you interrupted is my daughter. She was most upset."

The farmer shrugged, unconcerned.

"For another thing, the child you have accused is living in my home, so you have involved my family in your accusation. I came to find out why you thought Amos shot your turkey since he's a quiet child who plays alone most of the time. He's never in his life shot a gun."

"Well, I'll tell you," Ragsdill said. "Last night, a little past dusk, two boys were out by my turkeys. I saw 'em, but I didn't pay much attention. Young'uns walk by my place all the time. After I came into the house, there was a gunshot, and the turkeys raised a ruckus. I opened the curtains to find out what the devil was going on. Then one of the boys grabbed a dead turkey by the neck and jumped the fence with it, and they both ran off. I chased them, but they had too much of a head start. About fifteen minutes later, Amos Reese was out there." He pounded his fist on the end table to emphasize his point. "He was one of the boys that shot and stole the turkey."

"Wait a minute," Phineas said. "Any reasonable person knows that a boy who happens to walk by the scene of a crime fifteen minutes after it occurred has no relationship to the actual crime."

"All I know is that he was the same size as one of the boys that done it. That's good enough for me."

"Why don't we try to find the actual thieves instead of accusing an innocent kid who wanders by? Can you give me some details about those boys? I'm pretty good at finding culprits."

"I'm telling you, it was young Reese."

"It won't cost you anything to humor me," Phineas said. He pulled out his notebook and pencil, then licked the point. "Tell me everything you can remember about those two boys."

"You're wasting your time, but I suppose there's nothing to lose. Let's see. One was about five feet tall and skinny, like his mama don't feed him enough. That one was wearing dungarees and a white shirt."

"What was the color of his hair?"

"Nothing unusual. Brown, I guess."

Phineas wrote it all down.

"What about the other boy?"

"He was about my height and heavier. He was wearing dungarees, too, and I think his shirt was brown."

"Hair color?"

"I don't know for sure. He was wearing a straw hat."

"All right, that's good. Now, were they carrying anything?"

"Nothing but my dead turkey." Ragsdill began to get agitated all over again at the memory.

"You didn't see a pistol or a shotgun?"

"No, but I heard it."

"The fired shot — did it sound like a shotgun or a pistol?"

"A shotgun, for sure. . . Yes, it was a shotgun."

Phineas sighed, thinking the farmer should have seen at least the silhouette of a shotgun. They're not that easy to hide. He jotted down the details.

"Let's go outside and look at where all this took place."

The farmer agreed to show him where the turkey met its doom. The two men walked out to the road and around the corner, following the fence where the boys took the turkey.

"It was right about here," he said.

Phineas walked back and forth past the site, looking for any prints in the dirt. He was hopeful he would find something since there had been a light rain yesterday, but tall weeds hid any boot prints. He inspected the fence. Blood drippings and a bloody handprint marred the fence's top rail. Several medium-sized footprints were inside the fence enclosure with the turkeys, but so many overlapped that they were useless to an investigation.

Phineas leaned down to inspect one particular print without too many other tracks. Down on his knees, he sketched it out on his notepad as accurately as possible, including a small chip in the outer side of the heel. That may come in handy.

"Look at that unusual nick in the heel," he said, showing his sketch to Ragsdill. "If we find that boot, we'll have one of the boys."

For the first time, the farmer showed interest. He stared at the drawing with bushy eyebrows raised and ran his hand through his hair.

"I'm going to sketch out that bloody handprint and try to do it full-size. That could belong to the boy with the chipped boot, or it could belong to the other boy." He began sketching, and the farmer agreed that his sketch was accurate.

"You'll see that Amos fits either the boot or the handprint." The farmer still wasn't budging from his position.

"If he does, he'll be punished."

The farmer swore. "Yes, and he'll pay for the dead turkey."

"Thank you for your time, Mr. Ragsdill. I'll keep you informed."

"Hmph."

He pocketed his notes and pencil and walked back to his horse. "Let's head home, girl," he said. He mounted up and turned for home. It was a relief to be away from that farm.

At home, Phineas walked to the stream where Amos and Lizbeth were playing. "Amos," would you mind showing me the bottom of your boots?"

Amos sat on a rock and picked up his feet, one at a time. Phineas took note of the heels on both boots. Neither of them was nicked like the boot print in his sketch. "That's fine," Phineas said. "Now, let me put this sketch of a handprint beside your hand and see if they look the same."

This might be a problem, he thought. The hand was roughly the same size as the sketch, but an honest person would say it was inconclusive. On the other hand, a dishonest person looking to accuse Amos would swear it was a perfect fit no matter what. "Thank you, Amos."

"Sure," Amos said with a shrug.

It would be nice to be twelve years old and have no worries about the future, Phineas thought. He trudged back to the house slowly, trying to figure out his next step, then sat on the Chesterfield with his head in his hands, coming up with no ideas. Charlotte was in the kitchen peeling potatoes and turned in his direction. "Pa, what are you thinking? You look worried."

"I'm thinking about the possible consequences for Amos unless we can clear him of this ridiculous accusation."

Charlotte chewed her lip. "Can't you prove his innocence?"

"So far, I can prove one of the boys had a boot with a chip out of the heel. In addition to finding that, I found a bloody handprint on the fence, and Amos' hand is close to that size — close enough that someone trying to make a case against him will swear it's a perfect match . . . but of course, it's not."

"What's the worst that could happen?" she asked.

"If Ragsdill prefers charges, and the sheriff believes him, Amos could end up in jail, although the sheriff would not want to hold a twelve-year-old overnight. But if the town gossips learn of it, they will surely brand him a thief, even though he isn't, and taint his reputation. And he'd be charged for the cost of the turkey."

"We can't let that happen."

"No. We won't." Phineas only hoped he could keep that promise.

"Danny will be home soon. We'll tell him what happened. Maybe he'll have some ideas."

Danny arrived home after his shift at the general store. At the supper table, the whole family talked at once, telling the story. Danny couldn't believe his ears. "Who does that bully think he is? That's pure evil. What can we do to protect our family? We need to make sure the rest of the class is safe, too."

Phineas answered. "If he breaks into the school like that again, Charlotte, you need to send two of the older girls to get the sheriff. Keep the older boys there to help keep Ragsdill at bay."

"Good idea, Pa."

When the family rose from their beds the following day, Phineas got up at the same time. A plan had come to him during the night, and he wanted to carry it out as early as possible. He conferred with Charlotte. She agreed it was a good idea, so he hitched the horse to the carriage.

After Danny left for work, Phineas, Charlotte, and the children rode to school. They all walked into the school building together as a family.

As soon as Charlotte rang the school bell and the children entered, she made her announcement. "Children, we're going to do something different this morning. I want the boys over on that side of the room by the wall and the girls over on this side."

The children filed into their positions.

"Now, I want all of you to face the wall. Mr. Fletcher will inspect the boys' boots, and I'll examine the girls' shoes. Here's how you'll do it. When it's your turn, you'll put your hands on the wall and lift your right foot behind you until Mr. Fletcher or I can look at the bottom of your shoe. Then you'll put up your left foot. Then you'll be done."

One of the girls raised her hand. "Mrs. Reese, why are we doing this?"

"It's a secret experiment. We can't tell you right now, but we hope to tell you next week."

The entire class was cooperative. Some children were excited to participate in a secret plan, which went off without a hitch. Of course, Charlotte didn't expect to see anything from the girls' shoes, but checking them would keep the girls busy while the boys were being checked.

"Did you find out anything, Pa?" Charlotte whispered at the end of the 'experiment.'

"Yes, I did, dear. We won't discuss it now, but I'll tell you when you get home."

"All right. See you later."

Phineas left the classroom, certain of the identity of one of the boys. He wrote the name in his notebook: Wiley Rucker. The boy's reputation was well-known in the village.

Wiley was an angry, unruly boy whose home life was barely adequate. His Pa was abusive and loved to drink liquor more than he loved his family. His Ma was a timid woman who rarely left the house. Neither parent imposed any discipline on their son. Fortunately for the townfolk, he was the only offspring they ever produced.

A thought came to Phineas. Maybe Wiley shot the turkey because he was hungry. Theft wasn't the best way to handle hunger, but it would at least make sense to a desperate boy.

The most urgent question now was not why but with whom.

Phineas thought the easiest way to find out would be to interview Wiley, but not in the presence of his parents. And he would need enough time to gain the boy's trust before he would be willing to share any information. The best way to catch him alone would be after school. He would need Charlotte's cooperation in sending the rest of the students home while keeping Wiley behind.

When Charlotte and the children came home, the three youngsters went about their daily chores, and Phineas had a chance to talk to Charlotte alone.

"Did Mr. Ragsdill come back today?"

"He was hanging around outside the schoolhouse for a while, but I kept all three children close as we walked home. He stayed behind us at a distance, but he didn't try to approach."

"We need to learn the names of the two boys who stole the turkey, and we need to do it quickly, for Amos' sake," said Phineas. "I know who one of the boys was. It was Wiley Rucker."

"Oh, dear," Charlotte said. Her hand went to her head. "That boy doesn't have a chance in the world to make anything of himself. He gets no guidance at home. He thinks force and bullying are the only two ways to get what he wants. And it's a shame because he's smart. I'd like to help him, but I think he's beyond me."

"Who are the friends he spends time with?"

"He has two that are friendly with him sometimes, but I wouldn't call them close. He's too hard on them. Still, they admire the way he swaggers and gets what he wants, which seems to be what attracts them."

"Does Amos ever spend time with him?"

"I should say not. I think Amos is afraid of him."

"Can you give me the names of the two boys?"

"Yes, there's Paul Black and Augustus Jenkins. They call him Gus."

"I'm going to ask you one more question, dear, and I know you don't want to answer it, but for Amos's safety and yours, I'm hoping you'll tell me what I need to know. Where do Paul and Gus live?"

He was right; Charlotte had refused a similar request before, telling him it was against a teacher's policy to give out student addresses. But this time, the health and safety of her young brother-in-law were being threatened. She relented and gave up the information that her father needed.

"Good girl," Phineas said. "Now, one more favor. Is there some way to keep Wiley after school tomorrow after the rest of the children leave? I want to interview him alone."

"I can try, but if I stay with Wiley, that will leave Amos exposed on the way home from school."

"Hmm. You're right. Let me think on that a while longer."

This was a problem beyond Phineas. He needed extra help, so he retreated to his bedroom and bowed his head. "Father, here's another sticky problem. I need to find out who shot Ragsdill's turkey before the man can hurt Amos. So I ask for a cover of divine protection over Amos, and I ask you to clear the path for me to find out who the real culprit is. I want this mystery to end the way You want it to. So thank you, in Jesus' name."

He sat on the edge of his bed, suddenly realizing how weary his body was and how he could push himself no further mentally. He stretched out on his bed, right there in the middle of the day, and dropped off into a sound sleep. He didn't stir until Danny was home and supper was on the table. He heard voices downstairs and caught the aroma of beef and onions. He sat up, refreshed. He still didn't know his next step, but he was confident the Lord was working behind the scenes to answer his prayer.

The family gathered at the table for their evening meal. As Charlotte filled their bowls with pot roast, someone began beating on the door. The family's reaction was immediate. They all twisted their heads around to see what was happening, and Danny jumped up to find out who was there.

Phineas wasn't surprised that Ragsdill burst inside when Danny opened the door. He got up and rushed into the parlor to give Danny a hand with the aggressor.

"Where's Amos?" Ragsdill demanded, despite being confronted by two strong men. "He needs to be punished, and somebody's gonna pay for my turkey. You owe me two dollars, Reese. That was a big tom he shot."

Danny held his ground. "My little brother did not shoot your turkey, Ragsdill. There's no evidence that he did; you know there isn't."

"That's a lie. I saw him there."

"Any reasonable person would know that if Amos did shoot the turkey, he wouldn't hang around for fifteen minutes. He doesn't have a gun, for one thing, and for another, he wasn't carrying a turkey when you saw him."

"That don't matter. I know he done it."

Danny pushed his point. "You're not looking for the truth. You're just looking for someone to blame."

Phineas intervened. "Ragsdill, calm down. I'm actively working on finding out who those two boys were. I have the identity of one of them and intend to find out tomorrow who the other one was."

"Who was it?"

"If I tell you, you'll run over there and ruin any chance I have of talking to the boy and getting information out of him. So I'm not going to tell you, not yet."

"I have a right to know." He was still shouting.

"And so you shall, but not right now. Look, Charlotte has made a delicious pot roast for supper. Would you like to sit with us and have a nice meal?"

Ragsdill looked taken aback by the show of hospitality. "No. I need to get home to the missus. You'll give me the identity of the two rascals that robbed me of my turkey?"

"As soon as I find out."

Ragsdill nodded his head. "I guess I'll be going." Danny opened the door for him, and he left.

"Whew! That's a relief," Danny said. "I think I held my breath the whole time the man was here." He and Phineas chuckled nervously and returned to the table.

Amos' eyes were like saucers. "He was gonna hit me, wasn't he?"

"He wanted to," Danny said. "You stick close to Charlotte and William at school tomorrow, you hear me? I'll worry about you until Pop finds out who shot Mr. Ragsdill's turkey."

"He can stick close to me, too," said Lizbeth, her jaw set and fire in her eyes.

Charlotte grinned. "You're full of sauce and vinegar, young lady, but I don't think you'd be much protection in a fight."

"I know how to kick."

"I'm sure you do. Let's hope you don't get tempted."

An idea dropped into Phineas' mind. "Charlotte, I just had a germ of an idea. May I have a word after the dishes are done?"

"Sure, Pa."

After the kitchen chores were over and Lizbeth went to her room, Phineas came in for a private chat with his daughter.

"I haven't thought this all the way through, dear, but what if I had some whitewash and paintbrushes at the school after class is out tomorrow? You could tell Wiley and his two friends that you have a job for them to do—a paying job. You'll pay them each twenty cents to whitewash the fence for an hour. I'll supervise. I may get them to talk while we're working together."

"Where am I going to get the money?"

"Don't worry about it. I'll pay them myself. I got an unexpected windfall after solving the last case, so I'll bring the whitewash, too."

"Thanks, Pa. I'll take care of getting the boys to stay. And I'll tell William he needs to walk home with Amos tomorrow."

Phineas grinned. "You might have Lizbeth go with them, too. She knows how to kick."

Charlotte rolled her eyes.

The rising sun brought a new day that promised to be fruitful. The first task on Phineas' to-do list was visiting the home of Wiley's friend, Paul Black. He found the house at the address Charlotte gave him and rapped on the door. Mrs. Black opened it. She was a pleasant, slightly heavy woman with dark hair in a braid at the back of her head.

"Yes, sir?" she said.

"Mrs. Black, I'm Phineas Fletcher, here on a delicate matter, and I'm hoping you can help. Two boys shot and stole a turkey the other night from the Ragsdill farm, and I'm trying to figure out who they were. I was hoping you could give me some information. May I come in?"

Mrs. Black stepped back and crossed her arms. "You're not accusing my Paul, are you?"

Phineas hastened to put her at ease. "No, ma'am. I know who one of the boys was. I thought maybe he'd been bragging to Paul, and maybe Paul mentioned something to you."

She relaxed and opened the door wider. "Come on in. What did you say your name is?"

He stepped inside. "I'm Phineas Fletcher, ma'am." He handed her one of his cards.

121

"Have a seat, Mr. Fletcher. I read about you in the paper, didn't I? Would you like a cup of tea?"

"Yes, please. That would be very nice."

She went to the kitchen to brew the tea, giving Phineas a chance to look around the parlor. It was sparse but well cared for. A bookcase with several interesting volumes and a fiddle leaned against the wall. Paul was obviously from a better home than Wiley.

Mrs. Black brought in tea for both of them and sat in the chair opposite Phineas. "Who was it who shot and stole the turkey?" she asked.

Phineas rolled his options through his mind. He wouldn't usually tell her the name, but she might reveal some connection between the boys if he did. He decided to risk charging ahead.

"I'm reluctant to say. It would be best if you kept this strictly confidential until I find out who both boys are. Can you promise me that? Otherwise, you'll ruin my opportunity to talk to the boy first."

"Yes, I promise."

"All right…The boy was Wiley Rucker."

Mrs. Black's eyes flashed. "I've told Paul to stay away from that boy. He's a bad influence. Real bad. But my boy finds something in Wiley that draws him in."

"Has Paul said anything about a turkey in the last couple of days?"

"Not that I remember."

"Have you seen any evidence of anything, like maybe turkey feathers? I know that sounds silly."

"Well, I don't blame you for the asking. But no, I ain't seen nothing like that."

"Where was Paul two nights ago? I'm only asking because Farmer Ragsdill is blaming a young relative of mine who walked by his farm fifteen minutes after the shooting, but of course, he didn't do it."

"Paul didn't either. But to answer your question, he was with his friend—Gus. Gus Jenkins. They were tossing a ball at the park."

"Thank you. You've been very helpful." On the way out, he turned back toward Mrs. Black. "By the way, ma'am, the picket fence at the school needs whitewashing, and Mrs. Reese will ask some boys to stay after school today to help with that job. They'll get paid for their work. Paul may be one of the boys who is invited to stay. He may be home a little later than usual."

Her eyes lit up. "I hope he's chosen. That would be a good experience, earning something from his own labor."

"Yes, ma'am. Well, I'll be leaving now. I appreciate your help."

"Good luck finding your culprit, Mr. Fletcher."

He went outside and mounted his horse. Now off to visit the Jenkins house.

The Jenkins family lived several blocks away. The horse trotted along at a good pace, so it didn't take long to get there. After Phineas tied the horse to their rail, he knocked on the door, but it took a couple of attempts before he got a response. He expected to see Mrs. Jenkins, but it was Mr. Jenkins who answered.

"What can I do for you?" he asked. He was a pleasant-looking man, but his eyes drooped, making him look tired.

Phineas handed him one of his cards.

"I'm visiting some of the parents of school-age children, and you were on my list," said Phineas. "There was an incident the other night where two boys shot and stole a turkey, and I'm hoping that maybe one of the culprits has been bragging to the other boys."

"Come on in, sir. I can tell you my boy wouldn't do such a thing."

Phineas went inside and took the chair across from Mr. Jenkins.

"I'm not accusing anyone. I know who one of the boys was, and it wasn't Gus. But maybe your boy knows something. Has he mentioned anything about a turkey to you in the last couple of days?"

"No, but I don't see him much. I have an evening job. I'm the night watchman for some of the stores on Main Street since all that trouble at the bakery a couple of months ago, so when Gus gets home from school, I'm not often here."

"Perhaps I could talk to Mrs. Jenkins?"

Mr. Jenkins fidgeted and cast his eyes toward the floor. "My Betsy passed away two years ago."

"I'm sorry, Mr. Jenkins," said Phineas. He leaned forward in his chair and spoke in a more personal tone. "I lost my wife, too, so I know what you're going through. We had one child—a daughter. It's so difficult to raise a child on your own."

Jenkins sat with his head down and his hands folded between his knees. "You know it, don't you?"

Phineas wanted to reach out to this unhappy fellow. It was as if

123

they had an instant bond. They sat for a moment in the quiet of the house, not knowing what else to say.

Finally, Phineas broke the silence. "I wish you the best, Mr. Jenkins. By the way, the fence at the school needs to be whitewashed. It's going to be a paying job for some of the students. Your son may be one of the boys offered the job after school today. He may be home late."

Jenkins smiled. "I'd never know if he was late, but I hope he's offered that job. It would give him something constructive to do. And earning his own money, why, that would be a real blessing."

"So long, Jenkins." The men shook hands, and Phineas left, taking his horse to the general store. He thought about the loving parents he had talked to this morning and their need for their boys to have constructive, paying work. It tugged at his heart.

The next stop for Phineas was Link's General Store, where Danny worked. When he walked in, the bell jingled over the door. Danny glanced up, but he was busy helping another customer. "Hi, Pop. I'll be with you in a minute."

Phineas dawdled, looking at the jars of candy as if through the eyes of a child. He decided to buy a few pieces of the sweet treats and take them home for William, Amos, and Lizbeth. He scanned the jars, then reached in one after another, choosing pieces and dropping them into a bag.

Danny's customer paid for her purchases and left. Danny turned to Phineas. "You're getting a sweet tooth, Pop?"

Phineas laughed. "I'll take these home for the children. . . except maybe that piece of licorice." He popped it into his mouth. "Let me have that candy, and two buckets of whitewash, if you have it."

"I have some in the storeroom," Danny said. "What are you going to paint?"

Phineas lowered his voice and leaned over the counter in case other customers were within hearing. "I'm going to get some boys to whitewash the fence at the school so I can talk to them. One is the rascal that shot the turkey, and the others are suspects."

Danny considered that information and grinned. "That's not a bad idea. It's a much better idea than the time you faked a fever with hot coffee to find out if the doctor was a thief." He chortled all the way to the store room.

Phineas blushed at that embarrassing memory. "Just get the whitewash, Danny."

Danny was still chuckling when he came back with two buckets of whitewash.

"I'll need four brushes, too."

Danny got the brushes and laid them on the counter with the candy and whitewash. He added up the total, and Phineas handed over the payment.

"Good luck with that, Pop. Thanks for trying to clear Amos."

"You're welcome, son."

Phineas picked up his purchases and went outside. There it was — the enticing aroma of bread and cinnamon from the bakery next door. He parked his determination to slim down and turned toward the bakery to buy some fresh rolls and a pumpkin pie for supper. As he walked into the bakery, he thought, *I'll have to get some willpower. My britches are getting tight.*

When it was time for school to be out, Phineas hitched up the carriage, loaded the whitewash and brushes, and rode to the school. He arrived as the students streamed out the door, except three boys still inside with Charlotte. Phineas walked in as she explained the job that needed to be done and how much money they would get. All three of them were bright-eyed and eager to get started.

"Come outside, boys," Phineas said. "I'm going to help you. I have four brushes and two pails of whitewash. We probably won't be able to finish the fence today, but maybe we could finish it tomorrow."

Gus said, "We'll get paid by the hour, won't we? If we work an hour today and an hour tomorrow, will we get paid twice?"

"You can count on it."

The boys grinned and swapped glances, then turned to Phineas as he opened the cans. "Two of us can work out of each can," Phineas said. "Gus, why don't you and Paul take a pail and start at the far end of the fence? Wiley and I will start at this end and work toward the middle."

Gus grabbed a pail. "You get two brushes and help me with this, Paul. Let's go."

Phineas smiled as they ran to the far end of the fence, lugging the heavy pail between them. Once they were out of earshot, he said, "Let's you and I get started on this end, Wiley."

"Yes, sir."

They worked in silence for about three minutes. "Hey, Wiley, what do you like to do in your spare time? Do you play ball or anything?"

"Sure, sometimes I do, but that's not what I like best. I can find better stuff to do."

"Oh, yeah? What kind of stuff?"

"I practice shootin.' I shoot at bottles."

"Pretty good, are you?"

"Better'n most." He smiled and continued as if he'd decided a little bragging wouldn't hurt. "If you go behind my house, you'll see a pile of broken bottles. That was me. I did that." He paused in his painting to see if Phineas appreciated his skill. Phineas had adopted an admiring expression. He smiled and nodded at Wiley.

They worked in silence for a few more minutes.

"Do you have friends that practice shooting with you?"

"No. They're a bunch of sissies. They don't like guns much. Sometimes Paul watches me, but he don't shoot."

"Ever shoot anything but bottles?"

"Yep."

Phineas hesitated. "That skill can put food on the family's table. I'd be proud of that if I were you."

Wiley dipped his brush in the pail. "I am."

The two worked in silence for a while longer, pulling their brushes down, then up, down, then up, in a steady rhythm, moving toward the middle of the fence.

"You're a good painter, Wiley," Phineas said. "You might be able to earn some good money doing this kind of work."

"Where would I get a job?"

"Why, you'd run your own business. How old are you?"

"Fifteen, almost sixteen."

"You're almost out of school, then. Why don't you go into business for yourself? Look around town and see if you can find jobs that people would pay you to do. Say, I think you might be able to paint the new wall at the bakery. They put plaster on it, but it hasn't been painted yet. Go over there and talk to the owner. His name is John Reese."

"Is he related to my teacher?"

"He's her brother-in-law. I can recommend you."

Wiley thought about it, then swore. "If my Pa found out I had money, he'd take it and spend it on liquor. There's never enough money for food. It all goes to liquor."

Phineas stared at him. "How do you eat?"

Wiley turned his face away and kept painting. "I get food here and there."

Phineas paused his painting, and his heart ached for the boy. Guilty or not, he was forced into thieving to feed his belly. No boy should have to live like that, scrambling for every crumb in his mouth while his Pa drank their sustenance away.

"Wiley, I'd like more time to talk with you after we finish painting. Would you come to our house for supper this evening? That would make you late getting home."

"It don't matter. Pa don't care if I come home at all."

"So, will you come?"

"Sure, I'll do that."

The two continued painting until the hour was up. They were coming close to the middle and congratulated themselves on good progress. "Let's put the lids back on the pails, boys. I'll see you again tomorrow." He gave each of them their pay. Gus and Paul left with smiles, and Wiley climbed into Phineas' carriage.

"I don't know your name, sir," Wiley said. "Is your name Mr. Reese?"

"No. Reese is your teacher's married name. I'm Mr. Fletcher."

The boy nodded, and they rode to the house without further conversation.

At the house, Phineas and Wiley entered together. "Charlotte, we have a guest for dinner," Phineas called into the kitchen.

Charlotte came out to see who it was, and her eyebrows raised. "What a surprise, Wiley. Welcome. Supper will be ready in a few minutes. Why don't you come into the kitchen and wash up?"

Charlotte and Lizbeth put supper on the table for seven this time instead of six, and they all sat down. Wiley's eyes bugged at the sight of the food before him—ham, potatoes, and green beans, all in big bowls. Then there were yeast rolls with lots of butter.

Danny smiled. "Let's say grace." Wiley's eyes widened when he saw the family bow their heads. Danny asked for a blessing on the meal, and they all said, "Amen."

Everyone passed the food, and each put some on their plate. Wiley watched all this and did likewise. He was not accustomed to family dinners like this. On top of all this bounty, Charlotte served pumpkin pie for dessert.

After supper, Phineas invited Wiley onto the porch to sit in the rocking chairs.

"Did you get enough to eat?" Phineas asked pleasantly.

"I'd say I did. I haven't eat like that in a long time." He had a satisfied grin on his face.

"Could we talk man to man?" Phineas said.

"Sure. What do you have in mind?"

"I'd like to talk about your business, about you earning money and figuring out how to keep your Pa from spending it on liquor."

"All right."

"But first, can we talk about Farmer Ragsdill's turkey?"

Wiley's anger flashed. "Is that why you brought me here?"

"Only partly, Wiley. I'm interested in you. You have real potential. I can see you growing a business and learning to earn money, then eventually marrying a wife and having a family. I can see you taking your place as a respected citizen in the community. You have some big problems at home to overcome, but with the help of other people, you can do it, son. You can do it."

Wiley tilted his head to the side as if deep in thought. "Shoot, I wouldn't know how to go about that."

"The first thing you have to do is start building your integrity. You start by owning up to taking that turkey and see that Ragsdill is paid for it. People respect a man of integrity. I'll loan you the money to pay for the turkey, and I'll go with you to apologize and pay for the tom. You can pay me back out of your earnings."

"That's a tall order."

"Yes, but you can do it, and that's the first hurdle you have to climb. And I'll stand by you all the way. By the way, who was the other boy with you when you shot the turkey?"

"It was Paul. But he didn't have nothing to do with it. He just watched."

"That's fine. What happened to the bird?"

"Ma cooked it. She hasn't had much to eat lately. Pa takes

everything we have, and he hits her if she doesn't have supper cooked."

Phineas stared off into the distance and slowly wagged his head.

"Here's what I see. I see a young man in front of me who provided food for his Ma. That's an honorable thing for you to do as a boy. But you're a man now, so the way you went about it wasn't right. You stole from another man who worked to earn it for his own family. So now he has to be paid back. He also accused Amos of shooting the turkey and wanted to beat him. So you caused Amos to be in danger."

"I didn't mean to do that," Wiley said, looking at his shoes. "I'm sorry about that."

"I know you are. So you can apologize to Amos, too. That will cause the other boys to respect you."

"It will?"

"Yes. That shows integrity when you take responsibility for your actions. People respect integrity, no matter their age."

"I'll do that."

"Now, let's talk about keeping your earnings from your Pa."

"Do you know how I could do that?"

"Yes, I do. You said he hits your Ma?"

"All the time. He used to hit me, too, but I got stronger than him. He pretty much leaves me alone now. I stop him from hitting Ma when I'm home, but I'm not always there. He could be beating on her right now."

Phineas sighed over the hopeless situation the boy had been living in. "He's assaulting your Ma. Assault is illegal. We can file a complaint with the sheriff for assault and drunkenness. He'll be put in jail for a while. Are you willing to do that?"

"I'd hate to do him harm, but I admit it would make life easier for Ma and me. They'll feed him in jail, right?"

"Yes, and he'll have to sober up. While he's in jail, any money you earn can be spent wisely for food and other needs, not wasted on liquor."

"That's true. Do you really think I could earn a living?"

"I can tell you this, sir. Anyone your age who can hustle food for the family has enough hustle to earn a living honestly. Can you cipher?"

Wiley grinned. "Ask Mrs. Reese. I'm real good at it."

"Fine, then you can earn a living. Part of it will be painting, but you might find other needs you can fill, too. Are you ready to go make things right with Farmer Ragsdill?"

Wiley bit his lip. "Much as I hate to face him, I'd like to get it over with."

Phineas pulled two bank notes out of his pocket. "Here's a loan. You owe this back to me, understand? You need to earn your own way."

"Yes, sir."

Phineas went into the house to tell Charlotte they would be gone for a while. "If I'm not back in an hour, that could mean trouble, so send Danny to Ragsdill's farm, will you?"

"Yes, Pa. Be careful."

Phineas and Wiley traveled to the farm. Wiley had a stricken look, like he was going to his own wake. "You'll be fine, Wiley. Straighten your shoulders and go in as a man."

"Yes, sir."

"And if he insults you, pay no attention. He's just an unhappy man with a hateful personality. You're better than that."

"Yes, sir."

"If he insults you, answer him with kindness. That's important. It'll throw him off guard."

"Yes, sir."

They arrived at the house and knocked on the door. Ragsdill came to the door. He gaped from Phineas to Wiley and back again.

"Is this the rotten thief who shot my turkey?"

Phineas nudged Wiley, who spoke up. "Yes, sir, I am. I came to apologize and pay for the turkey. And I must say, it was the most delicious bird my Ma ever cooked. But I'm sorry I took it."

Ragsdill's eyebrows raised. He expected insolence, but he didn't get it.

"May we come in?" asked Phineas. The farmer showed them in, and Wiley handed over the two dollars.

"Where did you get that from?" asked Ragsdill. "Did you steal that, too?"

"He did not," said Phineas. "It was a loan he'll pay back from his painting business. Wiley is an excellent painter. I worked alongside him today and saw his painting style with my own eyes. I highly recommend him."

"Hmph," said Ragsdill. "He's just a boy."

"Not so. He's a man. He's been providing food for his family — admittedly, in the only desperate way he knew, but he's decided to go into business and learn to take his place as a man, doing it the right way."

Wiley spoke up. "Mr. Fletcher is right. He showed me how I could start earning. I have some things to work out, but I'm determined to make it a success. Do you know anyone who has any painting I could do?"

"Who would hire a thief?"

"I'd like to make a new reputation for myself. I have to start somewhere."

"If I hear of anything, I'll let Mr. Fletcher know. What's your name, boy?"

Wiley pulled himself up to his full height. "My name is Wiley Rucker."

Ragsdill's mouth formed an "O." He nodded as he made the connection. "You're Jeb Rucker's boy."

Wiley sucked in a breath. His hopeful momentum had just been reduced to despair. "I...I'm hoping to make my own way without being connected to my Pa's reputation."

"The nut don't fall far from the tree, I always say. Well, thank you for paying for the turkey. See that it don't happen again."

"Yes, sir."

With that, Wiley and Phineas took their leave. Wiley's shoulders sagged.

"I'll never make a success once people connect me with my Pa."

Phineas looked at Wiley's pinched face, and his arm reached around the boy's shoulders. "That's not true, Wiley. Respect is earned over time. If you show yourself to be honest and fair in your dealings with other people, they will eventually separate you from your Pa in their minds. But it will take some time."

"Are you taking me home now?"

"Yes. I'll take you there."

"Pa will want my money. Can I give it to you as payment on my two-dollar loan?"

"How will you get food tomorrow?"

"I don't know, but I don't want him to have today's pay. Tomorrow will take care of itself."

Phineas nodded and took the twenty cents from the boy. He dropped Wiley off at home and told him he would earnestly pray for him. Then they heard screaming and crashing from inside the house. Wiley ran toward the front door, crying, "He's beating Ma again! I have to stop him."

"I'm going for help," Phineas shouted back. He slapped the reins and headed for the sheriff's house at a gallop. He hated knocking on the door, knowing it Sheriff Lane's habit to go to bed early. But a crime was being committed.

Arriving at the sheriff's home, he jumped out of the carriage and banged on the door. "Lane! Lane! It's Phineas Fletcher."

It took a moment for the drowsy sheriff to come to the door. "What's going on, Fletcher?"

"Over at the Rucker house. Mr. Rucker is drunk and beating his wife. Again."

"She's his wife. I don't want to interfere in a man's marriage."

Phineas swore. "What's the matter with you? Didn't you hear me? He's drunk. He's always drunk. He's always beating the poor woman. Wife or not, if you don't put him in jail for a while, you'll have a murder on your hands, not just an assault. That wouldn't read very well in the paper, would it?"

"Give me a minute to get dressed. You have a way of showing up at the worst times." He shut the door, grumbling under his breath, and slipped on his shirt and trousers. He strapped on his weapon and hooked a length of rope to his belt to use as a restraint. "Let's go, Fletcher. I'll take my carriage, and you take yours. You lead the way."

Hooves pounded the road while two carriages clattered down the road in the twilight. The fighting was still in progress when they arrived at the Rucker house. The sheriff told Phineas to stay in his carriage, then he went to the door and rapped with the butt of his gun. "Open up! This is the sheriff."

There was immediate silence in the house, then Mrs. Rucker timidly opened the door just a crack.

"Open up, Mrs. Rucker. I had a complaint about some violence in this house."

"Everything is fine," she said.

"No, it's not. Now open the door."

She opened up, and the sheriff stepped inside. There was shouting. Momentarily Lane came back out, pushing Mr. Rucker in front of him. Rucker's hands were bound. The sheriff had a firm grip on the back of his shirt to hold the drunk steady. Rucker wiped his bloody nose with his sleeve as he stumbled to the carriage.

"This no-account is going to jail," said Lane. "You wouldn't believe what he's done to his wife. He beat his son pretty good, too. The boy won't take long to recover, but I need you to get the doctor for Mrs. Rucker."

"I'm on my way," shouted Phineas. He had rarely been as angry as he was at that moment. His stomach churned, and his hands shook.

It took some effort to get Doc Yarwood to come out at that hour, but he finally gathered himself to go to the Rucker house. Phineas gave him the address, then left him to stop by the house. "Everything went well at the Ragsdill farm, Danny, but I have to go to the Ruckers' and meet the doctor there. I'll explain when I get back."

"We'll wait up for you."

Phineas ran back to his carriage and was off again.

When he stepped inside the Rucker home, he first spotted Mrs. Rucker. He took a deep breath and tried to control himself as his stomach heaved. He wanted to look away from her, but he couldn't. Blood matted her hair, old bruises marred her face with the new, and one arm was broken. The doctor was still treating her. Phineas turned his attention to Wiley, who had a swollen jaw, bloody lip, and black eye.

Wiley was grinning. "I worked him over good, Mr. Fletcher, and he had to stop beating on Ma. I held him off her until the sheriff got here."

Phineas smiled grimly. "You look pretty rough. You might want to stay home from school tomorrow. I'll tell Mrs. Reese you won't be there."

"Could I come to your house, then, and work on a plan for my business?"

Phineas grinned and nodded. He had a new friend. "I'll see you in the morning. Oh — don't come before nine o'clock. I have a morning routine."

"Yes, sir. I'll see you after nine."

Phineas stepped over to talk to Mrs. Rucker. "You have a boy you can be proud of, ma'am. Best of luck recovering from your injuries. I hope you never have to deal with that again."

"I don't have much hope of that, but thank you for your help," she said.

"Don't you have relatives you can go live with? You need to get away from a man who beats you like that and breaks your bones."

"He's my husband, Mr. Fletcher. My duty is with him."

Phineas turned away from her. He admired her grit but would never understand why anyone would stay in a home where they were constantly attacked if they had an alternative. He wished fervently he could help her, but he didn't believe he could help a stubborn woman against her will.

He turned back to Wiley. "You're the man of the house now. Take good care of your Ma. I'll see you in the morning."

He tipped his hat to Mrs. Rucker and left them alone.

By morning Phineas had formed a plan. He and Wiley would start in Spencer's Mill, canvassing the merchants to see if anyone needed a painter. After that, depending on the time, they would go to Lamar and visit an investor in real estate who often bought properties that needed to be improved. There would surely be some work there. The man's name was Oliver Hardin, a man well-known in the county. The carriage ride to Lamar would be a perfect opportunity to pour wisdom into the boy's head.

Shortly after nine o'clock, boots thumped on the porch. It was Wiley, right on time, wearing a big grin on his bruised and swollen face.

"You look awful," said Phineas with a crooked smile. "Come on in."

"Morning, Mr. Fletcher."

"Have you had anything to eat today?"

"Not yet."

"Come on in the kitchen. I'll fry some eggs."

The two went into the kitchen. As he cooked, Phineas filled him in on the plan he had devised. "We need to stop and get you a paintbrush to stick in your pocket. It'll make you look more like a painter. And with a little luck, you'll need to use it today."

"In that case, sir," said Wiley with egg in his mouth, "can I borrow

134

back that twenty cents I gave you yesterday? I'll use it to buy a brush." He swallowed some coffee to wash down the egg and wiped his mouth on his sleeve.

"Yes. That will be your first investment in your business."

They stopped by the general store and picked up two brushes — one wide and one narrow — then went next door to the bakery, where Phineas asked to see John Reese.

John came into the salesroom, happy to see Phineas; then he glanced at the character beside him with the bruised and swollen face. "Oh, my, what happened to you?" he asked.

Phineas said, "John, I'd like you to meet my friend, Wiley Rucker. He was attacked by a drunk yesterday who's now sitting in jail. He'll get over his injuries, but he's looking for work. He's a painter. I worked with him yesterday, and I can tell you he's a good painter and a hard worker."

"Nice to meet you, Wiley," said John, and put his hand out for a shake.

Wiley shook his hand. "It's good to meet you, sir. Do you have any work I could do?"

"As a matter of fact, I have a recently plastered wall. It needs painting, but the work needs to be done at night so it doesn't interfere with the customers. Are you available for night work?"

"Yes, sir. What would be a good time for you?"

"Let's say seven o'clock. Is that good?"

Phineas interrupted. "John, if you're not in any hurry, could Wiley do your job tomorrow night? We have plans to go to Lamar and speak to Oliver Hardin today. He'll need some rest before he tackles your job."

"That works fine," said John. "That will give me until tomorrow to buy the paint. Do you have your equipment, Wiley?"

"I have brushes."

"That's fine. I think I can find some drop cloths around here. I'll see you tomorrow evening at seven. Just knock on the door when you get here."

"Thank you, sir. I'll see you tomorrow."

He shook John's hand and left with Phineas. They climbed into Phineas' carriage and headed toward the town of Lamar, fifteen miles east.

"We need to talk about the art of 'cutting in' and the necessity of using those drop cloths John was talking about." They had a long drive to talk about the finer points of painting, keeping the customer's floor clean, and other business topics. Phineas agreed to go to his first job with him.

The interview with Oliver Hardin went well. Mr. Hardin said he had just purchased a house on the edge of town that would need some painting, and the job would be ready for a painter next week. Wiley was hired.

"Let's stop and see Christian Wolf on the way home," Phineas said. "He's an attorney who may know of some work for you, too."

They found Wolf in his office, getting ready to go to lunch, but he invited Phineas and Wiley in.

"Mr. Wolf, I'd like you to meet Wiley Rucker. He's a painter looking for work. Wiley, this is Attorney Christian Wolf."

"Rucker? Are you related to Jeb Rucker? What happened to your face?"

After two successful interviews, Wiley's shoulders sagged, and his face fell.

"Jeb is my Pa," he said. "I didn't think he knew anybody in Lamar. My face? He beat me last night."

Wolf gave him a sympathetic nod. "I don't know him. He was brought into the county jail from Spencer's Mill this morning, and the judge assigned me to represent him. He did this to you?"

"He beat my Ma worse. He smashed her face up and broke her arm."

Wolf stared at him. "Sit down, son. Please, Fletcher, take a seat. I want to get more details."

Wiley told him the whole story about his Pa taking all the money that came into the house and using it for drink, then beating his Ma if she didn't provide a meal for him. Phineas told him about Wiley having to scrounge for whatever food he could get to feed the family, shooting the turkey, then taking responsibility.

Wolf listened to every word. "Well, I now have a better idea of how to represent your Pa. His hearing comes up in a few days. Since he's beating on his wife and son, drawing blood, and breaking bones, and he does it regularly, I'll be surprised if his sentence is less than a year. He'll be sitting in jail for quite a while."

Wiley lowered his head. "I'm sorry for him, but that's good news for Ma and me. I'll tell her when I get home. But that's not why we came, Mr. Wolf. I'm looking for painting jobs. Do you know of any work I could do?"

"He's a good painter, Mr. Wolf. I worked with him myself yesterday. I can vouch for him."

Wolf considered the question. "Tell you what, Wiley. I'll check with my wife this evening and find out if she has anything for you to do. I'll let you know the next time you come to town."

"Thanks, Mr. Wolf." Wiley shook his hand and left with Mr. Fletcher.

As they climbed into the carriage, Wiley said, "If we hurry back to Spencer's Mill, we'll get there in time to finish painting the fence."

"You're right. Let's go."

The following evening, Phineas arrived at the Crust & Crumb Bakery at seven o'clock with Wiley. The two spent four hours painting the wall together, enjoying each other's company. When Phineas arrived home exhausted, it was nearly half past eleven. His muscles ached.

Lying in his bed, Phineas reviewed the events since Farmer Ragsdill first burst into the classroom and threatened Amos. He had a deep sense of satisfaction. He had found the culprit who had shot and stolen the turkey, protecting Amos from a dangerous, irrational man. Then he made sure that the farmer was justly reimbursed.

With divine help, he pointed a young man's feet toward the right path. Wiley now had a better chance of becoming a successful adult, and Phineas believed their relationship would grow into something bigger. He liked the boy and looked forward to being a mentor.

He hoped to say one day that he had helped Wiley Rucker become the man he was.

BLESSINGS THROUGH THE FIRE

Phineas Fletcher stood in front of the letterbox, ripping the envelope. He unfolded the letter with eager hands and read it with mixed emotions. It was a summons to appear in court in Florissant on May 23rd to testify in the case of Carl Young, the murderer he had helped capture months ago. He was nervous about testifying in court but bursting with pride that he would be recognized as the investigator who fingered the criminal.

He was also excited to return to Mrs. Courtney's Rooming House in Florissant. Mrs. Courtney had become a bright spot in his life.

He wondered if Sheriff Lane had received the same summons. Lane had been the one to arrest Young in the bakery as he threatened the owners.

The urge to compare notes with the sheriff overcame him. He went out to the barn to hitch his horse to the carriage. It didn't take him long to get to the jail, where the sheriff sat at his desk.

"Phineas," said Sheriff Lane with a broad grin, shaking his hand. "Did you get a summons, too?"

"I did. I guess that means we go back to Florissant."

"A lot of people will be traveling this time of year," said Lane. "I would hate to get to Mrs. Courtney's Rooming House and find out she didn't have any vacancies. Should we send a telegram asking her to hold a couple of rooms?"

"That would be wise. I'll do that. Do you want to travel with me by carriage? We can review my notes on the trip."

"Sure," said Lane, "as long as you plan to return right away; otherwise, I can take the train. I know you're sweet on that rooming house lady." He grinned at Phineas, wiggling his eyebrows.

Phineas blushed. "I'd love to stay there a few extra days, but my daughter and son-in-law are getting ready to move to Illinois. I'm going with them. I'll have to come right back." He was painfully aware that this would probably be his last chance to spend time with Adelaide in person. After this, they would have only the mail service to keep them in touch. He tried to shove that fact to the back of his mind.

The following week, the two men climbed into the carriage with their bags and left Spencer's Mill, traveling fifteen miles to Lamar, a larger town to the east. Then they turned to the north, having another fifteen miles to go. The horses took them through the Ohio woodlands and farmlands. Horses and men alike were travel-weary as they arrived in Florissant.

Phineas and Sheriff Lane strolled into the lobby of Mrs. Courtney's Rooming House with their bags. Their business in town was solemn, but Phineas expected some happy moments, too.

Adelaide Courtney, the proprietor, was there to meet them, her eyes shining with delight. She stepped out from behind the front desk to grasp Phineas' hand. "Phineas, I'm so glad you could come again. I've been looking forward to this. And welcome to you, too, Sheriff Lane."

Phineas grinned like a wanderer who had finally come home. He gazed at her fondly. "Hello, Adelaide. I've missed you."

She smiled. "You gentlemen will be staying in rooms 2 and 5. You'll have to fight over which one gets the first pick." She grinned, held up a key in each hand, jiggled them on their rings, then held them out for the men to choose.

Lane took the key to room 2, knowing Phineas preferred the other one for its view of the front lawn. He started upstairs with his valise. The aging, red-flowered carpet padded his footsteps.

Phineas took the room 5 key and hesitated. "Do you have dinner plans this evening?"

She gave him a sly, confident grin. "I hope I'm going out with you."

He chuckled. "I'll take my bag upstairs and get freshened up. We'll be taking Lane with us. Shall I tell him six o'clock?"

"Sounds fine."

He surprised himself that he was as giddy as a boy on Christmas morning as he took his valise upstairs.

The evening was thoroughly enjoyable despite the stressful

business facing them the next day. They took the carriage to their favorite pub, where the light was low and the food was delicious. As they ate, Phineas and Adelaide touched fingers under the table, away from the eyes of the sheriff. The three made small talk and lingered over apple pie with whipped cream.

"It's probably time we should get back," Lane said. "I hate to rush us, but tomorrow is an important day." He rose from the table and started toward the exit, with Phineas and Adelaide reluctantly following.

"I didn't get a chance to tell you how lovely you look tonight," Phineas whispered, leaning toward Adelaide. She beamed at him.

The following day after one of Adelaide's breakfasts at the rooming house, Lane dabbed at his mouth with the napkin. "The trial starts in an hour, Phineas. Are you ready to go? I want to get there early and get my bearings."

Phineas stood. "We'll be back after the trial, Adelaide, probably this afternoon."

"Good luck, gentlemen." She waved at them as she cleared their table.

The men climbed into the carriage and headed to the courthouse. At the front steps, they chanced to meet Sheriff Milligan of Florissant.

"Fletcher and Lane," he said, shaking their hands. "Good to see you again. Come with me. I've already delivered the prisoner, so I'll show you where the courtroom is, and we can sit together." Phineas and the sheriff followed him in.

The small courtroom was jammed with jury members, witnesses, reporters, and citizens who had come out of morbid curiosity. Some people whispered to each other behind their hands and pointed to him and Sheriff Lane. Phineas was certain it was because of their role in the defendant's capture. He exchanged glances with Lane and grinned, never one to shy away from extra attention.

The judge took the bench, and the bailiff announced the case. "The State of Ohio versus Carl Young in the murder of Noah Taylor."

The trial began promptly at nine o'clock and moved smoothly. Phineas and Sheriff Lane were each called to the witness stand and gave detailed, convincing testimony, as did the victim's neighbors. Related documents Phineas had searched out at the courthouse were also entered. The defense attorney, resigned to his client's guilt, gave a feeble defense, and the jury took little time to deliberate.

The verdict: Guilty.

The sentence: Death by hanging.

At that moment, the shock of reality hit Phineas. The knowledge that his testimony had contributed to a man's death sentence was like a body slam. He sat numbly in his chair, slack-jawed.

The prisoner was hauled from the courtroom, kicking in his boots and screaming.

Finally, Sheriff Lane nudged his companion. "Phineas," he said, "let's go. It's all over."

"Poor sod," said Phineas. "He destroyed his own life, and he's so young."

"He made his choices. We can't have him running loose, threatening the citizenry, because we feel sorry for him."

Phineas nodded. "You're right, of course."

The two men stopped at a diner in town for a quick lunch. There was little conversation as each man was lost in his own thoughts. Phineas swallowed the last mouthful of chicken soup. "I'd like to get back to the rooming house," he said. "I need to talk with Adelaide."

"I'm ready to go," said Lane. "I'd like a good nap. We didn't do any physical work this morning, but testifying in court—well, I'm mentally and emotionally wrung out. I didn't expect that."

They climbed into the carriage. Phineas slapped the reins, and the horse pulled forward, clip-clopping along. Phineas was occupied watching the road and passing traffic, but as they got closer to the rooming house, Lane shaded his eyes with his hand and craned his neck.

"Phineas, something is wrong up there," he said. He grabbed Phineas' arm and pointed up ahead with jabbing motions in the air. "Something is wrong. I see smoke."

Phineas strained to see what was happening two blocks ahead. There was a crowd of people in the street in front of the rooming house, along with a horse-drawn pumper wagon painted bright red, its brass boiler tank glistening in the sun and its hose unreeled. Three firemen were working frantically, spraying a plume of water into the inferno as smoke billowed from the rooming house.

Phineas' eyes bulged. "No," he shouted, and urged the horses faster for the rest of the distance. His pulse pounded. He stopped the carriage at the edge of the crowd, jumped out, and ran toward the press of people.

"Adelaide, Adelaide," he shouted. He ran into the crowd, desperately searching for her, wondering if she had gotten out of the fire in time. He feared he would never see her alive again. "Adelaide," he shouted again. Finally, she emerged from the knot of spectators, broken and nearly hysterical, as orange flames danced in the kitchen. Smoke billowed out the windows.

"Phineas, the rooming house is everything I own. If they don't get this fire out quickly, I'm ruined. I don't know what I'll do."

He wrapped his arms around her without considering they were in public and wiped her tears from her cheeks with his thumb. "God is in charge, my dear. We need to trust Him to take care of this. Whatever the outcome, Adelaide, it's in His hands."

She nodded but continued to let the tears flow. Her shoulders shook with sobs.

After taking some calming breaths, her sobs began to subside. "My husband Winston and I bought this building when we were thirty. We ran it for fourteen years before he died, and I've kept it going alone since then. But this –" She turned to gaze at the fire. "I don't know how to handle this." She began to sniffle again.

"What happened?" he asked. "Where did the fire start?"

"It's hard to say." Her voice quivered. "I was cleaning one of the rooms upstairs when I smelled smoke. I knocked on all the guest doors and got everyone to leave, then came downstairs. Smoke was rolling out of my quarters. One of the guests went on horseback to fetch the fire brigade. They got here about fifteen minutes ago with the pumper, but the fire is—well, you can see for yourself." She waved an arm in the direction of the fire.

They stood by helplessly as the firefighters worked. Phineas paced back and forth furiously, then stopped short, waving his arms in the air. "Adelaide, I've never felt so worthless in my life. This tragedy is happening to you, and I can't do a thing about it."

She faced him with tears running down her cheeks, unable to speak. She could only reach out and grasp his hand.

In a few minutes, Sheriff Lane joined them at the front of the crowd. "I took care of the horses, Phineas. Is everything under control?"

"Not at all," Phineas said. "I don't know what's happening inside the house, but Adelaide is terrified. The fire is still burning, and the firemen have been here for a while."

They stared in horrified fascination for a few more minutes, then Lane said, "It looks like the smoke has stopped rolling."

The crowd stood quietly, watching and wondering. Presently the exhausted firemen came out of the building and began to roll up their hose. Phineas approached them. "Is it safe to go inside?" he asked.

"I'd wait for a while," the chief said. "It's still hot. Send someone for us again if it flares up."

"How much damage is there?"

"Well, it's not pretty. That looks like the owner's apartment in that wing of the building. The kitchen was burned the worst. The pantry is gone, along with the food. I think the stove survived, but it's covered in soot and water. Same with the pots. There was a lot of smoke and water damage. You'll have to see it for yourself. It's a shame. The owner of the place is a grand lady, but she doesn't have any family to rely on." He turned and went back to his work.

Phineas' heart broke. He dreaded passing the word on to Adelaide, but it wasn't necessary. She was standing behind him and heard it all herself.

"Phineas, I'm afraid I may pass out."

He guided her to the carriage and helped her into the seat. Once she had caught her breath, he said, "Rest here. I'll be right back. I need to speak to Sheriff Lane."

He searched the crowd for the sheriff and finally located him. "Lane, I need to talk to you. I know we're due to return to Spencer's Mill tomorrow, but I can't leave Adelaide here alone. She has no one to rely on. I'm going to stay with her for a few days."

Lane nodded. "I thought that's what you might do. If you'll take me to the railroad station, I'll buy a ticket for tomorrow."

"That would be a great relief to me, except can you take the carriage and get the ticket yourself? I can't think of leaving Adelaide alone right now."

"Of course."

"Thank you. And when you get back to Spencer's Mill, would you stop by my house and tell my daughter I've been delayed for a few days? Maybe as much as a week."

143

"I'll do that."

Phineas helped Adelaide get down from the carriage and sat with her on the boulders lining the entrance to the front walk, waiting for the embers to cool.

Within an hour, Lane was back with his railroad ticket.

Adelaide and the guests ventured back into the building, looking around in shock. Everything was covered in black soot. The Persian rug in the lobby was covered in ash and was so soggy that it squished dirty black water as they walked across it. One wall between the kitchen and Adelaide's private quarters had turned to charcoal, as was part of the kitchen and the food supplies. Her knees became weak at the sight of it, but there was no clean, dry place to sit.

The other guests gathered their belongings and checked out. The smoke in the guest rooms was minimal, but they all needed a good cleaning and airing out. The walls would probably need painting. It was an insurmountable problem for a widow to handle alone.

"Adelaide, I'll stay for a few days and help you with this," Phineas said. She was at the front desk checking out the guests and taking their payments.

She paused and turned to him with red-rimmed eyes. "Thank you. You don't know how much this means to me." She finished checking out the last guest.

Word traveled quickly in the small town as if it had been telegraphed from house to house. Soon friends began stopping by, bringing offers of help. Some volunteered to return the following day to clean up the fire damage. Other folks committed to bringing lunch for the workers. What a blessing to have caring friends.

Phineas had his belongings in room 5, his favorite room with a view of the front lawn. It would be livable with clean bedding from the upstairs linen closet and fresh air coming in an open window. Adelaide couldn't stay in her quarters until the smoke and ash were cleaned away and repairs were made. She moved into room 4, across the hall from Phineas.

"You've had quite a shock today," Phineas said. "Why don't you lie down and have a good nap this afternoon? When you wake up, the sheriff and I will take you to dinner at the pub. There's nothing left to eat in the kitchen anyway."

She smiled thinly. "That's one bright spot in a very dark day."

Early the following day, Phineas took Sheriff Lane to the train station. "This isn't how we envisioned this trip ending, is it? I'm glad there's a train leaving for Lamar today."

Lane nodded. "I can at least get that far. I don't know how I'll get the rest of the way to Spencer's Mill, but I'm sure someone will be going that way eventually."

"Attorney Wolf's office is in Lamar, but his home is halfway to Spencer's Mill, so he goes that way every evening after his office closes. Maybe you can get a ride with him. I know him well enough to believe he'd probably be willing to have his caretaker drive you the rest of the way."

"Thanks. I'll ask him about that." Lane hopped out of the carriage with his valise. "So long, Phineas, and good luck."

When Phineas returned, Adelaide was brewing coffee. "I found some coffee in a tin that survived the fire. This isn't much of a breakfast, Phineas, but this is all I have."

"Your friends will be bringing food soon. Maybe we can sneak a little before lunch."

Adelaide gave him a crooked grin and nodded. "I need to organize my thoughts so the volunteers' time won't be wasted. Help me make a work schedule, will you?"

The only chairs clean enough to sit on were in the guest rooms, so they carried their coffee upstairs. Phineas took the chair from his room into Adelaide's. They set themselves to the task of organizing projects for the volunteers as they sipped their coffee.

As the volunteers came in, they got their assignments and went to work. Phineas used his time to evaluate the burned kitchen walls and determine what repairs were needed. The walls weren't the only things burned. The parlor furnishings in Adelaide's apartment were scorched, as were two of the tables and several chairs in the guest dining room.

"I'm afraid, my dear, that the damage will take some time and money to repair. What is your financial situation? I'm sorry to ask since it's none of my business, but I won't know how to help unless I know what you need."

She hung her head. "Everything I have is tied up in this property.

I generally have only enough cash to operate the boarding house — to buy food and supplies for the guests, and cover my personal expenses. I don't keep much money here except for what I collect from guests checking out. I don't know if last week's money survived the fire. I haven't checked it yet."

"Where did you keep it?"

It was in a can in my nightstand drawer."

"Let's go downstairs and find out if it's there."

The two of them descended the stairs and went into her private quarters, where two young volunteers cleaned water and smoke off her wood furniture. She squished across the water-soaked rug to her dresser and pulled out a drawer. Everything inside was drenched, but the can where she kept her extra money was intact.

"Thank God," she whispered and opened up the can. She pulled out about twenty dollars in small bank notes and coins. "I wonder how far this will go toward getting me back in business."

Phineas shook his head. "This is not a good situation. This is a God-sized problem. He will have to provide for you. If He can use me to help, I'm willing, but I didn't bring a lot of cash. My money is in the bank in Lamar." He gazed into her eyes. They were dull and tired, unlike the sparkling eyes he had seen earlier.

"You have women washing the linens and men cleaning the walls upstairs. Let me concentrate on the kitchen. You can't reopen until the kitchen is in workable condition."

"You're right. Let me keep the other workers supplied with what they need while you do that."

Good, he thought. Her mind is beginning to click again.

He fished his trusted notebook out of his valise. He made a list of needs as he thought of them. The kitchen wall needed to be replaced, two windows were broken, and a layer of smoke and ash covered everything.

The damage could have been far worse, but Adelaide's twenty dollars would never cover the repairs and replacement of groceries.

In the lobby, two men rolled up the beautiful Persian rug, leaving a pool of water on the wood floor underneath. They took it out back to dry in the sun as one of the women chased the water out the door with a corn broom. The same men returned and took the mattress off Adelaide's bed to dry outside.

Several people had been working for only three hours, and

already the place was in much better condition.

"Time for lunch," Adelaide called to the crew of workers. She used the front desk as a buffet and laid out the dishes that friends had brought. The volunteers filled their plates and found places to sit, some on dining room chairs, but several on the floor. Common work creates camaraderie, so happy chatter filled the air as the group took lunch. People who had come in as strangers to each other went back to their tasks after lunch as friends.

"Adelaide, may I have a word?" asked Phineas.

She accompanied him into her private quarters. "What is it?"

"I've estimated how much it will cost to get you back in business. It's way beyond twenty dollars, but we can get started on the wall with that and buy some groceries."

She took a deep breath. "One day at a time," she said. "How long can you stay and help me?"

"I sent word to my family to expect me in a week. I should be there giving them a hand with their moving plans, but I'm sure they'll manage without me. They don't own any property that needs to be sold, so it's just a matter of crating a few belongings and loading them into a wagon."

She squeezed his hand. "Phineas, you're so gracious to be willing to stay here, but you should be with your family. I'm sure I'll manage somehow."

"I'm staying, Adelaide, until I feel the hand of God moving me on."

As the afternoon progressed, folks left, one by one, leaving Adelaide and Phineas alone.

"There's a little diner as you come into town from the south," Phineas said. "I ate there the first time I came to Florissant. Let's have dinner there. Then we'll come back and have a good rest."

"Let me wash my face first. I must look like a rag."

Phineas smiled. "Not at all. But go and wash up. You'll feel better. I'll meet you in the lobby in fifteen minutes."

Only two volunteers showed up to help the following day, a gentleman and an older lady, but their help was invaluable.

The man introduced himself to Phineas, extending his hand. "I'm Kingston Baker. A friend from the church told me that Mrs. Courtney's place burned. I came to see what I could do to help."

Phineas shook his hand. "Good to meet you, sir, and thank you for coming. I'm Phineas Fletcher, here helping Mrs. Courtney. Do you have any special skills?"

"I'm a carpenter by trade."

"Thank God, Baker. We have a wall badly burned here. Can you help me clear away the burned section, then frame in a new one?"

"I'd be glad to. Let me have a look."

The two men went to the kitchen and Baker evaluated the wall. "We need to cut away this burned part, remove the charred studs, and then we can start putting in a new wall."

"Do you have your tools with you?"

"No, I didn't anticipate doing anything like that, but I can go get them."

"While you're doing that, I'll go to the lumber yard and get what we need."

Adelaide and Miss Penelope, the woman who came to help, worked on cleaning the guest rooms.

In the meantime, Phineas had enough of his own money to pay for supplies to help Adelaide. He went to the lumber yard in his carriage. Loading the boards in his small passenger carriage was challenging, but he tied them down and got them to the rooming house to find Baker waiting.

"You're the expert, Baker. You tell me what I can do to help you."

"Tell you what. I'll make some measurements and mark the boards, then you and I can cut them. I brought two saws."

The men worked in tandem for most of the day, putting up studs and nailing up the lath. Adelaide took Phineas' carriage and went to the general store for food supplies. At day's end, the wall had been formed and only needed three coats of plaster. Adelaide and Miss Penelope had thoroughly cleaned three of the guest rooms, ready for someone to check in, but the faint smell of smoke was a lingering reminder of the tragedy.

That evening Adelaide moved around the kitchen, wearily chopping vegetables and roasting a small cut of beef for the first time since the fire. Often she leaned against the counter and took a deep breath to regain the strength to continue. Even though she was fatigued, cooking gave her a sense of normalcy and a hope that, eventually, things would be better.

She wiped the sweat from her face with her apron and called, "Phineas, dinner is ready." They sat at one of the guest tables together to eat. Since their first meeting, they had forged a bond, which had only grown stronger with each encounter. Now that they shared a tragedy and he was there to help her clean up, their sense of togetherness grew. They were building a short but intense history of shared experiences, even though their friendship was destined to end when Phineas returned to Spencer's Mill. It was a bittersweet time.

Over dinner, Phineas told Adelaide how much he enjoyed working with Kingston Baker.

"That's a coincidence," Adelaide said. "I was contacted by a young man named Baker recently. I don't remember his first name. I wonder if he's related to the carpenter who was here today."

"What did the young man want?"

"He wanted to partner with me and open a restaurant here in the rooming house. He wanted to open for lunch and dinner, as well as breakfast."

"You turned him down?"

"Of course. I told him I was too old to want confusion like that in my home. This is where I live. He did everything he could to persuade me to change my mind, but even if I had thought it was a good idea, something about the young man made me uncomfortable."

"Maybe he's not related to the carpenter, then. Kingston was a great guy. I enjoyed working with him. And Baker is a common name." They continued to enjoy their meal.

Phineas said, "I think the next project, in order of importance, is to get those two windows replaced. Do you have enough money to buy two windows and hire a glazier?"

"I don't know, Phineas. I don't know how much anything costs." She lowered her head. "Can we continue this in the morning? I'm exhausted right now, physically and mentally. I'd love to sit up and talk with you after the dishes are done. I would love that, especially since our time together is short. But tonight, I can't. My strength is gone. My home and business have been burned, my income has been interrupted, and my funds are gone. And when you leave at the end of the week, I'll never see you again." Tears began to flow down her cheeks. "I've held it together until now, but I can't keep going. I desperately need to sleep. I'm so sorry. Can you forgive me? Do you understand?" She burst into heaving sobs.

Phineas was moved to compassion. "Of course, my dear. You've done amazingly well." He moved toward her and wrapped his arms around her. "A good night's sleep is what you need. I could use some sleep, too. I'll help you with the dishes. Then, we'll both turn in early."

She wiped her wet face with the hem of her apron. "Thank you. I'll sleep downstairs in my apartment tonight since my mattress has dried out."

In room 5, Phineas changed into his nightshirt and laid back wearily on his bed. He prayed silently for Adelaide, thanking God for sparing her life and asking Him to provide the funds to keep her going since she presently had no income or savings. Eventually, he drifted off into sleep.

A while later—he didn't know precisely what time it was—he dreamed that someone was screaming downstairs. Was he dreaming? There it was again. Could that be Adelaide? His eyes flew open. There was a second shout, a man's voice, not a woman's.

Then a thump.

The hair on the back of his neck raised. He threw off his quilt, and his feet hit the floor. Scrambling down the stairs as fast as his bare feet could move, he sprinted into Adelaide's apartment just in time to see a slender form climb out one of the broken kitchen windows and scramble into the dark.

"Phineas," Adelaide cried and came running out of her bedroom. "He took all the rent money, every penny of it. I tried to stop him, but he hit me and pushed me back on the bed." She sobbed on his shoulder, and he wrapped his arms around her.

So now she had been involved in a physical struggle, and her little bit of money was gone. How could things get any worse? He stroked her hair and let her cry. "It looks black right now, my dear, but God is in this. He'll take care of all your needs. For now, tell me what happened."

"I don't know how long that man was in here. I woke up when my drawer opened next to the bed, and someone was there. In my sleepy state, I thought it was you. Then I woke enough to realize you wouldn't be in my room. When I realized it was a stranger I jumped out of bed to grab his arm. He swung at me with his fist. He got me

150

right here on my cheek; then he pushed me down. I started screaming, so he put his hand over my mouth, but I bit him. Hard. That's when he yelled. Then he turned tail and ran with the remains of my rent money in his hand. I grabbed a book and threw it at him, but missed."

"I got a look at his backside as he went through the window. All I saw in the moonlight was his britches."

"Let's go in the kitchen. I'll make some tea. I don't think I can sleep now, can you?"

"No, I can't. Let's light a lamp. Then I think a nice cup of tea is just what we need. In the morning, I'll make a report to the sheriff."

Adelaide put some water in the kettle on the stove while Phineas lit an oil lamp. She worked in her nightgown and realized how inappropriate other people would think this was. She started giggling.

"What's so funny?"

"Look at us. We're sitting together in the kitchen in our nightclothes. Can you imagine what people would say?"

Phineas smiled. "Yes, but God knows there's nothing untoward going on here."

"I'll pour the tea, then slip a robe on."

It was one more intense experience shared. They lingered for a while over their tea.

Adelaide yawned behind her hand. "I'd like to go back to bed now, Phineas. Would you mind going in there ahead of me to make sure no one is there? I know it must sound foolish . . ."

"Not at all. Stay here while I check. I'll be right back." He walked to her bedroom with the oil lamp and inspected behind the drapes and under the bed. No one was there, but he spotted a pocket knife on the floor. The blade was open. Thankful he hadn't stepped on it, he stooped to pick it up and turned it over.

"Adelaide, I found a knife by your bed. Is this yours?"

He took it into the kitchen and handed it to her.

"I still have my Papa's knife, but this isn't it. This must belong to the burglar. Take a look here. There's something scratched on the outside of it."

She handed it back to Phineas. He held his lamp closer and peered at it. "It looks like initials. Maybe J or I, then another letter. I can't tell whether it's a P or a B. Maybe we'll see it better in the morning light."

"What if the man realizes he dropped it and comes back to get it?"

Adelaide's eyes opened wide. "Phineas, I can't sleep down here. Would you take that knife to your room with you, and I'll stay in room 4 for the rest of the night."

"Good idea. You'll be safer upstairs until that window is replaced." They climbed the stairs, hand in hand. She went to her room, and he went to his, but he lay awake on his bed, staring at the ceiling and thinking about Adelaide. How could he leave and go back to Spencer's Mill, never to see her again? Being with her was like being at home. Finally, at around 4:30, he fell asleep.

He awakened three hours later to the aroma of eggs and coffee. He and Adelaide enjoyed breakfast together, then Phineas took the pocket knife to Sheriff Milligan's office. He described the whole incident.

"I need to question Adelaide myself," said Milligan.

"Of course. I'll be there putting a coat of plaster on the lath. Say, do you know who in Florissant replaces windows?"

"I think Ed over at the lumber yard does that as an evening job after he closes for the day."

"Thanks. I'll check with him before I go back to the rooming house. I'll see you when I get there."

The lumber yard was a short ride away.

"Mr. Fletcher, you're back. Did you forget something?"

"I did, Ed. We need to have two windows replaced. Sheriff Milligan said you might be able to help us out."

"I could come about six o'clock this evening. Did you measure the windows?"

"Yes, I did." He pulled his notebook out of his pocket and quoted the dimensions to Ed. "We need the glass installed as quickly as possible. Someone got in through the open window last night and stole all the rent money."

"Oh, no. Poor Mrs. Courtney. She's already been through such an ordeal. I'll put the windows in this evening." He turned away, wagging his head.

"Thanks, Ed. See you later."

Phineas drove back to the rooming house slowly, thinking and praying. Since Adelaide was out of money, he could finance the windows himself, but she was still without income. What would she do when he went home? Her difficult situation was complicating his thinking. He didn't want a relationship with her built on a foundation of tragedy. He didn't want her to think of him only as the proverbial knight on a white horse. Deep down, he didn't believe she did. She was strong and resourceful, taking care of herself since her husband's death and getting along fine.

His mind wandered back to the sound of her laughter when they ran out of that sleazy bar on one of his investigations. He remembered their long dinner conversations, their ride in the moonlight, and how she waited for hours one night to give him dinner when he worked with Milligan on a stakeout. She had even given shelter to the prisoner's little daughter.

He approached the rooming house but still needed time with his thoughts, so he slowly circled the block. If he took her back to Spencer's Mill for a few days to withdraw some money and put his home up for sale, they could get married there, and when his property sold, they would have money to make all the repairs needed in the rooming house. It would be glorious to spend every day with her, hearing her voice and seeing her face. He could continue his investigative career in Florissant, and Adelaide could still run the rooming house.

He would miss Charlotte, but his daughter didn't need him anymore. Adelaide did.

This was a life-changing decision that would affect his whole family. He wanted God's will in this, not his own, since God could see into the future and wanted the best for him and Adelaide, whether together or separately. He stopped the carriage by the side of the road and spent a few moments in prayer, hoping to hear a yes or no from God. He didn't get an immediate answer but was confident his answer would come at the right time.

He tied his horse to the rail in front of the boarding house and went inside. Sheriff Milligan was already there, looking around Adelaide's apartment and getting a list of everyone inside the building since the fire. She gave him the names of all the friends who volunteered.

"Oh, good, Phineas is back," she said.

Phineas asked, "Did you find anything else to help nail the perpetrator?"

"Well, the only evidence I could find was a piece of torn brown cloth sticking to one of the glass shards in the window frame," said

Milligan. "If we find a fellow whose first name starts with I or J, and the last name begins with B or P, with a torn brown shirt and a bite mark on his hand, we have our man. There are three people on this list of volunteers whose initials fit the clue, but I hate to think that a person willing to volunteer is the same one who's a thief. It's probably someone else."

"That seems likely. Thanks for being on the case. By the way, Ed is coming to replace the glass in the windows this evening."

"Good. I'll see you later." Milligan went his way.

Phineas had been so preoccupied with the fire cleanup that he hadn't considered how he might find the thief. Maybe the thief had set the fire. He went outside the kitchen window where the burglar had made his escape and found a complete footprint on the ground. It was a perfect footprint on top of many others that firefighters had probably left when the mud was still wet. The one on top had to be the one left by the burglar. He measured it carefully, then sketched it to the exact size, including the little knicks on the boot heel and one on the toe. He would make sure the sheriff got his sketch.

He turned to Adelaide. "What's on the schedule of repairs today?"

She sat on a towel placed on one of the wing chairs in the lobby to have a clean place to sit. "Have a seat in that other chair, Phineas. I'm so tired mentally that I don't know which direction to go, and I'm flat out of money anyway. I don't know how I'll ever get this place reopened. I think I'll just sell it at a bargain price and go live in a cabin. Maybe I should sell it to Mr. Baker for a restaurant." Her weary body slumped, and her arms hung limply over the chair.

"I'm trying to work on a solution to that problem. I don't think selling at a low price is best for you."

"Or maybe I could get a loan from the bank, enough to pay for new furniture to replace the burned pieces, and enough to paint the walls and put a new rug in the lobby."

"That would be one solution, but then you would have loan payments on top of your other expenses. Don't do anything in haste, Adelaide. Please."

"How I would love to get away from here for a few days," she said. "I haven't had a vacation in years. I think it would give me the break my mind needs. But I don't know how I could do that. I've never been down to no money at all before. I feel trapped in a big problem with no solution." She leaned forward with her elbows on her knees and her face in her hands.

He slid his chair next to hers and reached for her shoulder. "Adelaide, funny you should mention that. I'd like to take you to Spencer's Mill for a few days. I've been living in my daughter's house. You could stay in my room at her house, and I could go to my own home at night, then spend days with you."

She straightened up and stared at his face with her mouth agape. He noted that her eyes had taken on a sparkle. "Your daughter and son-in-law don't know me, Phineas. They might feel uncomfortable with a stranger. And you said they're getting ready to move."

He smiled. "I also told you they have nothing to take with them except their clothes and a few trinkets. It's going to be an easy move for them. And they are both outgoing people. They will love you."

Adelaide thought in silence for a while, her eyes averted, and finally nodded her head. "If you're serious about this, I would like to take you up on your invitation. How would I get home?"

"I'll bring you back. We'll come together."

Phineas grinned at her, his smile going from one ear to the other. "We can leave in the morning."

"Oh, Phineas. I can't believe we're really going to do this. I'll go pack now." She moved out of her chair with more energy. Her face was radiant.

A tingling thrill surged through Phineas' chest. He was sure that sometime during the trip, he would get the answer to the question he had asked of God.

That afternoon was a busy one as they made their preparations. One of Phineas' concerns was the security of the building during their absence.

"Adelaide, do you know anyone who would agree to stay here and watch the property while you're gone?"

She studied the matter for a few minutes and finally thought of someone. "A young married couple, the Bronsons, were here as volunteers. They don't have children, so they may be able to stay."

"Good. Do you want to take the carriage and ask them to move in for a few days?"

Within a half-hour, Adelaide was back with the news that the

155

Bronsons would be there in the morning.

"Let's celebrate our decision by going out for an early supper. We'll need to be back by six o'clock so Ed can put glass in the windows."

"I'm not accustomed to being pampered so much, but I won't turn it down."

The following day Adelaide and Phineas rose early for a breakfast that would last them until they got as far as Lamar, marking the halfway point to Spencer's Mill. Adelaide packed biscuits and cheese for the trip.

At eight o'clock, Isaac and Betsy Bronson were there as promised. Adelaide showed them around and tacked a sign on the door: "Closed Temporarily for Repairs." Phineas asked them to be on the lookout for intruders. Then they were ready to go.

The weather was glorious. The yellow sun shot out its morning rays over the earth, unhindered by clouds, as a light breeze tempered the warm air. Phineas helped Adelaide into the carriage and climbed beside her, thinking how lovely she was, inside and out. His heart thumped. He slapped the reins, and they were off. Adelaide reached toward him and curled a hand under his arm. The day couldn't have been better.

They reached the edge of town and continued south through the Ohio farmland, past cattle grazing in pastures and fields plowed by hard-working farmers behind teams of draft horses.

Adelaide had been in thought for a while. "Phineas, I've been praying about the future of the rooming house, but I honestly don't know what's going to happen."

"God only reveals one step at a time."

"I wish I didn't have to do it by myself."

His heart skipped a beat. "I wish you didn't either, Adelaide."

She turned her face away from him. Finally, Phineas believed he had just received his answer from God.

"Adelaide . . . are you thinking the same thing I'm thinking?"

She turned toward him, her lips slightly parted and her brow furrowed. "I hope so."

"Adelaide, would you marry me?"

"Absolutely."

Phineas pulled on the reins and cried, "Whoa, whoa!" He stopped the horse in the road and turned toward Adelaide as she threw her arms around his neck.

They sat there for a few minutes, laughing, tears streaming.

He wrapped his arms around her. "My dear, I want to be sure you know I didn't ask you this only because of the fire. I've longed to be with you, even when we were apart."

"I understand that," she said. "And when you were in Spencer's Mill, I still thought about you every day and prayed for you to come back."

"We have a lot to talk about, don't we?" he asked.

Their conversation the rest of the way to Lamar was quite animated. They decided to stop in Lamar, have lunch at the Old English Tea Room, draw some money from the bank, then get married in Spencer's Mill after talking to Charlotte and Danny. They would also go to Phineas' house and do what needed to be done to put it up for sale before returning to Florissant.

They pulled up to Danny and Charlotte's home in Spencer's Mill at about dinner time. Phineas left the carriage in front of the house and helped Adelaide down.

"This is where you live, Phineas?" she asked. 'It's such a large home."

"It's where I've been living with my daughter, son-in-law, and his three young siblings. My own house is unoccupied right now, a few blocks away. Come on in, and I'll introduce you." He led her through the front door. "Charlotte? Danny? Is anyone home?"

"We're in the kitchen, Pa. You're home earlier than we expected. Come and get something to eat."

Phineas peeked around the kitchen door. The family was sitting at the table in the middle of supper. "I have a surprise."

Danny glanced up with a curious smile. "What is it, Pop?"

Phineas pulled Adelaide through the doorway into the kitchen. "It's Adelaide Courtney, my fiancée."

The faces of everyone at the table changed in concert. Their mouths dropped, and they stared at Adelaide.

She smiled shyly. "It's very nice to meet you all."

"Is there enough food for two extra?" Phineas asked.

That shook Charlotte out of her shock. She jumped up to get two more plates. "Of course, Pa. Excuse my manners. Please come and grab a chair, both of you." The family members scooted their chairs closer to one another to make more room.

Danny regained his composure and gave Adelaide a polite smile. "Miss Courtney, how long have you known Pop?"

Phineas was tempted to answer for her but allowed her to speak for herself. "Oh," she said, "I've known Phineas for months since he first stayed in my rooming house in Florissant. We've had the most wonderful time each time he has come there. Except for this time, that is. My rooming house had a little fire, but Phineas has been helping me get it back in shape. For the short time we've known each other, we've been through a lot together." She glanced at Phineas. He smiled and nodded, surveying the bowls of food.

Charlotte scurried around, getting silverware. "Have you set a date for the wedding?"

Phineas helped himself to a piece of chicken. "We thought tomorrow would be a good day. I'm sorry, baby, but I won't be going to Illinois with you. This is a bad way to spring it on you, but there's so little time. Lizbeth, would you pass me the sweet potatoes?"

Lizbeth passed the sweet potatoes and sat wide-eyed.

"We had a little lunch in Lamar, but I'm still famished," Phineas said, with his mouth full.

Danny and Charlotte weren't eating much. They were still trying to absorb this new wrinkle in their lives. The three youngsters continued eating, then asked to be dismissed from the table. When they left, the adults were free to say whatever was on their minds.

"Pop, she looks like a lovely lady, but this is a bit reckless, don't you think?" Danny spoke freely, even though Adelaide was sitting right there.

"No, Danny, this isn't reckless. I've prayed about this. We've both prayed about this. This is our opportunity for companionship and love for the rest of our lives. I'd like to go to Illinois and stay with you and watch my grandchildren grow up, but Charlotte . . . you don't need me anymore. Adelaide needs me. I need Adelaide. I can't imagine the rest of my life without her."

Adelaide sat quietly, looking down, with a Mona Lisa smile and hands folded in her lap. Her manner was calm and gracious. Charlotte eyed her soon-to-be stepmother with interest.

Phineas continued. "So here's the plan. We'll get married

tomorrow and put my house up for sale. Then we need to return to Florissant and finish getting the rooming house ready for guests. There's still painting and refurbishing that needs to be done. . . Danny, can you and Charlotte come through Florissant and stay for a few days on your way to Illinois?"

"It's a little out of the way, but that could be arranged. There's only one more week until William, Amos, and Lizbeth go back to live with Ma. After we drop them off, we could head up to Florissant."

"Miss Courtney, may I ask you a question?" Charlotte said.

"It's Mrs. Courtney," said Adelaide. "My husband passed away several years ago."

"I'm sorry. Mrs. Courtney. Pa said you've been through a lot together. Do you have stories to tell?"

Adelaide's face broke into a wide smile. "Where shall we start, Phineas? Shall we start with the day you discovered a murder had been committed, and we went out to dinner that evening, and the sheriff came looking for you later to tell you he found the body? Or should we tell her about going into that awful pub on one of your investigations where people told bawdy jokes too shameful to mention?" She started giggling, and her laugh was infectious.

Charlotte's eyes sparkled, and curiosity danced across her face as she reached for Adelaide's hand across the table. "Please, if you're going to be my stepmother, I want to hear all the details."

Adelaide leaned in, smiling, and began to relate the whole story to Charlotte.

Danny was the only one still withholding judgment. Phineas valued Danny's opinion, but he had made his decision. Danny would have to live with it. He hoped he would resolve his angst before they left for Illinois.

"What shall we do about sleeping arrangements tonight?" Danny whispered discreetly as Adelaide chatted with Charlotte. "We don't have an extra bedroom."

"Adelaide can sleep in my room tonight if you don't mind," Phineas said. "I'll go to my old house and stay. It may need to be aired out anyway."

"Probably not," Danny said. "Wiley has been over there every day painting. He said you asked him to paint the house to get it ready to sell."

"Yes, quite right," Phineas said. "I did ask him to do that. I'll have to settle his bill before we leave Spencer's Mill. I've been thinking of hiring Oliver Hardin to sell the house. He knows the property business better than anyone."

"He'd be a good choice," said Danny.

Adelaide turned to Danny. "Is that the same man who will be selling your house?"

"This is where I grew up, but it isn't my house. My Pa died, so now it belongs to my mother. She remarried a few months ago — to her attorney, a fine man. I don't know what they plan to do with the house when we move out. We're only here to keep my siblings in their old familiar school until the end of the school year."

Phineas was getting restless. "I'd like to take Adelaide to my house and show it to her this evening. It's still early enough."

"Phineas, let me help Charlotte clean the kitchen before we go."

Charlotte intervened. "Mrs. Courtney, I wouldn't hear of it. You're a guest. Lizbeth will help me."

"Nonsense, and you can call me Adelaide. By tomorrow this time, we'll be family. Hand me a dish towel."

Charlotte grinned, and the two ladies made quick work of the dishes.

Phineas and Adelaide drove to his vacant house on Willow Street. The shadows lengthened as they walked up the cobblestones toward the door and entered the parlor. "This is a cute little house, Phineas." Adelaide walked from room to room. "Could we take some of this furniture back to Florissant? It would replace some of the pieces that were burned. What do you think?"

"I promised Charlotte she could have her pick of her mother's things, but we can take the rest. We'll have to hire someone to haul it to Florissant." He wandered from room to room, looking at the newly painted walls. "Wiley did a good job. We could save time if we went to his house and took care of his bill. Are you ready to go?"

Ten minutes later, they knocked on the door at Wiley Rucker's house. The young man answered the door and beamed. "Mr. Fletcher, come on in."

"You did a good job on the house, Wiley, and I want to pay you." As the money changed hands, Phineas continued. "Now, there's another job I want to ask you about. It would mean going out of town for a few days. Are you up for that?"

Wiley grinned with excitement registering in his eyes. "Tell me about this job."

"Well, it starts with a wedding. I'm going to marry Mrs. Courtney here tomorrow — "

"Congratulations, Mr. Fletcher." He grabbed Phineas' hand and pumped it up and down. "And congratulations to you, Mrs. Fletcher."

She blushed. "It's still Mrs. Courtney today."

"What about that job?" Wiley asked.

"Mrs. Courtney has a rooming house in Florissant, about a four-hour drive by carriage north of Lamar. There was a fire in it a few days ago, and we have the walls washed of the smoke, but they need to be painted. There are five guest rooms upstairs, a main lobby, a kitchen, a dining room downstairs, and Mrs. Courtney's private apartment. Are you interested in taking on a job that big?"

"Yes, sir. Yes, sir, I am. Since you helped me start my painting business, I bought myself a horse. Ma has had plenty to eat and even got a new dress. I'll leave her with some money to buy food for a week. When will this job start?"

"Let's see. We'll get married tomorrow, then go to Lamar to see Oliver Hardin about selling the house. We'll stay at the Lamar Hotel tomorrow night, then travel home the day after. So the following morning — let's see, that would be Monday, right? — that's the day you can start the job. Let me give you the address . . ."

The arrangements were made, and Wiley agreed to travel there on Monday or Tuesday, depending on another painting job he had already lined up.

After a fitful sleep in his own house, Phineas rose early and went to Charlotte's home to rejoin his fiancée and have breakfast with the family. "Let's all go find the pastor and ask if he'll perform a wedding this morning," said Phineas. "If he can't do that, we'll find the pastor of the other church or someone else in Lamar."

They took two carriages to the pastor's modest home decorated with gingerbread trim. Pastor Buchanan was indeed willing and invited them in. They all — Phineas and Adelaide, Danny and Charlotte, and Danny's three siblings — stepped into the cozy living room.

"Mrs. Buchanan, would you bring in three more chairs for young people to sit on," the pastor asked, "and then we'd like to hear a rendition of the Wedding March."

William helped Mrs. Buchanan bring in the chairs from the kitchen, and then she seated herself on the piano stool. She raised her hands over the keys and began the wedding music on the slightly out-of-tune piano.

Phineas and Adelaide took their places in front of the pastor. By some miracle, the sun streamed in the windows, spotlighting Phineas and Adelaide as if it were a blessing from the Almighty. As the pastor went through the short ceremony, Adelaide trembled from the excitement and tears formed in her eyes. She said her vows, and Phineas said his. He beamed with joy. Then the pastor pronounced them man and wife. They shared a shy kiss, and the rest of the family applauded and hugged them.

"Adelaide, you're one of us now," said Danny. "Welcome to the family." Overcome with emotion, Phineas embraced his son-in-law.

After the short ceremony, they stopped by the Crust & Crumb Bakery, where they announced their marriage to Danny's brother, John, and his wife, Katie.

"We'd like to buy your best chocolate cake to celebrate," Phineas said.

Kate laughed. "I wouldn't hear of it. Here, you take this cake as a wedding gift from us. And congratulations."

Back at the house, over cake and tea, Phineas asked Danny if he could bring some of his furniture to Florissant when they came. "Are you buying a wagon to take to Illinois instead of your carriage?"

"Yes. Charlotte wants some of her mother's things. A carriage wouldn't be big enough to bring it all. So we'll bring up whatever furniture you need for the rooming house."

Adelaide's eyes softened. "Charlotte, we won't take anything you want. Phineas says you'll have the first pick of everything in the house. And something else…I know this sudden change in your life would be an opportunity for you to be jealous of me, but you haven't been. I can't thank you enough."

"Please don't think too highly of me," said Charlotte. "Frankly, I've been concerned about Pa coming to Illinois with us and not having friends or familiar surroundings this late in his life. I've been praying about it. You look like God's answer to me."

Adelaide's eyes teared up, and she smiled.

"We should pack up and get ready to go to Lamar, dear wife," said Phineas. "We'll see Charlotte and Danny in a week or two."

Adelaide went upstairs to get her valise. Phineas went with her to collect all his personal things from the bedroom to take to his new home. They made their goodbyes, then pulled away in the carriage. Four hours later, they were in Lamar, knocking on the door of Oliver Hardin's home. Phineas arranged for him to sell the house in Spencer's Mill and left him the key.

By Sunday afternoon, the Fletchers were back in Florissant. This time Phineas didn't need a room key. He moved into the owner's apartment with his wife. After they paid the Bronsons for standing guard over the rooming house they had a little privacy.

"Welcome home, Phineas," Adelaide said. He grinned and embraced her.

"Thank you, my dear. This is wonderful, isn't it?"

A knock on the front door interrupted them. "I'll see who's here and tell them the rooming house is closed," Phineas said. He went to the door to find Sheriff Milligan.

"May I come in? I have some news," he said.

"Come on in," Phineas said with a grin. "I have some news, too. What's yours?"

"I'm still looking for the fellow who broke in, but I was passing by and saw your carriage out front. I wanted to tell you that Adelaide's friends took up a collection, and I have twenty-three dollars here to replace the stolen money."

Phineas was taken aback by the generosity of his wife's friends. "Adelaide," he called. "Sheriff Milligan has something for you."

"Be right there."

"While Adelaide is coming, I'll tell you our news. We got married yesterday morning. I'm here to stay."

Milligan's eyes sparkled, and his face broke into a wide smile as he grabbed Phineas' hand for a shake. "Congratulations, man. I wish you both many years of happiness."

"Thank you. I don't know how many years we'll have at our age, but I'm looking forward to spending whatever I have left with

Adelaide. Oh, here she is."

"Mrs. Fletcher, how good to see you."

Adelaide blushed. "So Phineas gave you the good news."

"Yes, and I'm not surprised. Listen, I brought you some money to replace what was stolen. Your friends and neighbors took up a collection." He handed her an envelope with the money.

Tears came into her eyes. "I am so blessed. First, a new husband, and now this. God is pouring out more blessings on me than I deserve. That reminds me of the verse in Psalm 66 that Phineas and I read this morning: "…we went through fire and water, but you brought us to a place of abundance.""

Milligan smiled. "You've certainly been through fire and water. And look at how abundant your life has just become. Well, I'll leave you folks alone to enjoy the evening. Congratulations again."

"One more thing before you leave, Milligan. I almost forgot."

Milligan turned back to see what Phineas wanted. Phineas went to the front desk and retrieved his drawing of the footprint by the kitchen window.

"Here's a footprint of the rascal who stole the money. If we find him, we may find he was the same one who started the fire in the rooming house."

"Hm, I hadn't thought of that," said Milligan. "Good thinking. I'll keep this in case we find a suspect." He went out the door and was gone.

When it was time to turn in for the night, Adelaide took the money envelope into the bedroom and opened the drawer to put it away. "Phineas, you won't believe what I'm about to tell you," she said.

"What is it?"

"The stolen money is back."

"You're talking about the money Sheriff Milligan just gave you."

"No, Phineas. The money that was stolen. It's all here. Like it came home again." She chuckled. "How do you suppose it got here?"

He peered into the drawer to confirm her story with his own eyes. There was the actual rent money—dollar banknotes and coins—in addition to the envelope the sheriff brought. "I'm as astonished as you. Let's think about this. The only people in the apartment since we left were the Bronsons, as far as we know."

They gazed at each other with puzzled expressions. As they

changed into their nightclothes, Phineas said, "I don't think I'll get much sleep tonight. My mind will be busy trying to solve this latest mystery."

Adelaide chuckled. "I guess the honeymoon is over."

The weather turned wet overnight. Rain fell steadily, watering the spring foliage. By morning, the clouds cleared, and the sun came out. It would be a beautiful day.

After breakfast, Phineas said, "I won't rest until I visit the Bronsons and ask if they know anything about that money. As much as I hate to think ill of someone as kind as they are, consider the knife we found after the intruder escaped. The initials scratched on the knife could be IB – Isaac Bronson."

Adelaide's expression clouded. "Oh, Phineas, I don't want to believe that. They're such a sweet couple."

"Yes, but we can't ignore the evidence. I'll talk to them today. I'll be kind and give them the benefit of the doubt, but I need to satisfy myself."

He left Adelaide in the kitchen and went to visit the Bronsons. They were surprised to see him on their doorstep and invited him in.

"Did you find everything in good order at the rooming house, Mr. Fletcher?" Betsy asked.

"Everything was in excellent order. Thank you again. Your willingness to help was a real blessing to Mrs. Fletcher. It allowed her to take a break from worrying about the fire. We even got married while we were gone."

The Bronsons expressed delight.

"By the way," Phineas continued, "some missing money was returned during our absence. That mystifies us. Do you know anything about it?"

Isaac's eyebrows went up. "Money was returned? How could that happen?" He shot a glance at Betsy and pushed some unruly hair away from his eyes.

"I don't know," Phineas said. "I wondered if you had any idea. Did anything odd happen while we were away? Was anyone else in there for even a few minutes? Did you hear anything strange at night?" He studied Isaac's expression as he talked but couldn't read him.

"Not that I know of. How about you, Betsy? Did anything odd

happen that you know of?"

"No. Are you sure the money was really missing in the first place?"

"Oh, yes. Adelaide and I both searched for it, and it was gone. But now it's back. If you folks don't know anything, maybe it will always be a mystery. Thank you again for being so kind as to watch the property while we were away."

He left them, still dissatisfied. This question was going to nag at him until he had the answer. Were the initials on the knife "IB," or were they something else?

When he returned to the rooming house, there was a visitor. Adelaide was at the front desk listening to a young man who spoke intensely, using his hands to illustrate his point.

"Here is my husband now," she said. "Why don't you talk to him?"

Phineas walked into the lobby, wondering what was going on.

"Phineas, this is Mr. Jeremiah Baker, the young man I told you about who wants to open a restaurant here. Mr. Baker, this is Mr. Fletcher."

"Nice to meet you, sir," said Baker. "Congratulations on your marriage."

"Thank you. What can we do for you?"

"I think your wife mentioned that I presented a plan to her for opening a restaurant in this facility. I'm a trained chef — studied at a culinary school in France. I apprenticed under the famous chef, Georges Auguste Escoffier. I'm sure you know of his reputation." He paused, apparently waiting for some sign that Phineas and Adelaide were properly impressed, but they only stared at him with blank expressions.

He continued. "I'm looking for a place to open a fine restaurant here in my hometown. I think Florissant could use a boost in culture, don't you?"

He chuckled, expecting them to agree, but again, their faces were expressionless.

"This rooming house is a prime location," he said. "It would be the top restaurant in Florissant. Why, I could fill this place with people every day. They would come from miles around. We would be so crowded that the clientele would have to make reservations. I could make a lot of money here, and we can negotiate a healthy percentage for you and your wife. Does this sound interesting to you?"

Phineas searched the man's face, looking for any signs of duplicity. The taller man peered down at Phineas with his chin tilted up ever so slightly. *I can't be sure of duplicity, but the man reeks of arrogance,* he thought.

"Mr. Baker, let me show you around, and we'll talk."

Baker beamed and squared his shoulders. Adelaide stood behind the front desk with eyes wide and her mouth agape. Phineas turned his face toward her and, unseen by Baker, gave her a wink. Her features relaxed.

"Have you seen the kitchen?"

"I'd be very interested," said Baker, and followed Phineas. "Ah, yes," he said. "This isn't big enough for a professional kitchen. We'll have to expand. We can move that wall two feet that way." He pointed toward Adelaide's parlor. "Another stove can go here, another icebox. We'll need to build another work surface with storage in the center of the room."

"It's almost like you had this all planned already. I thought you said you were never here."

"I haven't been. But don't you think those ideas are valid? Listen, I know you're probably strapped for funds after that fire. We can work it out that I will pay for the renovation to the kitchen as part of our deal."

"I need to talk it over with my wife, of course. Now let me show you the garden in the back. Do you think there would be a possibility of opening up outside dining during the summer?"

Baker followed him out enthusiastically. "That's an idea I hadn't considered," he said. "Yes, look at these beautiful trees. We could hang lanterns at night to give it some romantic ambiance. Maybe hire a violinist or a concertina player."

Phineas smiled thinly and led him through the rain-soaked grass to a bare spot under the window. "What do you think about using this window as a pass-through? Come on over and get a good look at it."

Baker walked closer to the window to humor Phineas, then nodded his approval. "Yes, it would make a good pass-through, wouldn't it?"

The chat continued for a few more moments until Phineas said he would have to speak to Adelaide. After all, this was her property, and he was only the new husband. By this time, Baker was bubbling with excitement as if he anticipated that the deal was all but sealed. He shook Phineas' hand and said he would see him in a few days, as he had to go out of town.

Phineas went back inside, where Adelaide was waiting with questioning eyes. "Adelaide, do you have a clean piece of paper handy?"

She scrounged at the front desk and found a piece of paper and a pencil. "What's going on, Phineas?" Her voice betrayed uncertainty.

He chuckled. "I got him to leave us a good footprint in the wet ground, thanks to last night's rain. I'm going out to sketch it, and I'll take the sketch over to Milligan's office. We'll compare it to the footprint left outside the window after the fire. Do you want to go with me?"

"Of course." She jumped at the chance to be included in the investigation. She went outside with him and stood in rapt attention as he measured and sketched the footprint in detail.

"I enjoy having you work with me, Adelaide."

She grinned.

He put the final details on his sketch. "Let's take this to Milligan."

The sheriff rose from his chair as they came in. "Welcome, Fletchers," he said. "What can I do for you?"

"I have another footprint for you," said Phineas. "This one was left by Jeremiah Baker, initials 'JB,' who just left this print less than an hour ago. He may be the owner of the knife, the one who broke in and stole the money. He may even be the one who started the fire. His motivation to commit a crime against Adelaide is that he wants to open a restaurant in the rooming house, and she refuses."

"I see. Let's compare that footprint with the other one. We'll see if he's the man who broke in after the fire."

Milligan took the original print from the file and laid it beside the new one. There were some obvious differences. "Baker's footprint is much larger than the first one. They can't be from the same person."

"What a disappointment," said Phineas. "So he's not the man who broke in through the window."

"No," said Adelaide. "But couldn't he still be the one who set the fire? He might have reasoned that the fire would make me want to sell the building, then he could buy it cheap and refurbish the kitchen for his own use."

"Hmm. That's a theory I hadn't considered," Phineas said. Milligan nodded thoughtfully.

"If that's true, he's lucky the fire didn't consume the whole building and ruin his plans," Milligan said.

"Think about it," Phineas said. "The fire was started during the day when someone was there who could report it and stop it from spreading too far."

Milligan stroked his chin. "Hmm. But his initials were on the knife. That would make him the burglar, not the arsonist."

"Not necessarily. There must be many men whose first initial is I or J and whose last initial is P or B. But, I found it interesting that he already had planned what he wanted to do to the kitchen, including moving a wall two feet and placing the appliances. He claimed to have never been there. I didn't believe him. I think he had been there before, at some time."

"We'll have to keep an eye on him."

"Adelaide and I have some decisions to make, so we'll go back home now," Phineas said. "Keep me informed if you get more information, will you?"

"Of course, and thanks for the new footprint. It will be in the file when we need it."

In the carriage on the way home, Phineas was preoccupied.

"We've only been married for two days, and I've already lost your attention." Adelaide gave him a sly smile. "What's up, Phineas? Spill it."

Phineas ducked and winced. "Ouch, I didn't mean to ignore you. I was preoccupied. Will you forgive me?"

"Only if you tell me what you're thinking."

Phineas grinned. "I don't want to overstep, my dear, since this is your rooming house, but I've had some ideas."

"This is our rooming house now, Phineas. You're not only my husband; you're my business partner. So what are your ideas?"

"Here's the idea. We don't bring the rooming house back to its original condition; we improve on it. We put in new paint colors, new curtains, and bigger mirrors in the guest rooms, that kind of thing. We completely redecorate. What do you think?"

"We don't have any money to do that."

"When my house is sold, we'll invest a large percentage of it in the rooming house. We can even rename it. We could put up new signs saying, "Florissant Bed and Breakfast." And we would raise the rates."

Adelaide laughed. "What about "Fletcher House Bed and Breakfast?"

"Fletcher House? Of course." He grinned. "We'll make it a first-class place. We'll have a new front desk built, a bigger one. The lobby will look spectacular, and we'll decorate the guest rooms fancier than the bedrooms people have in their homes."

"Oh, Phineas, this will be so much fun!"

"Maybe we'll even take that large necessary room upstairs and divide it into two, each with a new bathtub, one for men and one for ladies. We'll even install toilets."

She stared at him, wide-eyed and slack-jawed.

He wasn't through laying out ideas. "Then, if you ever wanted to open for lunch, we could hire a cook and other staff and increase our income. We could do that without Jeremiah Baker. But that would be a step not taken lightly."

"Since we're in it together, that may be something we would consider. Reluctantly."

Phineas chuckled. "We'll not do anything you're reluctant to do. Life is too short."

They listened to the horse's hooves thud rhythmically against the road all the way home.

Wiley arrived late Tuesday with his brushes and drop cloths. Phineas and Adelaide had selected some paint colors and ordered wallpaper for the lobby. Phineas had mentored Wiley in his painting business; now, he would teach him how to hang wallpaper.

Wiley went to work early with his brushes. He went to work on the upstairs rooms first so that they could welcome guests. Their residence apartment could wait until last.

Adelaide was short of some supplies in the kitchen. "Would you take me to the general store, Phineas? I need to restock some things."

They left Wiley at his work and took the carriage to the general store.

"Morning, Mrs. Courtney," said the store owner.

"Good morning, Mr. McGinty," Adelaide said. "I have a bit of news. I'm no longer Mrs. Courtney. You can call me Mrs. Fletcher now, and this is my husband, Phineas."

McGinty beamed and came around the counter to shake Phineas' hand. "Best wishes for a long and happy life. Say, are you the Phineas Fletcher what caught that murderer?"

"I am, sir."

"I made a good deal on that shovel what dug up the body."

Phineas gave him a sly smile. "Yes, Sheriff Milligan told me about that. He said you left the mud on it, doubled your price, and made a fast sale."

"I did." McGinty leaned over, laughing, and slapped his knee. "If you ever go looking for another body, let me know if I can help."

"I'll do that. And if you hear of anyone who needs a mystery investigated, will you tell them to contact me at Adelaide's rooming house?"

"Yes, sir, I'll do it."

Adelaide left them chatting and went about the store, picking up items and putting them in her basket.

McGinty lowered his voice to a whisper. "Someone said you had a break-in after that fire. Well, I overheard two people talkin' in the store here the other day. I might have a bit o' information for you."

"Is that right?"

"Yes, sir. Now, I don't know the names o' those folks, but they were arguin'. The girl said to the young man, 'I know we needed the money Jeremiah paid you, but you shouldn't ha' done it. And you really shouldn't ha' took that money.' Then the man said, 'Shhh,' like he didn't want nobody to hear."

Phineas' brain snapped to attention. "Can you tell me what they looked like? How old were they?"

McGinty put his finger to his chin. "Let me think. I'd guess 'em to be in their early twenties, fresh-faced, y'know. The young man was shorter than me, and the girl was a bit shorter than him."

"Do you remember what they bought that day?"

"Nothin' outta the ordinary. Sugar, tea, a tin o' yeast. Maybe somethin' else; I don't recall."

"Thank you very much, McGinty. You've been an enormous help." Phineas took his notebook from his pocket and jotted down this new information.

Adelaide came to the cash register to pay for her purchases. On the way home, Phineas filled her in on what he had learned.

"It sounds to me like Jeremiah Baker may have paid someone to come in that night," she said.

"But the way McGinty said it, stealing the money was not part of the deal, like he hired them to do something else. I wonder if he hired them to measure the kitchen."

"In the dark? That sounds crazy. But that would explain how he already knew where he wanted the wall and where the stoves and iceboxes would sit."

Phineas pondered this new wrinkle. "He could have measured the kitchen in the lamplight. You would never have seen it from your bedroom. I'd like to talk to some of Jeremiah's friends and see if any of them know what he was up to. We might get some fresh evidence. How can we find out who's in his circle of acquaintances?"

Adelaide said, "Do you remember my thought that he might be related to the carpenter, Kingston Baker? I wonder how we could get any information from him."

"Adelaide, all those folks came from your church. Can you talk to someone who knows everybody — maybe a person with the reputation of a gossip — and make some inquiries?"

The horse clip-clopped along. They were almost home.

Adelaide's lips formed into a crooked smile. "One particular woman in the church, Lillian Dobbins, the doctor's wife, seems to know everyone and their business. I'll invite her to tea tomorrow."

At precisely ten o'clock the next day, Lillian entered the rooming house lobby. Adelaide had a pot of tea and some warm cookies fresh from the oven. The two ladies sat at one of the guest dining room tables and began their chat. Lillian loved to gossip. They discussed the business of one person after another and eventually got around to Kingston Baker and his family.

"Poor Kingston," Lillian said. "His wife passed two years ago, and all he has left is his daughter. She's a comfort to him, of course, but then she married that boy Kingston thought wasn't good enough for her. You know how that goes with doting fathers."

Adelaide nodded. "That's a shame. What's his daughter's name?"

"Elizabeth is her given name. He calls her Betsy. Lovely girl."

Adelaide sat a little straighter in her seat. "You say Kingston wasn't keen on the young man. What do you think of him?"

"Isaac? Oh, he seems nice enough. Not much ambition, sad to say. I think Betsy could have done better."

Adelaide's brow arched. So Isaac Bronson was the son-in-law of Kingston Baker.

She took a sip of her tea. "Did you ever hear anything about a Jeremiah Baker?"

Lillian rolled her eyes. "Don't get me started on him. What a pretentious boob. He thinks he can cook better than any woman who's been doing it all her life."

"Is he related to Kingston?"

"I don't think Kingston would claim him, but he's his nephew."

Adelaide commiserated with Lillian. "It sounds like poor Kingston has enough trouble without the likes of him lurking about the family tree."

Lilian let out a hearty laugh. "I say. That's a good one, Adelaide. Well, it's time I should be getting back home. I have to make dinner for my family. Of course, I probably can't do it as well as Jeremiah." She chortled again, picked up her purse, and stood. "We'll have to do this again sometime."

Adelaide waved at her as she drove away. Then she became aware of footsteps coming down the stairs.

"I listened to as much as possible from upstairs," Phineas said, "but I couldn't hear it all. You're quite a clever investigator, my dear."

"Yes, and I have some fascinating information. Sit here with me. Have a cookie, and I'll tell you all of it."

He took a chair and popped a cookie into his mouth. Adelaide's eyes sparkled. "If you're looking for an assistant, I'm for hire," she said.

Phineas grinned. "You're hired. What have you got?"

"To boil it all down, Kingston Baker is the father of Betsy Bronson. He thinks Isaac isn't good enough for her. Kingston is also Jeremiah Baker's uncle, making Jeremiah a cousin to Betsy. So they all know each other very well."

A slow smile spread over Phineas' face. He nodded, mulling over this new information. "So, according to what the store owner told me, Jeremiah could have hired Isaac Bronson to enter the rooming house at night and measure the kitchen, but Isaac decided to search for money while he was there. He dropped his knife in your bedroom."

"Yes, with the initials IB."

"And he left the smaller footprint. Since he's a short man, that makes sense. Then Betsy's conscience got the best of her, and when you asked Isaac and Betsy to mind the rooming house for a few days, Betsy put the money back."

Adelaide's brow creased. "But who set the fire?"

"We still don't know for sure. It could have been Jeremiah. We don't have a good footprint from the fire. We may never know for sure who set it. We only know that Jeremiah had the best motive."

Adelaide leaned back in her chair. "You know, I could still be in danger from that man. I'm so grateful you're here now. He'll be less likely to attack me with a man in the house."

Phineas smiled as his chest puffed out a little, and he reassured her of her safety.

Adelaide continued, "That reminds me—we haven't seen Jeremiah since last Monday. I was sure he'd be here Tuesday, bothering you about his fancy restaurant here in this building."

Phineas rubbed the back of his neck. "No, he said he was going out of town. I'm sure he'll be here within the next few days."

"On another topic, how is Wiley coming along with the painting?"

"He's almost finished with the guest rooms and will be ready to start the downstairs tomorrow. The wallpaper will be delivered on Monday, so he'll paint the apartment, kitchen, and dining room over the weekend before the wallpaper comes in."

Adelaide climbed the stairs to inspect the freshly painted guest rooms. Wiley's work satisfied her critical eye. She put a sign in the front window, "Open for Business."

"I must talk to the Bronsons," Phineas said over breakfast. "My heart can't rest until I do. I think they must know who set the fire. And while I'm out, I'll order a fancy new sign that says 'Fletcher House.' Then I'll put an ad in the paper saying that the new Fletcher House Bed and Breakfast is open for guests."

He finished his coffee and left to visit the Bronsons. Within a few minutes, Phineas was knocking on their door. Betsy opened it and invited him in. He doffed his bowler and stepped inside.

"What can I do for you, Mr. Fletcher?"

"Is Isaac here? I need to talk to him."

"I'm sorry," she said. "He's at the neighbor's house helping with some repairs. He's good with his hands."

"Then may I speak with you? You might have the answers I'm looking for."

Betsy began to fidget. "I guess it would be all right. Would you like to sit down?"

"Yes, thank you, dear." He lowered himself into an old stuffed chair and leaned forward, folding his hands.

"Betsy, I need you to be honest about what happened at the rooming house."

Betsy dropped her head and stared at the floor. "What are you talking about?"

"I think you know. I need you to tell me if Isaac had anything to do with the fire."

"No, sir." She was still looking at the floor and tapping her feet as she sat in the chair.

"Betsy, look at me."

Betsy raised her eyes.

"Did Isaac have anything to do with that fire?"

"No, sir, he didn't. Honest."

"Do you know who did?"

"Yes, sir. But I'm not going to tell you. I can't." Her eyes filled with tears.

Phineas leaned back and decided to speak gently to the young girl. "I can see you're protecting someone. What if we played a game?" He smiled at her as if they were conspiring in some deep plot. "If I guess who it was, will you nod? That way, you won't have to say it."

"I guess." She rubbed the toe of her shoe on the floor.

"All right," Phineas said. "Let's see... Was it Sheriff Milligan?"

She smiled thinly and wagged her head.

"Was it your Pa?"

She gave him a cross look. "Don't be silly."

"How about your cousin Jeremiah?"

She gasped, and her eyes grew large.

"You don't even need to nod, Betsy. That's fine. You can honestly tell your family you didn't tell me who did it. Thank you for your time, dear." He put on his bowler, adjusted it to a proper angle, and left, heading straight for Sheriff Milligan's office.

Phineas burst into the sheriff's office. "I know who did it, Sheriff. I know who set the fire."

Milligan was at his desk. He raised his eyes from his paperwork and grinned. "Take a chair, Fletcher. Tell me what you know."

"I don't have hard evidence, but it was Jeremiah Baker. It was confirmed by his cousin, Betsy Bronson. He fancies himself an expert chef. He wants to open a new restaurant in town and sees the potential of the rooming house. He's been pressuring Adelaide to let him go into business in her kitchen. When she refused, not once but several times, he decided to burn the place just enough to discourage her. Whether she moved out and sold it to him cheap, or stayed and let him do what he wanted for a percentage, it didn't matter to him. He'd get his restaurant one way or another. He chose the kitchen to start the fire to refurbish it to his own design."

Milligan cocked his head. "Go on."

"Once the kitchen was burned, he hired his cousin's young husband to break in. I believe he wanted him to take measurements in the kitchen so he could make his plans. But Isaac thought that while he was already there, he'd help himself to Adelaide's money. I remember that he and Betsy were working as volunteers in Adelaide's bedroom when we checked on the rent money, so he knew where it was. Unfortunately for him, Adelaide woke up when he opened the drawer beside her bed. She screamed. He pushed her down on her bed, snatched the money, and ran, but not before she bit him hard on the hand. You may find that Isaac Bronson still has the marks."

"Isaac Bronson? He seems like such a quiet boy."

"He's lucky to have a wife with morals. When we asked them to watch the rooming house while we went to Spencer's Mill, his wife returned the money to the canister in Adelaide's bedroom. It was there when we got home."

Milligan threw his head back and belly-laughed. "That's a kick in the pants for a thief, isn't it? He sneaks around, risks getting caught, and then his wife gives back the loot."

Phineas joined in the laughter. "I'll talk to Adelaide. She may be reluctant to press charges against Isaac, seeing that the money has been returned, but he needs to be held accountable. The embarrassment of a stained reputation — and pressure from a morally upright wife — may give him the incentive to straighten up. But Jeremiah Baker — that's another story. That fellow needs to spend some serious time getting familiar with the walls inside your jail."

"I agree, Phineas." Milligan grinned. "Who can verify the details of what you just told me? You're only speculating about the motivation, right?"

"Yes, sir, but I'd lay odds. You can interview Jeremiah and Isaac, of course, then Mr. McGinty from the general store. Betsy Bronson will be slow to talk, but you'll be able to persuade her. And you can get more details from Adelaide. The firemen may be able to verify some of the details, too."

Milligan leaned back, satisfied. "I say, you can add one more case to your list of mysteries solved, can't you?"

"I believe I will, when the scoundrel confesses or is convicted."

"Then I'll go bring the scoundrel in, my friend. You go home and enjoy your wife while I do the work necessary to wrap up this case and tie the bow on it."

The next few weeks were a flurry of activity. Phineas taught Wiley to hang wallpaper, transforming the lobby. The house in Spencer's Mill was sold to Oliver Hardin, who wanted it himself for a rental property. Adelaide and Phineas took the train to Chicago to shop for new curtains, rugs, lamps, and furnishings. Upon their return, a team of workers installed one of those innovative septic tanks behind the building. Then Phineas hired a local fellow to remodel the upstairs, including two bathrooms with tubs and toilets. They set new nightly rates, then advertised the grand opening of the Fletcher House in the Lamar and Toledo newspapers.

It was a success. Guests filled the rooms and spread the word to their friends. Soon it became possible to hire a breakfast cook, housekeeper, and front desk clerk to help Adelaide, giving her some rest and time to accompany Phineas on various investigations.

It wasn't long until another case came up, the most important one Phineas had ever undertaken, a case that would impact both of them for the rest of their lives.

THE FOUNDLING

Danny came home from work at the general store with good news for Charlotte. "Mr. Link may have found someone to replace me as store manager. I hope he makes his decision soon. I'm itching to pack up and head west."

Danny and Charlotte had looked forward to this adventure for months. Now that school was out, William, Amos, and Lizbeth had moved to their mother's new home seven miles away. Phineas had remarried, so Danny and Charlotte were alone for the first time in their short marriage.

Charlotte's eyes sparkled. "I'm just as excited to get going as you are—moving clear to Illinois and finding that farm you always wanted. I'm only sorry Pa won't be going with us. I feel like I'm abandoning him."

"Abandoning him? He's the one who got married on one day's notice, then moved out of town to his wife's rooming house. I don't think you need to feel guilty about leaving him."

Charlotte grinned. "Maybe it's more that I'll miss him, the old grouch. By the way, they're advertising Adelaide's place as the Fletcher House Bed and Breakfast now."

Danny grinned. "That sounds higher-class than a rooming house. I hope they raised the rates."

"I've started looking at what we'll need to take when we move. Pa said I could take my pick of Ma's things from his old house. I want to keep her china, at least one bed, and those two dressers."

Danny's mind calculated the wagon space needed for a bed and two dressers. "My Ma said we could have anything from her barn we want. I'll take the plow and all of Pa's tools. The first thing we need to do is sell our carriage and buy a wagon."

Charlotte tilted her head, thinking. "I have an idea. What about those people who just moved here from Indiana and bought your brother's house? They probably don't need that big wagon anymore."

"Good idea. They're both working at the bakery. If I go now, I might catch them before they go home."

"All right. I may have supper ready by the time you get back."

Charlotte put on her apron and busied herself in the kitchen, firing up the woodstove and peeling potatoes from the garden. In an hour, she was keeping supper warm and waiting for Danny.

He returned with a smile on his face. "I worked a deal with George. He'll trade his wagon and one of his horses for our carriage and twenty dollars."

Charlotte's jaw dropped. "That's a lot of money, isn't it?"

"I think it's a fair deal," Danny said.

The two of them sat at the table and said grace. The meal was strangely quiet. For the last few months, there had been six mouths to feed. Now the number of chairs around the table had suddenly dropped to two.

Charlotte glanced at the empty places at the table and giggled. "We need some noise and confusion here to feel at home, don't we, Danny?"

He chuckled and kept eating. "No, I could get used to this."

That night Charlotte tossed restlessly in her bed. A packing list rolled through her head. Images of the anticipated trip followed—the rolling hills, the tilled farmland, small towns they would pass through, railroad crossings and covered bridges—she imagined it all. Finally, afraid she would wake Danny with her tossing about, she went downstairs, thinking a good book might make her drowsy.

She chose a book from the bookcase, then snuggled into the Chesterfield sofa under a quilt, reading by the light of the oil lamp. Her eyelids became heavy. She was about to doze off when she thought she detected light footsteps outside on the veranda. Her ears perked up. *I must be dreaming,* she thought. *The grandfather clock says it's not quite four o'clock in the morning.*

But there it was again, light footsteps like someone tip-toeing across the veranda. She went to the window and pulled back the curtain, but nothing was visible in the blackness. The oak trees and massive blue spruce in the yard hid any light from the gaslight on the street. Her reflection in the window glass also blocked her view. She returned to the sofa to resume her interrupted sleep.

Later—she didn't know how much later—there was a second

sound. It sounded like a baby's cooing, so she must be having some vivid dreams. She smiled and dropped into a twilight sleep, half awake, half asleep. Having a baby with Danny would be so lovely. She would touch its tiny nose, its little fingers and toes, its rosebud lips. She would feel its soft breath on her neck. What a pleasant dream. She drifted off again.

Then, it couldn't be denied. It was the cry of an infant somewhere near. She flew off the Chesterfield and ran upstairs. "Danny, wake up," she said, trying to jiggle him out of a sound sleep. "Somebody is outside with a baby. Wake up."

"Hmmph."

"Danny, come downstairs. I think there's someone outside with a baby."

"Hmmph." He rolled over with his back to her and resumed snoring.

Charlotte gave up, put on a robe, and went downstairs. Crossing the rug barefoot, she opened the door just a crack.

"Who's there?" she asked.

A squeal came from near her feet. There was no one else—just a baby wrapped in a thin blanket, resting in a wicker basket. Charlotte's hand flew to her chest, and her jaw dropped.

She stooped to pick up the basket and checked to see if anyone was around. The bearer of this gift had left in a hurry. She brought it in and set it on the Chesterfield, lifting the baby gently. Its britches were dripping.

"No wonder you're crying, little one," she said, bouncing it up and down. Let's see what we can do for you." Nothing else was in the basket except a blanket and a glass bottle with a leather nipple. At least someone had thought to leave that. In the absence of diapers, she found a dishtowel in the kitchen. She undid the baby's diaper and cleaned up his mess. "Ah, you're a boy," she said. "We'll have to find your Mama." She dusted his little bottom with cornstarch. Once the dishtowel was in place, she climbed the stairs with the child in her arms.

"Danny," she whispered. "Look what I found."

Now Danny was awake. "Whose baby is that?"

"I guess he's ours for now." Charlotte smiled. "Someone put him on our porch and left."

"No, no, a baby doesn't fit into our plans. We have to find his mother. Then we're going to Illinois."

180

"His mother doesn't want him. He looks to be only a few days old. We don't have anything to feed him but cow's milk. Do you have any of that Liebig's infant food at the store? And we'll need some nappies until we find his Ma. Do you stock those?"

Danny sighed. "Yes, we have Leibig's and some diapers on the shelf. You can pick them up at the store in the morning. But you'll need to find someone else to take him so we can get on with our plans."

"I will, Danny. Right now, I'll try to feed him and get some sleep. I'm dead tired."

Charlotte carried the infant to the kitchen and found some milk. That meant heating the stove. In the meantime, the baby kicked and squirmed. When the milk was at the right temperature, she cuddled the little thing in her arms and put the bottle in his mouth. He sucked at it heartily, looking at her through bright blue eyes.

"I'll call you Michael," she said, "because you're like one of God's angels."

After the feeding, he urped a lot of what had gone down, so she was obliged to clean up another mess and change his dishtowel again. She loved cuddling him in her arms. Once he was clean and dry, she sank back on the Chesterfield with the baby on her chest, and the two went sound asleep.

She was still there when Danny got up to go to work. Since she hadn't slept much that night, he wasn't willing to wake her. He brewed a pot of coffee, ate some bread with apple butter, and tip-toed out of the house.

When Charlotte woke, she found that Danny was already gone. *I can't let that get to be a habit,* she thought. Michael was ready for another feeding, so she repeated the process.

Who might be willing to take a baby until his mother was found? She went through her mental list of friends and acquaintances. There was Marie Beavey, her mother-in-law's closest friend. She didn't think it would be fair to ask a woman in her fifties to take charge of an infant. Her sister-in-law Katie couldn't do it because she and her husband had just opened a bakery. She didn't want to ask her other sister-in-law, Mary, because her husband was going through a bad patch and probably wouldn't tolerate the extra stress of someone else's child. She thought of one friend after another, but no one was suitable. Maybe Danny would have an idea.

She found a deeper basket she usually used for vegetables, cleaned it out, and lined it with blankets to use as a baby bed. Michael slept for another two hours while she packed small, lesser-used items in crates for moving.

When he woke again, she remembered the family across the street. They had just moved in recently. She didn't know them yet, but maybe they could take the baby. If not, perhaps they had seen someone in the night and could help find the mother. She gave him another bottle, cleaned him up, and then carried him to the neighbor's house.

She rapped on the door and waited, jiggling Michael up and down to keep him happy. A little girl opened the door.

"Ma," she said, "it's a lady with a baby."

The girl's mother came to the door, a tired-looking woman. She didn't look well. "What can I do for you?" she asked.

Charlotte said, "Someone left this baby on my veranda last night and—"

"Ma," the little girl said, "that's the same baby that was on our step."

The woman, already pale, became white and almost swooned. Alarmed, Charlotte stepped forward. "Can I help you to a chair?"

The woman recovered and fanned herself. "I'm sorry. I may as well confess now that Nettie here has already opened her mouth. The baby was left on our doorstep last night, and I'm not well enough to care for another child. I simply can't do it. So I picked up the poor little thing and took him to your porch. I'm sorry, missus. I just can't take care of him. But I peeked through the window to make sure he was all right until you carried him into your house."

Charlotte's heart was touched. This sickly woman was indeed in no condition to take another child. "Did you see who left the baby there?"

"No, ma'am. When I realized someone had been on the step, I quick ran to the window. A man was driving away in a buckboard. It was too dark to see his face, but I'd say he was a big guy, bigger than most men. He headed in the direction of Lamar."

That wasn't much to go on. "Thank you. I'm Charlotte, by the way." She smiled at the woman.

"I'm Eleanor. Nice to meet you, ma'am. Maybe we can become friends, living across the street."

"We're getting ready to move to Illinois in a few days, so I'm sure

182

someone else will be moving into our house soon. But if you need anything before we leave, be sure and let me know."

"Thank you. I will. I hope you find a good home for the baby."

"I do, too."

Charlotte turned and walked back to her own house, chuckling. *Maybe Danny will find someone else's doorstep where we can leave the baby tonight.*

The neighbor called her back. "Wait, missus. I have something you might use." Charlotte turned around, and the woman disappeared from the open door momentarily. She returned with an armful of infant-sized blankets and an old silver pot.

"My children used these blankets and this bubby-pot. You can have them. Sometimes babies don't like the taste of those leather nipples."

"How do you use that thing?" She had never cared for a child before, so she turned the unfamiliar pot around, trying to figure out how it worked.

"Oh, you put the baby's milk in the pot and then stuff a clean rag in the spout. The baby sucks the milk out of the rag."

"Thank you, Eleanor. I'll put them to good use."

She hugged the baby close. She thought she could get used to having a little one around. It would be wonderful to start their own family in Illinois. But she knew she would have to find a home for this baby to get on with their plans. Still, she didn't want him to go to just anyone. It would have to be the finest parents possible.

"Lord," she prayed, "please put Your hand on Michael's life. Help me find the parents You want him to have."

Most of her day was spent taking care of the baby. After his shift at the store, Danny came home carrying infant formula and diapers. He hoped to find that Charlotte had been able to find a home for the baby, but of course, she hadn't. She told him the story about the baby being left first at the neighbor's house and the neighbor immediately dropping him off at their house.

Danny shook his head. "That poor baby. I think we should contact your Pa and have him come back to Spencer's Mill. He does a good job of finding people and solving mysteries."

"That's a good idea. He can stay here with us while he does his search. Hopefully, he could find the mother quickly. By the way, I'm calling the baby 'Michael.' Can you hold him while I get supper ready?"

Danny took the wiggly bundle. "I'll go to the telegraph office in the morning before I go to work. I'll send a telegram to your Pa."

The following morning, Charlotte put the baby in the carriage, drove Danny to the telegraph office, and then delivered him to the general store. She took the carriage to make some inquiries around town. Her first visit was to the pastor of her church. She carried Michael through the church door, where the pastor studied for his sermon.

"Mrs. Reese, what have you there?" he asked, grinning.

"Good morning, Pastor Buchanan," she said. "Meet Michael. He's a foundling that was dropped on our doorstep. We need to find a home for him so we can move to Illinois. Danny doesn't want to take the child that far away, or his mother will never be able to find him."

"Have you considered that maybe the mother doesn't want him?" he asked gently. He opened the blanket and peeked at the tiny face. The baby slumbered peacefully, making sucking motions with his little lips.

"That may be true," Charlotte said, "but Danny doesn't want to take him. We're making a big enough life change without the unexpected burden of a little one. So can you think of anyone willing to take him in?"

The pastor adjusted his spectacles and frowned. "I can't think of anyone off-hand. Our church members are either too old to take in a child, or not financially able to take another one. But I'll let you know if I think of someone."

"Thank you, Pastor." Charlotte's shoulders sank. She took the baby back to the carriage and tucked him into his basket. "Let's go see Sheriff Lane," she said.

It took only moments to get to their destination. She gathered the baby up and went into the office.

"Good morning, Sheriff," she said. "Do you remember me? I'm Charlotte, the daughter of Phineas Fletcher."

"Of course, I remember you," said the sheriff, rushing around his desk to move a chair in position for her. "Your help with that runaway child was invaluable. Please have a seat. What can I do for you? Say, is this Phineas' grandchild?"

Charlotte smiled and took a seat. "No such luck, Sheriff. This is a foundling that showed up on our porch yesterday morning. I call him Michael. Look at this face. How could a mother give up a child like this?"

Lane fastened his gaze on the sleeping baby. "It's hard to imagine," he said. "Maybe she couldn't afford to take care of him. Maybe she doesn't have a husband. Those things happen, you know. You must want me to help you in some way. What can I do for you?"

"Do you know anyone who could be the mother of this child? You know about a lot of things in town."

"No, there hasn't been any news like that lately. And gossip like that travels like lightning."

"Do you know anyone who might be willing to take in a cute little guy like this?" She jiggled the baby gently.

"I'm sorry, Mrs. Reese, I can't think of anyone. But they have that orphanage over in Lamar. You could take the little thing over there."

Charlotte made a face. "There are stories about that orphanage. The staff workers probably mean well, but they don't have the time each child needs. I wouldn't take this baby there if you paid me. That's unthinkable." She hugged the baby a little closer.

"Well, do you think your Pa could help you with this? I know he moved out of town—"

She smiled. "We sent him a telegram this morning. We're hoping he'll be here tomorrow. I'm sure he'll want to come by and say hello to you while he's here."

"That would be good. I'll look forward to it."

The next afternoon, while Danny was still at work, there was a knock at the door, and Phineas Fletcher arrived with a small valise.

"Pa!" Charlotte opened the door for him, baby in her arms. Her Pa hugged her.

"What's this?" he asked and took the baby.

"That's Michael," Charlotte said. "I don't know what name his mother gave him. He showed up at our door in the night. Danny doesn't want to go to Illinois until we find his mother or someone else to care for him. Since you've developed a reputation as an investigator, we hoped you could have a go at finding the baby's mum."

Phineas' eyebrows raised. "Hmm. What do we have to go on?"

"The woman across the street saw a man in a buckboard drive

185

away in the direction of Lamar right after the baby was left. Going by his silhouette under the gaslights, she said he was a large man, bigger than most. That's all we know."

"That's certainly not much. Let's go into the kitchen and think this over. Can you make me a cup of coffee? It's been a long trip."

"Give me the baby, and you take your valise upstairs to your bedroom. I'll brew some coffee while you're doing that."

In a few minutes, they sat at the kitchen table together. Phineas blew on his coffee to cool it and said, "It wasn't the mother who left him. It could've been the pa. I wonder where the mother is. She could have died in childbirth, or maybe the baby was too much for the father, and he decided to get rid of it. In that case, there could be a mother somewhere frantic to know where her child is.

"What a tragic situation that would be," said Charlotte. "I would rather think they didn't have enough money to care for the little guy and decided to give him a better chance at a good life."

"I think my best plan for tracking down the parents would be to go to Lamar since that was the direction he went. There's no town for miles in the other direction, anyway. I'll check with the churches to find out if there have been any inconvenient pregnancies lately."

"That may give you some good leads. But Lamar is such a big town...."

"On the other hand, the solution may be found in the seedier parts of town. If I can't find an answer at the churches, I'll visit the pubs to see if I can get a lead there. There are a lot of loose lips at pubs."

Charlotte shivered. "Whatever the situation, I suspect the baby would be better off with us. I wish Danny would consent to take him to Illinois."

"That's asking a lot of a young husband pulling up roots and starting a new life. He'll have to clear at least ten acres the first year by himself, build a house, dig a well, and plant crops to make a go of it. That's a gigantic bite for a man to chew. A baby was never part of your plan, was it?"

"Not until we get settled. We want to start a family eventually."

"My advice, daughter, is not to push Danny into being the father of another man's child. Not right now, anyway."

Charlotte nodded. That bit of advice sounded wise. She jiggled the baby in her lap and hugged him close.

"It's been a long trip from Florissant, and I'm road-weary. I'd like to stay here tonight, then go to Lamar tomorrow to look for the mother. I'll be at the hotel if I'm not back tomorrow night. Say, I almost forgot. On the way here, I passed a nice farm with a For Sale sign out front. It's sixty-eight acres with a house and barn. The owners have died, and the heirs want a quick sale. I wish you wouldn't go all the way to Illinois. Do you think Danny would take a look at that property?"

Her eyes sparkled at the thought of staying in Ohio, then she quickly realized it probably wouldn't happen. "I doubt it, Pa. He's had his heart set on Illinois for quite a while. The railroad is selling forty-acre tracts of land for cheap. There's a small down payment, then nothing more due until the crops come in. He just has to clear ten acres and plant crops the first year."

"Clearing it is hard work," said Phineas. "Real hard. And he'll have to put up a cabin, too. He'll need your help. You won't have time for a baby." He stood. "Thank you for the coffee. I'm going upstairs to take a nap before supper."

In the morning, Phineas rose early to make the trip to Lamar. He said goodbye to Danny and Charlotte and kissed the baby. "I'll try to find your mama today, Michael."

It took him nearly four hours by carriage to get to his destination. He made the rounds of the churches near the center of town, asking about any recent pregnancies where the mother was distressed. By late afternoon none of the pastors had any leads for him.

He decided to treat himself to dinner at the Old English Tea Room, his favorite restaurant in Lamar. Then he planned to try a couple of pubs, hang around, and keep his ears open. Maybe he would have some luck.

His first stop after dinner was the Two Roosters Tavern, a rough establishment where fighting often broke out. Just as often, there were spilled confidences among the drinkers. He took a stool at the bar and called for a pint of ale. As he sipped at it, the faces around him changed regularly. He chatted with all of them, asking if they knew anything about someone getting rid of a baby. No one had, so he eventually left.

His next stop was the Golden Lamb, a few blocks away. "They name their pubs after farm animals in this town," he muttered as his carriage rolled over the dark brick-paved streets. Bright light streamed from the tavern windows, and the sounds of music and raucous laughter spilled onto the sidewalk. Phineas opened the door and stepped inside. There was live music that evening, so the crowd was heavy. He found a spare chair at a table occupied by three other men and took a seat.

"Do you gentlemen mind if I join you?"

"Course not, friend," one of them said. His breath betrayed the length of time he had been sitting there. The gentlemen applauded the singer, who warbled a tune at the front of the room, then the conversation turned to various inane subjects as the next song started.

Phineas still had the search for Michael's mama on his mind, but his approach had lacked finesse at the last pub. He decided to come at it from another direction.

"Say, you'll never guess what happened to my daughter," Phineas said in a confidential tone. His table companions leaned in to hear the secret.

"She found a baby on her doorstep the other day. Can you imagine? It was in the middle of the night." He lifted his mug and took a sip.

The semi-sober man across the table asked, "What's she gonna do with it?"

"Why, I think she wants to keep it unless the Ma shows up."

The drunk to Phineas' right was lost in thought. "Say, you know, there was a fellow in here last night braggin' about gettin' rid of a baby."

"Anyone you know?" Phineas asked.

"I don't know him for a personal friend, but I've seen him here a lot. I overheard him tell somebody he had to come through Cosmopolis to get here. It sounded like he lived in a cabin a couple of miles west of Cosmopolis. I got the impression he's hard on his woman."

"Is that right? That's too bad."

The man to his left chimed in. "Oh, you're talking about that big guy that comes in here. Big, nasty guy. Hard drinker."

"And you say he bragged about getting rid of a baby. Quite an upstanding gentleman." Phineas wagged his head.

"I'm surprised he's not here tonight," said the drunk. "He's here nearly every night."

Phineas wondered how long he should stay in case the big guy showed up. But it was already late. He would surely have been there by now. Phineas pulled his pocket watch out and made a show of looking at the time. "I've enjoyed your company, gentlemen, but I need to get to my hotel now. Long day tomorrow."

He left the Golden Lamb, but instead of going to his hotel, he decided he had time for one more stop. Down a side street full of trash cans and old barrels casting shadows under the gaslights, he spotted a barroom he hadn't been to. The sign said it was Fitzpatrick's Tavern. He decided to take a chance on it.

The same rowdy sounds greeted him as he had encountered at the Golden Lamb, but the musicians played slow music with a hard beat. Scantily clad girls wrapped their bodies seductively around a brass pole. Phineas took a seat at the bar. "Give me a Pabst."

The bartender brought his beer. He took it and swiveled around in his seat to scan the hard-looking crowd of men, many of them already drunk and loud. The gentleman in the seat beside him slumped over his drink, and his cap slid to the floor. He was too intoxicated to care.

As Phineas surveyed the crowd, he spotted a big man at a table who could fit the description he was given at the Golden Lamb. He took his beer and wandered among the tables, finding a seat at the table adjacent to where the big man drank his ale.

The conversation at the next table was crude. The men discussed the anatomy of the pole dancer and bragged about what they would do with her. Phineas averted his eyes from their table and listened. The band ended that song, and the girl left the stage for an intermission. Then one of the man's companions asked, "How is your woman doing without her papoose, Jube?"

The man smirked. "She's all broke up, but she'll get over it. I couldn't stand that kid bawling all night long."

Phineas turned his head away as if he could unhear that comment. He couldn't imagine the brutality of a father giving away his own child because he cried.

The men at his table turned their attention to other topics more important than an unhappy woman, so Phineas took his leave and returned to his room at the Lamar Hotel.

He stretched his weary bones over the mattress, praying for God's grace and mercy for Charlotte, Danny, the baby, and the baby's mother. He breathed a request for blessings on his wife. As a last request, he asked God to touch the pole dancer's heart and lift her out of that debasing situation. Then he sank into a deep sleep.

Phineas allowed himself the luxury of sleeping late the following day. Once he coaxed himself out of bed, he grabbed a cup of coffee in the Tea Room. He roamed the streets of downtown Lamar, formulating a plan in his mind. After hearing that conversation in the tavern, he was certain that giving up the baby was not the mother's choice.

But if he found her, what would her reaction be? Did she want to stay with the man she was living with? He couldn't return the baby to a home where his drunken father wanted to get rid of him. If he could find the mother when the man called Jube wasn't around, she would have to be willing to leave with Phineas. But then what?

She probably had no income to take care of the baby and no other home to go to, or she would have run off to her people. He would have to find her a place to stay and maybe a job to support herself. And if she had to go to work, who would watch over the baby?

So many obstacles to deal with. Phineas decided those problems were God's business, and he should try to find the mother anyway. Maybe she needed saving. He would rescue her if she wanted to be saved and leave if she didn't. Either way, she wasn't in a good position to care for a baby.

He planned to look for her that evening when Jube was at the bars, so he returned to his hotel room and gave himself an afternoon sleep.

Later, when he judged the time to be right, he drove his carriage south to an intersection with a group of five houses. A fancy sign by the road announced the name: "Cosmopolis." He took a right turn.

The sun was dropping toward the horizon. He didn't want to pass Jube on his way to the cabin for fear of arousing suspicion. He continued his travel. When he finally glimpsed a rough cabin back from the road in the woods, he scanned the property, looking for a horse or a carriage. He didn't see either. In an abundance of caution, he drove a quarter-mile farther to the other side of a rise. No one at the little cabin would be able to spot him there.

He waited until the stars were bright, then cautiously approached. Not seeing anyone around, he pulled his carriage up to the front of the house and knocked on the door. A waif of a woman in a dirty dress and bare feet answered. Her panic at his presence showed in her eyes, even as she tried to hide the bruises covering her arms. "What may I do for you, sir?"

She sounded like a cultured young woman, but her appearance didn't bear evidence.

"Is your husband here with you?"

"No, sir, and you shouldn't be here, either. Jube has a mean temper."

"Then let me speak quickly. Are you the mother of a little boy?"

Her hand flew to her mouth, and tears squeezed from her eyes.

"Do you know where my baby is?"

"Yes, but I know you can't care for him alone, and I couldn't bring him back here in good conscience. Would you like me to help you escape from Jube?"

Her eyes darted back and forth in fear. "If he catches me, he'll beat me. And you, too."

"Then we need to hurry. Get your things as fast as you can, and let's go."

She took a last look at the house she had endured for the past year. Her eyes carried the pain of all the beatings. "This place has been full of horrors. I don't have anything of value now that the baby is gone. I'll go with you now."

"Where are your shoes?"

"Jube burned them so I wouldn't run off."

Anger stirred inside Phineas' gut, and he swallowed hard. "At least bring a quilt. If you have to huddle on the floor of the carriage, you'll need something to hide under."

She ran to the bed and pulled the quilt off. "Let's go," she said, her eyes revealing fear mixed with hope, and they dashed to the carriage. "Usually, Jube goes to the bars this time of night, but if he sees you between here and the next town, he'll suspect I'm with you. There are no other houses out here, and no other reason for anyone to be here."

"I brought my revolver, and it's loaded." Phineas lit the gas lamps on the carriage and told the woman to sit in the back seat under the canopy to be better hidden. "We can talk to one another as we drive. What's your name?"

She pulled the quilt up to her neck even though there was no one to hide from at present. "My name is Emma ... I mean Marta. Marta Randolph. And you?"

"I'm Phineas Fletcher, my dear. You weren't sure of your name?"

"I've been called Emma since I was kidnapped. He wanted to erase my past."

She squirmed in her seat. "I'm in a disgraceful position. I'm not married to him. He kidnapped me as I was about to marry the man I love, and took me to that God-forsaken cabin, where he forced me to act as his wife. No one in my family knows where I am. I don't even know where I am."

The blood in Phineas' veins froze as he pictured the terrors she must have experienced. His heart broke for her. "You're near Lamar, Ohio. Where are you from?

"Celina."

"That's quite a distance from here. How long have you been gone?"

"I don't know what day this is, but I'm sure it's been over a year. I haven't even heard the sound of my name. Jube calls me 'Emma' to make me forget who I was. I recited Bible verses in my head to keep my sanity."

"It's nice to meet you, Marta."

A wide smile lit up her face.

The horse trotted on, making good speed. When they reached Cosmopolis, Phineas spotted a horse and wagon headed their way from the direction of Lamar.

"Duck down and cover yourself up," he said. "We'll keep going east and not turn toward Lamar until that other wagon passes." He slapped the reins and kept the horse on course until they came to a farmhouse with a place to park vehicles in front of the barn. "Thank God, here's a place where we can turn the carriage around and get back on our route."

They had managed to avoid the other traveler. Phineas mopped the sweat off his brow while Marta exhaled slowly.

It was a full hour later that they arrived in Lamar.

"This could be the most dangerous part of our trip," Phineas said. "Jube frequents the taverns close to my hotel. I'll get you a room while you wait in the carriage. I'll register you as Anna Fletcher, my daughter. When I come to get you, slip into the hotel as fast as you can so no one sees you. I don't want your clothes to give you away."

A few minutes later, he returned to the carriage to get her. He put his coat around her shoulders and shielded her from view as best he could while they ran upstairs. "Your room is down the hall from mine. There are some towels in your room, so you can use the washroom to take a bath. Be sure and lock the door. I'll bring you some breakfast in the morning."

She thanked him profusely and headed down the hall to the washroom. Phineas went to his room but couldn't sleep. He was bewildered about what he should do for Marta. He bowed his head, spent time praying, and went to bed, still not knowing what the next day held. But Marta was safe, at least for now.

Early in the morning, Phineas slipped over to the Tea Room and ordered two breakfasts to take with him. He carried them upstairs to his room and went to wake Marta.

She was awake and dressed in the only rag she had. No one was in the hall, so Phineas told her to come to his room. "I know this wouldn't be considered proper, my dear, but we must keep you safe."

She padded down the hall barefoot and slipped into his room. Her eyes lit up at two plates of food on the dresser. Phineas smiled. "Dig in," he said.

She took a plate, sat in the only chair in the room, bowed her head, and thanked God for Phineas and the food. He marveled at the courageous character of this young woman, as beaten down as she had been over the past year. He joined her in saying "Amen," and then they enjoyed their bacon and eggs. She ate like she hadn't seen enough food for a long time.

"If you'll stay here," he said, "I'm going to the thrift shop to buy you a dress and some shoes, so you'll be comfortable in public. I wish I had something to occupy you while I'm gone, but I'm sorry, I don't."

She smiled a contented smile. "For the first time in over a year, I feel safe and well-fed. You don't know what a blessing that is. I can't complain that I have nothing for entertainment."

Phineas smiled, nodded, and slipped down the hall. He returned in forty-five minutes with a dress, underthings, a shawl, a purse, and shoes. "We can thank the fine lady at the thrift shop for suggesting these other things," he said. "I explained your situation, and she took charge of finding you some proper clothes. She said the church that runs the store wouldn't have her charge for them. She said to cover your bruised arms with this shawl."

Marta's jaw dropped, and she smiled. "I had forgotten that people could be kind," she said. "I'm so grateful. I'll take these to my room and change."

"I'm sorry, your room is no longer available. I had to check you out so they could clean for the next guest. I'll go down to the lobby and wait while you change. Throw your old dress in the trash can."

Phineas began descending the stairs to the lobby when he realized there was a disturbance. An angry man ranted and shouted profanity. "My woman was gone when I got home last night. Her name is Emma. She must be in Lamar somewhere. I want to know if any women checked into the hotel alone." Phineas crept further down the stairs, far enough to see Jube bellowing at the front desk clerk. He froze in place.

"The only single woman I've seen lately was the daughter of another guest. I'm sorry, sir, her name wasn't Emma, and she already checked out."

"Where did she go?"

"Guests don't tell me where they're going, sir. I haven't any idea."

Phineas backed up the stairs slowly, trying to conceal himself. He managed to get upstairs to warn Marta to stay in the room. She trembled and prayed for safety.

When all was quiet downstairs, they went through the lobby. Marta was like a different person, wearing a beautiful, clean dress. For all she had been through, she was a woman of grace.

They stepped into the carriage. "Is my baby safe? When can I see him?" she asked.

Phineas put the reins down and turned to her. "Your baby is in the loving care of my daughter. But we need to make some decisions. You can't take care of a baby until you can care for yourself, don't you agree?"

She lowered her head and nodded. "So, what do you suggest?"

"I'll take you to your baby, but you can't take him yet. And my daughter and her husband are getting ready to move away."

She clutched her chest in alarm. "They can't take him away with them."

"We haven't been able to find anyone else willing to take him."

"So I need to find a job, and quickly."

"I have an idea. I know the folks who own the bakery in Spencer's Mill. They may need some help. We'll go there first, then decide what to do about the baby. I promise he's safe and well cared for."

"I suppose I'll have to wait a few more hours to see him." Tears ran down her cheeks.

"Sit behind me, my dear, where you won't be so easily spotted, and we're off to Spencer's Mill."

The carriage rolled forward. In the next block, they spotted Jube clomping down the sidewalk in a foul mood. In terror, Marta pressed herself into the back of the carriage until they were past him. By the grace of God, he paid no attention to the road traffic. Relieved, Marta broke down sobbing. The stress had finally caught up with her.

The carriage turned west. The two had a few hours of traveling to get acquainted. Phineas' opinion of Marta increased the more he learned about her. Hers was a shocking story, having been kidnapped the day she was to marry and forced into slavery by that brute. She had lost hope that her sweetheart would want her after all she had been through. Since it had been a year since her disappearance, he may have even believed her dead.

That afternoon they arrived in the village and went directly to the Crust & Crumb Bakery.

"Is John in?" asked Phineas. The clerk at the cash register went to get his employer.

"Mr. Fletcher," John greeted him with an outstretched hand.

They shook hands, and Phineas introduced Marta. "This is Marta Randolph. I met her yesterday, and we've had a good chance to become acquainted. She's a fine young woman in a hopeless situation, the victim of a brutal crime. She needs a job and a place to live, being in as much distress as anyone I've ever known. Do you have any openings here?"

"Do you have any baking experience, Marta?" John asked.

"Yes, sir, I cooked for my family ever since Ma died when I was small. I know how to bake bread, cookies…you name it."

"My wife does the hiring in the kitchen. Let's go talk to her."

John escorted Phineas and Marta to the kitchen. "Katie, this is Marta. She's desperate to find a job and a place to stay. Do you need any help?"

Kate turned away from her bread dough. "Yes, I do. Do you have any recommendations, Marta?"

"Only Mr. Fletcher. My family in Celina could vouch for me if I could reach them."

"She'd be good in your kitchen, Kate," said Phineas. "She has overcome difficulties I hope you and I never face and has remained a woman of integrity."

Kate smiled. "Then we'll hire you on a trial basis if you can accept the same wages as the other kitchen help." She shook her hand.

John said, "Our apartment upstairs is currently empty. Can we let her stay there for a couple of weeks while she finds permanent accommodations?"

"Yes, we can do that. Do you want to bring in your things, Marta?"

Marta spread her skirt. "This is all I have, missus, and I didn't even have this until Mr. Fletcher bought it for me this morning.

Kate's left eyebrow raised, and she glanced at Phineas. He nodded his confirmation. "Then let me show you the apartment. I'll have to hear about your recent trials and tribulations."

Marta hesitated.

"It's all right, Marta," said Phineas. "Go ahead. I'll wait for you here."

He turned to John. "Would it be acceptable if she starts work tomorrow? She's the mother of the foundling left on Charlotte and Danny's doorstep. The baby was stolen from her, and she hasn't known where he was for almost a week—a terrible situation. I'll have to explain it to you later. But she's aching to see her baby. I promised to take her there. She knows she's not ready to care for him until she's established."

John shook his head slowly. "It's amazing, the fixes people get themselves into."

"She didn't get herself into this one. She's a victim, kidnapped right before her wedding. I don't suppose her intended would want her now."

The ladies came downstairs together. "Thank you, ma'am," Marta said. "Mr. Fletcher is going to take me to see my baby now. I'll return later this evening and start work in the morning."

Outside, Phineas helped Marta into the carriage. Soon they were at Charlotte's home. As they crossed the lawn, Marta's excitement increased. Her eyes sparkled. Phineas opened the door and let Marta in ahead of him.

"Charlotte?" he called out.

"In the kitchen feeding the baby."

Phineas escorted Marta to the kitchen. "Charlotte, meet Marta. She's the baby's mother."

A look of panic flashed across Charlotte's face. She recovered quickly and became a gracious hostess. "Marta, it's nice to meet you. You must want to see him."

Marta came closer and reached for the baby. Charlotte slowly extended her arms and gave him up. Marta shuddered with joy, and tears cascaded down her face. She put her face close to his and tickled his nose and chin. "Oh, little Jube. I have missed you so much."

"Jube? Is that what you call him?" Charlotte's eyebrows raised. "I call him Michael, like the angel."

"His father named him Jube, but I can call him anything I want now, can't I? And I think Michael is a perfect name." She cooed and cuddled the baby. "Michael. My angel."

Phineas intervened. "I'll tell you Marta's story later. She can't care for Michael yet, so she'll have dinner with us, then I'll take her back to the Crust & Crumb. She has a job there and will stay in the upstairs apartment for the next two weeks. Michael will have to stay here."

Charlotte rubbed the back of her neck. "You'll have to explain all this to Danny when he gets home."

Phineas nodded. "Marta, would you like to take Michael into the parlor and get reacquainted while Charlotte cooks dinner?"

Marta had tears in her eyes. "Charlotte, thank you for taking such good care of my baby. Normally I would help in the kitchen, but—"

"Nonsense. Pa says you've been through a traumatic experience. You enjoy the baby. I have the kitchen duties under control."

Marta found a comfortable wing chair in the parlor and settled in to enjoy her son. Phineas returned to the kitchen and spoke to Charlotte in low tones. "You wouldn't believe what she's been through. She was kidnapped when she was about to be married, forced to live with a brute and perform as his wife, bore this child, then he stole the child and brought him here."

Charlotte's jaw dropped, and her hand flew to her chest. "She seems like such a nice girl."

"That's quite a triumph, I'd say, for what she's been through. She said it was her faith that sustained her."

Charlotte nodded. "I imagine that's the only thing that could have done it."

Danny arrived home at his usual time. Privately, Phineas explained the whole situation, including the danger from the kidnapper and Marta's current inability to take care of her baby.

Danny pounded his fist on the table, and his jaw tightened. "Mr. Link found a replacement for me today. I thought we could leave. Now, this."

"I'm sorry, Danny, but I'm still glad I rescued the girl. She was in a hellish place. She's been beaten, raped, and otherwise abused for a year and forced to bear a child out of wedlock. Now she's carrying that shame for the rest of her life."

Danny took a long breath and nodded reluctantly before stomping upstairs to his bedroom in a foul mood. Phineas had a heavy heart for his part in delaying Danny and Charlotte's plans to move away. He knew how badly Danny wanted to leave Spencer's Mill and start their new life. This baby was ruining his chance at buying the best land in Illinois before other farmers chose their parcels.

Danny was absent at the dinner table. Charlotte took a plate upstairs to him.

After dinner, Marta kissed her baby goodbye. Phineas took her to the apartment over the bakery for a good night's sleep, then returned to Charlotte and Danny's house. By this time, Danny had come back downstairs.

"I'm sorry about my behavior," he said. "I needed some time to wrestle with my emotions. This is almost as hard to deal with as my Pa's death."

Charlotte grasped his hand to reassure him.

"Let's talk about options, Danny," Phineas said. "While waiting for Marta to take Michael back, why don't you pack up your wagon and come to Florissant? Adelaide and I could use some help getting Fletcher House in shape. Then you could bring Michael back here and be on your way."

"That would help us fill the time, wouldn't it, Pop?"

"Yes, it would. And selfishly, I would like the extra time with you and Charlotte."

Danny smiled weakly. "Then that's what we'll do. Only I want to make sure we get to Illinois before the best properties are sold."

The following day Phineas prepared to return home. "You'll need to stop by the bakery and tell Marta you'll have the baby out of town for a few days, but you'll bring him back when she's ready."

"That's fine, Pa. We'll pack up the wagon today and see you either tomorrow evening or the next."

Phineas kissed his daughter, said goodbye to Danny, and left.

Charlotte snugged the baby into his basket and turned to Danny. "What do we do first, my dear?"

"First, I'm going to the bakery to ask John to help load the furniture. Adelaide wants some things from your Pa's house before he sells it."

"There are only a few pieces they want for Fletcher House, right?"

"Yes. Don't worry; they won't take the bed or dressers you want. The rest shouldn't take long to load."

Danny went to the bakery to ask for his brother's help. John willingly agreed and said he had time to spare later in the afternoon.

"How is Marta working out?" Danny asked.

"She's picking it up quickly. What a delight she is. She'll be a real asset to the bakery."

A slow smile spread over Danny's face, and he nodded. The sooner she got established, the sooner they could get to Illinois.

"Thanks, John. I'll see you this afternoon."

Florissant was a day's drive from Spencer's Mill. Danny and Charlotte bundled up Michael and started early. It was a beautiful day, and they were in high spirits. They enjoyed the mild June weather, the sunny skies, and the beautiful foliage along the way. The trees were in full leaf—oaks, maples, black walnuts, and buckeye trees.

Michael was restless and kept Charlotte busy as they rolled down the road. They stopped several times to rest, have lunch, and care for the horses. The afternoon's scenery was less woodsy. There were large fields of corn and soybeans. Farmers worked the crops, and livestock grazed in fenced pastures. They passed farm after farm, mostly in full sun without the benefit of many shade trees.

About an hour before they expected to arrive in Florissant, they came to the For Sale sign on the farm that Phineas told them about. "Danny, could we stop and peek in the windows?" Charlotte asked. "Pa says it's sixty-eight acres, already cleared. And the house and barn are already built."

"Maybe on the way back, Charlotte. I'm getting tired. I want to get to Florissant."

She sighed. "All right."

It was getting late when they found the building with the fancy new sign, FLETCHER HOUSE BED & BREAKFAST.

"This is a beautiful place, Danny."

"It's more than I expected. You get Michael. I'll grab the bags, and we'll go inside."

Adelaide was behind the front desk as they entered.

"Welcome, family," she said. "I'm glad you're here. We have a room ready for you."

She hugged them and took the baby from Charlotte's arms. "Oh, little Michael. You're already famous, young man. You've been quite the topic of conversation." She jiggled him up and down.

"Be careful, Adelaide. He just ate."

Michael's dinner came up all over the front of Adelaide. She giggled and gave him back to Charlotte. "It's been years since that happened to me. Excuse me while I get cleaned up." She handed them the key to room 5. "It's your father's favorite room. You have a view of the front lawn from there."

Phineas emerged from the owner's apartment. "Glad you made it. Let me take you upstairs to your room. After you get settled, you can come down here and see our apartment."

Danny and Charlotte enjoyed visiting Phineas and Adelaide for a week, helping the renovations take shape after the fire, and meeting the guests as they came and went. At the end of the week, Danny was eager to get on with their plans, so they packed up their belongings, took some food and drink for the journey, and said a final goodbye. Charlotte clung to her father for a long minute and said goodbye with tears in her eyes. It may be a long time before she would see him again after they settled in Illinois. They started toward Spencer's Mill.

An hour later, as Michael was napping, they came to that farmhouse with the sixty-eight acres for sale.

"Please, Danny, let's stop and look. It will give us a chance to stretch our legs, and it will satisfy my curiosity."

Danny relented and pulled up in front of the house. The son of the deceased property owners lived next door and happened to be at the house, checking on things.

"Can I help you folks?" he asked.

Danny shook his hand. "We're here to look at the property — mostly to satisfy my wife's curiosity. If all goes well, we plan to move to Illinois and buy a farm there in about a week."

The man nodded. "I'm Eb, and this was my Pa's place. Go ahead and look around. Ma and Pa kept it up real nice. There are three bedrooms and a bathroom upstairs, a parlor, a kitchen, a dining room downstairs, and a cellar below. There's a barn out back and a couple more storage buildings." Eb motioned toward the field, now lying fallow. "The land is all cleared and fenced for farming. Pa had a crop of corn last year before he died. My sisters want to sell it quickly, but living next door as I do, I'm going to be particular who buys it, if you know what I mean."

Danny grinned. "Yes, I do. My name's Danny, and this is my wife, Charlotte."

Charlotte was busy looking at the big windows that let in the light, the high ceilings, and the spotless kitchen with more storage space than she had ever dreamed of. "Danny, look at this. There's even a bathroom with a tub."

Danny walked around the house with her. "I'll admit, this is very nice. While Charlotte looks at the bedrooms upstairs, could we look at the barn?"

Danny and Eb walked to the barn together, talking like old friends. The barn was in good shape, with stalls for livestock and a large hayloft.

"Why are you going all the way to Illinois?" asked Eb. "Do you have people there?"

"No, we're going out because the Illinois Central Railroad is offering farmland at a favorable price. All I have to do is buy forty acres, make a down payment that covers a year's interest, and I can take possession. I have to agree to clear and plant at least ten acres in the first year. Then nothing else is due until the crops come in. Of course, I'd have to build a cabin and sink a well, too."

"Hmm, that is a good deal financially, but you're taking on an almost impossible task that first year. We could probably work out a similar financial arrangement if you want to stay in Ohio. You can see that the land is already cleared and ready for planting. You don't have to build a house, and the well is already sunk. What do you think?"

201

Danny paused. He agreed that the amount of work necessary for the first year in Illinois would be daunting. He was strangely at home on that Ohio farm, even though he had never seen it before. "It's strange, but I feel like I've been in a rowboat, rowing as hard as I could to get to a particular spot, and now I'm thinking of turning around and rowing in the other direction. This idea would take some getting used to, but I admit, this farm is appealing."

Eb laughed. "I'm sure we can agree on the price and terms. Do you honestly think this is something you might like to do? If it is, we'll go back in the house and talk this over."

Danny paused, gazing at the large farm, the house that pleased Charlotte, the barn, and the outbuildings. "If we stay here, we'll be closer to our family. That would make my Ma happy, and Charlotte would be close to her Pa. Let's go inside and talk about this. I'm not promising anything, you understand."

"Of course. Neither am I."

They found Charlotte in the kitchen with the baby lying on the counter.

"Charlotte, do you think you would be happy living here?"

Her eyes flooded with tears. "I would be so happy living here, Danny."

"Don't get your hopes up too high, but Eb and I are going to his house to discuss terms. If you want to rest, you can sit in the wagon."

"I'll stay here until the baby cries," she said, with a grin that lit up her entire face. "Maybe I'll look around the house some more."

After an hour, the men had negotiated an agreement, pending Danny's inspection of the acreage and doing some research at the courthouse to ensure there weren't any liens on the property. The two shook hands, and Danny took Charlotte back to the wagon.

She was as excited as a schoolgirl. Her eyes sparkled. Danny recognized a bounce in her step he used to see during their courtship days. He grinned.

"It's too late to continue on home now. We still have another seven hours of travel. Instead, let's return to Florissant and stay with your Pa one more day. This afternoon I'll go to the courthouse and do the research that needs to be done, and we'll go back home tomorrow."

He turned the wagon around. They were back at Fletcher House by early afternoon, surprising Phineas and Adelaide. As Danny pulled up to the rail, Charlotte hopped down and ran inside with the baby.

"Pa—Adelaide—you'll never guess what. We're buying that piece of property with the sixty-eight acres. We won't be going to Illinois after all."

Phineas grabbed his daughter and the baby, and danced round and round with them, laughing.

"Give me that child," Adelaide said, grinning and taking Michael. "I don't want you two to squash him."

Phineas was well known at the courthouse and accompanied Danny on his quest. They found the property to be clear of liens.

"I'd like to go with you tomorrow when you visit Eb to finalize the deal," Phineas said.

"You're welcome to come with us, Pop," Danny said, "but how will you get back home? We won't be returning to Florissant."

"I'll take my carriage right behind your wagon. Charlotte and Michael can ride with me until we get to your new house. Then after I satisfy my nosy curiosity, Charlotte and the baby can continue to Spencer's Mill with you, and I'll return home to Adelaide."

"That sounds like a good idea. You can walk the land with me and give us some ideas about painting and sprucing up the house, though it's in pretty decent shape."

The following day, they traveled down the road in the carriage and wagon, enjoying the fresh air and sunshine. After an hour's drive, they arrived at the new house. Danny went next door to find Eb and finalize the deal while Phineas and Charlotte headed to the house, brimming with excitement.

"When you have children of your own, we'll be able to see them often," Phineas said. "That's what I've been praying for."

"Thanks for that, Pa," she said. "I was willing to go to Illinois. I would do anything for Danny, but my heart is more content to stay close to you."

Eb brought the key and let them back into the house. They took another tour of the house and barn, then Danny and Charlotte left to get back to Spencer's Mill at a decent hour. Phineas continued to walk the property alone. He did a close inspection of the barn, the water pump, and the outbuildings. Grinning with delight, he turned his carriage toward Florissant.

Travel went easier for Danny and Charlotte since the wagon had been emptied of the furniture they delivered to Fletcher House. The horses stepped more smartly. Michael traveled in his basket behind the driver's seat, relieving Charlotte of having to hold him as much. Life was full of promise.

"If we get to Spencer's Mill at a decent hour," said Charlotte, "let's stop and tell John and Kate the good news — that we're not going as far as Illinois."

"Yes, and we can let Marta see Michael for a few minutes. She'll be off work by that time."

"She might want to keep him overnight. We could pick him up in the morning."

Danny's jaw dropped, and he swiveled his head in her direction. "That's a very generous offer, seeing how attached you are to the baby."

She smiled sadly. "I know I'm going to have to give him up eventually. I need to start getting used to it. That will break my heart."

"I must admit I've gotten used to the little guy," Danny said.

Charlotte laughed. "It's my turn to be surprised. Maybe we can start our family when we get established on the farm."

"That would be good, wouldn't it? Especially now that I'm used to having a baby around."

Charlotte pursed her lips into a crooked smile.

A few hours down the road, the wagon pulled up in front of the Crust & Crumb Bakery. Inside, they asked to see John. He and Danny greeted each other with a hug.

"We came to tell you the good news," Danny said. John's preoccupied reaction puzzled Danny, but he continued. "We're not going to Illinois. We found a farm between Lamar and Florissant. We'll be moving within the next few days."

John nodded grimly. "Good news, Danny, but we have a problem with Marta. Come to my office. I need to explain what's going on."

Dread rose in Danny's chest. Charlotte's reaction was similar to his own. She reached for his arm, and they glanced at each other as they walked to John's desk.

"What's happening, John? Isn't Marta working out?"

They pulled up two chairs in front of John's desk and took their seats. Charlotte jiggled Michael to keep him quiet.

"We had a visitor here yesterday. It was a big, nasty man named

Jube, Marta's kidnapper. Somehow he tracked her down through the hotel's front desk clerk and came looking for her. He created quite a disruption, shouting and cursing in front of the customers, demanding that Marta come with him, except he called her Emma. I kept him at bay with a revolver while one of the customers went for the sheriff. Not something I enjoyed doing. Jube is locked up in jail now for kidnapping and creating a disturbance, but he's raising all Hades in his cell. As soon as he gets out, Marta will be in danger again. She's terrified. She managed to get a telegram through to her father. He's coming to get her. Should be here tomorrow."

Charlotte hugged Michael closely.

"Can we talk to her?" she asked.

He left the room and returned momentarily with Marta. She walked straight to Charlotte and reached out for Michael. Charlotte put the baby in her arms, noticing the tears rolling down her cheeks.

"Marta, I'm so sorry about what is happening to you," she said.

"I thought the nightmare was over when your father rescued me. But Jube found me somehow." She buried her face in the baby's blankets. "That means Michael isn't safe with me."

She kissed the baby's face and hands before continuing. "I need to ask you something I never thought I'd ask anyone." Her shoulders shook, and she broke down in sobs.

Charlotte was moved with compassion. She reached out to Marta and put her arm around the girl's shoulders. "What can we do for you?"

"Would you take Michael and raise him? Keep him out of Jube's reach?" Her knees buckled, and her body sagged. Danny reached out to hold her up.

"Sit here in this chair."

"We need to give this some serious thought," Charlotte said. "Of course, we love him, but as hard as it would be for you, we would need you to give him to us legally. I believe Danny would agree that he would be told you're his mother, but it would be best for Michael if he had our name."

Marta's face had drained of color. She nodded.

"I have a different suggestion," Danny said. "Why don't we refer to Marta as his aunt? It would be a more natural relationship to someone who doesn't live in the same house but sends letters and maybe gifts once in a while."

Marta's tears flowed freely. She dabbed at her face with a handkerchief and hugged the baby to her chest. "Michael, Michael, my sweet baby, I would do anything to keep you safe." She turned to Danny. "I would agree to that. It would give me a chance to be a part of his life from whatever distance, without putting any stress on him as he grows up."

"I can't imagine the depth of grief you're experiencing," Charlotte said. "I'm not sure I could think so clearly if I were in your position."

"I've had to force myself to think clearly for the past year. I never expected to ever go through anything like that. I hope no one else ever does."

The atmosphere was heavy. Finally, Danny spoke. "Time is short since your father will be here tomorrow. My stepfather is an attorney. I have very little time to get to his house. I'd like him to draw up papers for you to sign, giving Michael to us and naming us his parents. If I can get that tonight, would you sign it tomorrow before you leave?"

Marta nodded.

"Would you like us to leave Michael with you overnight?" Charlotte asked.

"Oh, yes, please. One last night with my beautiful boy."

Charlotte went to the wagon to get Michael's diapers and other paraphernalia. When she returned, Kate had come in from the kitchen.

"Danny and Charlotte must leave quickly, Katie, but they'll be back tomorrow. I'll fill you in on all the details when they go."

Kate gave Charlotte a quick hug. "I'll see you tomorrow."

John had one more thought. "Danny, give your horses a rest and take my carriage. I don't think pushing animals that hard is good."

"Thanks, John. I wasn't thinking."

It had been a long, weary day, and here they were, off again on another long drive.

The sun at their backs had dropped to the horizon when they reached the home of Christian and Susannah Wolf. Susannah went running to her son and threw her arms around him.

"Hi, Ma," he said. "We have a lot to tell you. Can we all sit down together? I want Christian to hear this, too. We need his legal services — tonight, if it's not too much to ask. It's an emergency."

"Have you had your dinner? If not, we'll talk in the parlor while

Hannah makes something for us to eat."

Danny realized they hadn't had more than a snack since breakfast. "No, Ma, we haven't eaten."

Susannah gave instructions for dinner, then she and Christian each sat in the wingback chairs. Danny and Charlotte sat on the Chesterfield opposite them. Danny related the story of Marta and Michael. He moved through the story quickly, telling only the essential points. He wanted to make Christian understand enough of the situation so he could draw up the necessary adoption papers.

During his discourse, Susannah's expression changed from horror to compassion. Upon learning that she was to have another grandson, her hand went to her chest, and her mouth formed an "O."

Christian listened intently. "You know that as long as you have this man's son, you're at risk, too. The thing in your favor is that his name is not on any birth record as the father, and he's not married to the mother, so he has no legal way to enforce a father's rights. Marta's signature on a document is all that is needed. With witnesses, of course."

Danny thought about their level of danger. "Since this Jube is the one who stole the baby from Marta and left him miles away on a stranger's doorstep, I don't think he'll come after Michael. I think our risk from him is low. Marta is the one at risk."

Christian nodded. "That's true. Let's have our dinner, and then I'll go to my study to draw up the documents. I'll finish them before I go to bed. You can have them in the morning."

"Thank you, sir. This means so much to us."

Christian grinned mischievously. "I'm not doing it for you. I'm doing it to gain myself a grandson."

In the morning, the adoption papers were ready to be signed. Danny and Charlotte left early to be in Spencer's Mill before Marta's father arrived.

The pre-dawn air was damp and cool as they traveled the familiar road, carrying the precious documents. Charlotte snuggled against Danny to soak in his warmth.

"You're a good man, Danny. You're willing to take another man's child and raise him as your own. I love you more now than I ever have."

"I'm not taking another man's child. That's our child. He's ours. You're his mother, and I'm his Pa. We'll do right by our son."

As Charlotte turned her face toward his, tears ran down her cheeks. "I thank God for you, Danny."

He put his arm around her shoulder and held her. "And I thank God for you." He kissed her forehead and drove on.

They arrived at Spencer's Mill as the bakery opened. They waited for Marta in John's office. Presently she came in with Michael, trembling and pale.

"I'm ready to sign the papers." She took a seat in front of the desk. Danny put three copies of the document before her: one for her, one for Danny and Charlotte, and one for Attorney Wolf. She took time to read it. Then, with her hand shaking, she penned her signature on all three. John signed as a witness and pressed his blotter over the fresh ink. Marta folded her copy slowly, dropping tears on it.

She kissed the baby, then hugged him close for the last time. Her face was drained and full of anguish. Finally, she held Michael out toward Charlotte. "Do you want to take your son?" she whispered.

"Thank you, Aunt Marta," Charlotte replied, taking the sleeping infant. "Do you want your father to see him when he comes?"

"Oh, no. He knows I had a baby, but it won't be so real in his mind if he doesn't see him. I want to spare him having to give up his first grandchild."

Charlotte swallowed. "That's wise."

"Would you take him home now? My heart is bursting in my chest." She could barely breathe.

"Of course. You'll stay in touch?"

"I would lose my mind if I didn't."

The couple took their son, leaving Marta grief-stricken at the bakery.

Danny and Charlotte settled into farm life with Michael. The years passed quickly. Danny had good business sense, so the farm was prosperous, except for the one year of drought. Two more children were born into the family. A boy, Curtis, was two years younger than Michael, and Vanessa was born two years after Curtis.

Letters frequently came from Aunt Marta. The sweetheart she intended to marry before her kidnapping had married someone else. Marta couldn't blame him. She met a tenderhearted man fifteen years her senior and fell in love. When she nervously confessed to him about the out-of-wedlock child, he wanted to marry her anyway. In a sacrificial act of kindness, he moved her to a town on the edge of Grand Lake after the wedding to protect her from the shame of her past.

Charlotte always replied to her letters, telling her about Michael's achievements in school and how he helped his father on the farm.

When Michael was ten years old, the letters stopped. Alarmed, Charlotte sent a telegram to Marta's home. A reply came back that Marta was suffering from enteritis, a debilitating disease, and wasn't expected to live. She had a request: to see Michael before she died.

Charlotte was torn. She had the responsibility for the house and the other two children. She couldn't make a trip like that on a whim. But neither could she deny Marta.

Danny had a solution. "I'll take you to Florissant, where you and Michael can catch the train to Lamar. Once there, you can walk to Christian's office, and he'll take you to Ma's house after work. It will be a long day's drive from Ma's house to Grand Lake. She might want to go with you in the carriage. You can get a hotel room at the lake for two nights, then come back."

"That's quite an adventure for a homebody," Charlotte said, relieved that the trip was possible. "I'll pack some things. Can we go tomorrow?"

Charlotte and Michael bought tickets to Lamar the following day. This was their first train trip. Michael's eyes darted this way and that, trying to take in the whole experience. They checked their luggage and boarded the train. After they settled into comfortable seats by the window, the conductor came by to punch their tickets, and the train started slowly, with a chug...chug...chug. The chugging went faster and faster until they were at top speed. Michael's attention was glued to the window.

"Ma, why does the train rock back and forth?"

"I don't know, but isn't it fun?" She enjoyed it as much as her son. They listened to the wheels' mesmerizing clickety-clack and the whistle's wail as the train wound across the rolling plain. Michael couldn't sit still. He wanted to go to the dining car and explore the other passenger coaches. Some had sleeping accommodations, and others were for seating, like their own coach. Weary from lack of sleep, Charlotte allowed the boy to wander the train at will while she napped. He had always been a well-behaved child.

Eventually, the train huffed to a stop in Lamar, bell clanging, while the wheels screeched to a halt on the rails. Steam billowed from below the engine with a long hiss. They collected their luggage and stepped onto the train platform.

Charlotte smiled. This was familiar territory.

"This way, Michael," she said, strolling north along Main Street. "We have to walk to Grandpa Wolf's office. It's about a mile. Can you carry your bag that far?"

"I think so, Ma."

Entering the lobby of Christian Wolf, Attorney, they were dismayed to find he wasn't in. His clerk said he had just walked to the Old English Tea Room for lunch. If they left their bags in the lobby, they might be able to catch up to him.

Charlotte and the boy took off at a good pace. "Grandpa, Grandpa," Michael called when he spotted the familiar form on the sidewalk ahead.

Christian turned to the sound of his voice. "Mikey, what a surprise." He stopped, waited for them to catch up with him, and gave Michael a bear hug. "Can you join me for lunch? This is quite a treat."

"Don't call me Mikey, Grandpa. I'm too old for that."

Christian chuckled. "All right, Michael."

They found a table in the noisy Tea Room at the height of the lunch hour. It was jammed with patrons. They ordered their lunch while Charlotte explained that Michael's Aunt Marta wasn't well and wanted to see him.

Christian nodded thoughtfully. "I'm sorry to hear that."

"I've never met her," said Michael, "but she sends gifts. She must be a very nice lady."

Christian's gaze fastened on his face. "I know for certain she's an exceptional lady. I'm sure we'll meet her in heaven one day."

Charlotte asked Christian if he could help them get to Grand Lake.

"It's about a day's drive from our house. I'll see if Susannah wants to go with you, but you'll need to drive the carriage. If she isn't up to a trip like that, I'll send our caretaker to drive you. He enjoys travel and would love to have a boy to talk to." Christian reached over and ruffled Michael's hair.

Michael grinned and slurped his soup.

"Michael, don't do that," Charlotte said.

He ducked his head and stifled another grin.

As it turned out, Susannah was delighted to be invited on a trip to Grand Lake. The caretaker hitched up the horses and gave them directions to their destination. The three travelers began their journey. Clip-clop, clip-clop, clip-clop.

Michael was interested in everything along the way, even though it was similar to their own farm. Hours later, the scenery changed from farmhouses to cabins and fishing huts. They were nearing their destination. At last, the lakeshore was in sight.

"Look at the boats, Ma," Michael said with his eyes sparkling. "Wouldn't it be fun to take a boat ride?"

She smiled. "I suppose it would. I've never been, but yes, I suppose it would."

Michael shielded his eyes with his hand and scanned the horizon. A small sailboat with white sails made a crisp outline against the blue sky. "That's so pretty, Ma. See that sailboat out there?" He could hardly contain himself. His head swiveled around, trying to take in all the scenery.

"Maybe we'll spend some time looking at the lake later. We need to find our hotel."

"The sign said it's down that street, dear," said Susannah, pointing away from the lake. They took a right turn, found their hotel, and checked in. Michael was wired and eager to go anywhere within view of the lake.

"Calm down, love," Susannah said, smiling wearily. "We're going to have a little rest, something to eat, and then visit Aunt Marta. After that, we'll look at the lake."

Michael reluctantly found a book in his valise and snuggled into a reading chair while the ladies napped.

An hour later, Charlotte and Susannah found a restaurant, had a leisurely meal with Michael, then prepared to visit Marta. "I believe her address is within walking distance of here. Shall we go on foot?"

After the long day in the carriage, that sounded appealing, so they stretched their legs and made their way to Marta's house. Charlotte rapped on the door. A tall, distinguished-looking man with white hair opened it, and his eyes opened wide. "Let me guess," he said. "Could this be Michael Reese?"

Michael responded. "Yes, sir."

"Come in, all of you," their host said. "I'm Carson Iverson, Marta's husband. You must be Charlotte." He smiled, then turned to Susannah. "I'm sorry, I can't guess who you are."

"I'm Michael's grandmother, Susannah Wolf."

Iverson nodded at her. "Please have a seat. I'll tell Marta you're here. She might want to spruce up a bit before I bring you into her room. Those long days of suffering do take their toll on one's grooming habits."

The three visitors found chairs and waited while Marta's husband disappeared into a side room. There was quiet shuffling and muffled voices on the other side of the door, then Iverson opened it. "Would you like to come in now? Marta is ready for you."

Charlotte put her hand on Michael's shoulder and guided him into the room. She caught her breath at the sight of Marta. The poor woman was barely recognizable. It took Charlotte great effort to keep the shock from registering on her face.

The woman was lying in her bed, hollow-eyed and thin as a stick. Her form was barely noticeable under the quilt. Her husband touched her arm tenderly. "Marta, Michael is here to see you."

With effort, Marta rolled her head to look at her baby, now ten years old. She managed a smile with tears in her eyes. "Michael, I'm so glad you made it. This is an answer to my prayer. Can you come a little closer?"

Michael turned to Charlotte with questions in his eyes. "It's fine, Michael. Aunt Marta is sick with enteritis. It's not catching." She nudged the boy closer to the bed.

Marta grasped his hand. "Michael. I've loved you since the day you were born."

Michael didn't understand how that was possible, but summoned the maturity to be gracious. "Thank you for all the gifts you sent, Aunt Marta. I enjoyed every one of them."

"I've enjoyed sending them." Her eyes drooped. She forced them open again and took a deep breath. "Do you help your Pa on the farm?"

Michael smiled. "Yes, ma'am. He lets me help plant seeds, collect eggs, take care of the horses, and all kinds of things. I plan to farm when I grow up, just like Pa."

"Good boy, Michael." She closed her eyes again but never took her hand away from his. Opening her eyes, she asked, "Do you think you'd like to take a boat ride on the lake?"

Michael's mouth dropped open. Marta caught a glimpse of the sparkle in his eyes. Her free hand went to her chest, and a broad smile covered her weary face. "Mr. Iverson has a son Benjamin who owns a boat. He agreed to take you for a ride if you want to go. Your Ma and Grandma can go, too."

"I'd love to take a ride." Michael quivered with excitement. "What kind of boat is it?"

Marta took a deep breath, turned her head away, and coughed. A pinched look of pain crossed her face. Her free hand clutched at her stomach. "It's a boat Benjamin uses for fishing. Michael, I'm afraid that will be my last gift to you. I'm going to see Jesus soon. Do you understand that?"

"Yes, ma'am, I do. I asked Jesus to be my savior, so I'll see Him someday, too."

Marta stifled a wave of nausea. "Thank God. And thank you, Charlotte. God couldn't have chosen a better mother for my —"

She cut her sentence short.

Charlotte cut in. "God's hand is on Michael. And on you, too, Marta. We should go and let you rest."

"After your boat trip tomorrow, would you bring Michael back for just a few more minutes?" She gazed lovingly at the boy.

"Of course."

"Michael, would you let me hug you?"

Michael shyly moved closer and leaned over this lady he had never met. Her thin arms wrapped around him, and tears flooded her eyes. She kissed his face.

"You rest now," Charlotte said. "We'll see you tomorrow."

"Goodbye, Aunt Marta, and thanks for the boat ride."

"You're welcome, son." Her eyelids closed.

Mr. Iverson escorted them into the parlor and gave them directions to the boat. "I can't thank you enough for coming. Marta has longed to see the boy for years, and now she can go peacefully. She's been a wonderful wife. I'm not ready to lose her, but she's in God's hands." His head bowed to his chest, and his eyes had the glassy look of grief.

Susannah touched his arm lightly. "Mr. Iverson, you will both be in our prayers."

He nodded. His lips moved in a silent "thank you" as he let them out the door.

They walked solemnly in the direction of the lake. Michael sighed. "I don't feel like looking at the boat tonight. I feel so sad for Aunt Marta. Let's walk along the lake to the hotel, but we'll look at the boat tomorrow. Can we do that, Ma?"

"For a young man of ten years, Michael, you have such wonderful sensitivity and compassion. Yes, we can do that."

They all slept soundly through the night, as tired as they were from the day's journey. In the morning, Michael woke early, too excited to stay in bed. He woke his mother and grandmother. They agreed to head to the lake. "I don't see any point in trying to slow him down," said Susannah, laughing. "He won't stop until he gets that boat ride."

They dressed hurriedly and walked to the lakefront. The boat was right where Mr. Iverson had told them. His son Benjamin, wearing a flat cap and beard, was sorting his fishing equipment. As the trio approached, he broke out in a smile.

"You must be Michael," he said. "Welcome. And this is your Ma and Grandma?"

"Yes, sir," he said. "We came for a boat ride."

"I know you did. And I have just the spot to take you. Come on, let's all get in the boat."

The boat was a wooden skiff with enough seating for five. Susannah eyed it suspiciously.

"If you don't mind, I'll wait here on the shore. I've never been in a boat."

"Mother Wolf, I think it will be fun."

"It probably will, dear, but my poor nerves wouldn't be able to take it."

"We'll see you later then, Grandma." Michael was ready to go.

Benjamin helped Charlotte into the middle seat. He assigned Michael the seat closest to the bow and pulled the ropes off the cleats. Taking the seat at the stern, Benjamin used one oar to push away from the dock. Charlotte nervously grabbed the sides as the boat wobbled.

Iverson rowed with powerful strokes. They skimmed across the rippled lake. What a sensation. Michael was giddy with excitement, constantly talking about the seaweed under the hull, the fish swimming in the clear water, and every other thing that was a new experience for a farm boy. "The air smells like fish, doesn't it?" Benjamin grinned and let him prattle on.

"Could I try those oars?" Michael asked.

Charlotte objected. "It's too dangerous, Michael."

"He'll be fine, Mrs. Reese," Benjamin said. He passed one of the oars to Charlotte, who handed it to Michael.

"You paddle out the left side of the boat. I'll paddle out of the right."

Michael dipped his oar in the water. "It feels harder than I thought. Oops, it's dragging." He struggled to get the oar out of the water, and the boat spun slowly. He giggled. Benjamin turned his oar to correct the boat's direction.

"Give it another try," he said.

Michael dug the oar too deep into the lake's surface but couldn't lift it as easily as he expected. The movement of the water dragged it out of his hand. It fell into the water lilies, smacking the wooden hull as it fell. Michael's face fell in dismay.

"No worries," said Benjamin. "It floats. Reach in the water and pull it out."

Michael stretched his small frame over the side of the boat and reached as far as he could. Benjamin paddled closer. Michael grabbed the end of the stray oar with one hand. Water ran up his arms as he raised it into the boat. "Here, Mr. Iverson, you better take both oars."

Iverson chuckled. "You come back in a couple of years, boy, and we'll have you rowing all over this lake."

Michael turned and shot his mother a glance. She smiled, enjoying his delight.

"It's probably time we should head back," Benjamin said. "My arms tell me they're half done." He turned the boat toward the shore, rowing steadily. Michael grinned all the way. As they skimmed across the ripples, he trailed his hand in the lake, watching the water splash off his fingers.

Susannah waited by the shore, sitting on a bench under the shade of a buckeye tree. She stood and waved her wide-brimmed straw hat at them.

Reaching the dock, Michael's eyes were still sparkling. "Thank you, Mr. Iverson. I never expected to get a boat ride when we left home yesterday morning."

"You can thank your Aunt Marta. I had a lot of fun, too. I hope you come back another time. I'd like to take you fishing."

Susannah was ready to go. "If we go see Marta now, we'll be back at the hotel in time for dinner, giving us the evening to relax. We can get a good night's sleep before the trip home tomorrow."

That plan sounded good to Charlotte. They walked to the Iverson house and asked to see Marta.

"Please come in," Mr. Iverson said. His face was pale, and his eyes flooded with tears. "I'm afraid I have bad news."

Susannah's hand went to her mouth. Charlotte put her arm around Michael's shoulders.

"Marta went to be with Jesus about a half-hour ago." He stifled a sob. He was a shrunken version of himself, helpless, like someone who needed to be told what to do next.

Susannah stepped toward him. "Mr. Iverson . . ."

Michael's jaw had gone limp. "Ma, would it be all right if I went in to see her?"

"We need to be respectful of Mr. Iverson."

Iverson nodded and took the boy's hand. He led him into the bedroom, with Charlotte and Susannah following. Marta's face was relaxed and peaceful.

"She's not sick anymore, is she, Ma?"

"No, son. She doesn't need the body she left behind on that bed. Her spirit burst right out of that body and went to heaven. She's probably dancing right now."

Michael's eyes went moist. "I liked her. She was a nice lady."

Iverson kissed his wife's forehead and pulled the sheet over her face. Then the group left the bedroom and closed the door. "I've sent for the undertaker," he said. "Thank you for coming. I hope Marta knows you were here today."

Susannah smiled. "If she doesn't, we'll tell her the next time we see her."

Iverson smiled and wiped his tears with the back of his hand.

The ride back to Susannah's house the next day was more subdued. Michael was consumed with his thoughts, only breaking out of his

216

reverie for short periods. At one point, Charlotte tried to draw him out.

"I'm sad for Aunt Marta," he said, "but sometimes I'm happy for her, too. I didn't know whether to tell you that. It sounds weird."

"No, that's not weird at all," Charlotte said. "That's one of the blessings of belonging to God's family. We're sad for ourselves because we lost someone dear to us. But we're happy for the one who is now enjoying life in heaven."

Michael nodded. "That makes sense." After another pause, he asked, "Why did Aunt Marta want to see me, not Curtis or Vanessa?"

"She didn't know them, honey. You were the only one she held when you were a baby."

That evening they had a good night's sleep at the Wolf house. In the morning, after breakfast, Michael and Charlotte said goodbye to Susannah, then drove back to Lamar with Christian. There they caught the train to Florissant.

Phineas was at the train station with the carriage when they arrived. Michael spotted him through the train window, grabbed his bag, and ran onto the platform to meet him. "Grandpa, we took a boat ride."

Phineas grinned and waited for Charlotte to catch up with them. "You'll have to tell me about it on the way to Fletcher House. We'll have time for every detail. Your Pa is going to pick you up tomorrow.

He turned to Charlotte. "And how are you doing, dear?"

"I'm weary, Pa, but it was a worthwhile trip. So much emotion. So many experiences."

Adelaide had a hearty dinner waiting when they arrived. The evening was spent chiefly listening to Michael recount the trip's events, with Charlotte occasionally breaking in to add details.

After the children were shuffled off to bed, Phineas and Charlotte had a chance to talk together. Adelaide brought in cups of tea and joined them.

"How is your investigative work going, Pa?"

"I'm slowing down some. I still love it, and I'm still in demand, but I'm sixty-two years old. I'm not as spry as I used to be."

Adelaide smiled gently and adjusted her spectacles. "You can say that again."

Charlotte asked, "Looking back on ten years of investigations, which case would you say was the most profitable?"

Phineas leaned back and clasped his hands behind his neck. "Well, if you're talking about profit in terms of money, I'd have to say the case where I found out my client had an inheritance she didn't know about. But if you're talking about profit in personal rewards, hands down, it was the case where I found the mother of the foundling. I didn't get any cash payment for that, but I gained a first-class grandson."

OTHER BOOKS BY THIS AUTHOR

TEACUPS AND LIES

Susannah Reese, an Ohio wife and mother in 1886, faces the most overwhelming crisis imaginable—the loss of her husband. She still has three children to raise and no income. How can she feed her family? She runs out of options. Then, just when she thinks she has found a solution, Susannah is sabotaged by a most unlikely source.

She leans on her faith to conquer impossible obstacles and finds joy even after tragedy.

TEACUPS AND LIES is a story of romance and drama, illustrating God's strength, faithfulness, and provision in desperate times.

THE RIPPLING EFFECT

Two brothers, John and Eli Reese of Spencer's Mill, Ohio are torn apart in 1887 by John's betrayal and Eli's bitter refusal to forgive. As John realizes his wrong and tries to pick up the pieces of his life, danger threatens his family, and obstacles block his path. His mother warned him of the rippling effect of his actions, but he doesn't realize the full weight of what he has done until Eli shocks the whole family.

THE RIPPLING EFFECT is the story of the power of God to heal hardened hearts and restore family relationships.

Visit the author's website:
www.CherieHarbridgeWilliams.com

www.ingramcontent.com/pod-product-compliance
Lightning Source LLC
Chambersburg PA
CBHW072235170626
46813CB00003B/1239